AFTERMATH

MURDER · ADVENTURE · REVENGE IN LAKE TAHOE

LISA PARSONS

To Michelle,
Thanks for being a fun
kayak buddy..
Kayak like a Girl!

Lisa

CONFLUENCE
ADVENTURES LLC

ISBN-13: 979-8-9861986-1-3

Cover design by: Lisa Parsons

Paramedic photo: shutterstock.com: 1878018100

Mountain Biker Photo: Joey Or

Back Cover Photo: Lisa Parsons

Library of Congress Control Number: 2022908123

Printed in the United States of America

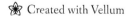 Created with Vellum

To my husband, David, my amazing adventure partner.

In memory of Taz, our adventure dog.

CONTENTS

PROLOGUE

PARAMEDIC MAYA MURPHY was working her normal shift near Seattle, Washington. She'd just been joking with her younger partner, Jeff, about the fact that people knew when they worked with her anything could happen. She was known as the 'shit magnet' at work.

During Maya's first year as a rookie paramedic, she had counted over forty-five cardiac arrests where she had overseen the coordination of the lifesaving efforts. A month after she graduated paramedic training, she was the lead paramedic on a six-person head-on car crash on a rural country road. That, along with countless car crashes, shootings, and complex medical emergencies, had set her reputation in stone. She was a shit magnet.

They were laughing as she shared her stories, when their pagers started beeping and the overhead alarms chimed in, followed by the dispatcher's announcement: respond to 240th and Pacific Highway south for officer down. Shots fired; suspect has fled the scene. Scene is not secure.

The laughter stopped, and Jeff looked at her with that look

that said, 'I should have called in sick today'. Officer down. They jumped up and ran to the medic unit. Outside, the night air was cold, but the feeling in Maya's gut was even colder.

They jumped into their rig and donned their headphones. As Jeff started the engine, Maya pressed the responding button on their dispatch computer. She was the officer in charge of the upcoming call. The door of the garage opened, and they drove out into the night with their lights and sirens ablaze, driving faster than they normally would. This was one of their own police officers shot and dying on the street.

When they arrived, police cars and emergency vehicles were coming in from all directions. Maya let dispatch and the battalion chief know they were on scene; she recognized the battalion chief's voice as he directed them in just ahead of the fire engine. It was Danielson. He was by far the best battalion (bat) chief to have on a call like this.

Danielson and his team of firefighters had the police officer on a backboard, ready to carry him to the back of the medic unit. Two other firefighters opened the doors of their medic unit and removed the stretcher, as Jeff and Maya jumped in the back. The firefighters started loading him into the rig.

Suddenly, gunfire rang out around them. Everyone dove inside the medic unit. They grabbed the doors and shut them and ducked down, waiting as they heard the police return fire. Even though the medic unit was made of steel and aluminum, it wasn't bulletproof. Maya knew that and felt extremely vulnerable.

She asked a seasoned firefighter, Dan, to gauge the situation. "When you think it is safe enough, drive us to a place where we can safely work." In the meantime, everyone cautiously went to work disrobing the police officer, setting up a bag-valve-mask, and spiking IV bags.

Once his uniform was off, they realized that this was clearly an attempted execution. He was wearing a bulletproof vest. The gunshots, probably from a 9mm handgun, entered at his groin and neck, just below and above his bullet proof vest. This was strategic!

Outside was chaos, shouting, and more gunfire. There was the sound of rapid pop pops from a possible automatic weapon. Dan informed them they were being ambushed from two sides. One shooter was somewhere in a four-story apartment complex to their right. There was another shooter on the other side of the highway.

Jeff set up to place a breathing tube into the officer's mouth as Maya placed an IV into his right arm. He was losing a lot of blood and his pulse was weak. After Jeff placed the breathing tube, a firefighter trained in basic lifesaving skills took over, pushing air from the bag-valve-mask through the breathing tube. Then Jeff placed two more large IVs into the officer's left arm.

Maya drew up some morphine and Valium to make sure that the officer was not in any pain. With a lull in the shooting, Maya turned to Dan. "Do you think it's safe to get out of here?"

"Yes, I'm on it," he replied without hesitating.

They had a life to save! He jumped into the driver's seat and hit the throttle, just as a bullet penetrated the box of the medic unit above their heads. He kept driving. They were in a race to get to Harborview Medical Center. The firefighter merged onto the freeway, using the lights and sirens.

Jeff monitored the officer's vital signs. He echoed Maya's fears. "His blood pressure and heart rate are dropping." They checked for a pulse and could barely feel one. Jeff rechecked the officer's blood pressure. "Too low!" They looked at each other. They both knew time was running out.

Maya gave directions to the firefighters to start CPR. One of the younger ones took off his firefighting jacket and started chest compressions. She gave another young firefighter the job of squeezing the IV fluid bags.

Maya called up to the driver. "Go faster, if you can!" She dialed up the emergency department medical control to let them know they were coming in with a gunshot wound, what they referred to as a GSW, and ongoing CPR. She added, "It's one of our officers."

Upon arrival at Harborview, the emergency department staff was waiting to help them bring in the officer. An officer was dying, and everyone needed to do everything right in the moment to save his life. The pressure was palpable.

They wheeled him into the trauma room and moved him over onto the bed. Maya yelled out the report.

"Thirty-year-old police officer shot in the groin and neck, possibly with a 9mm handgun. Patient found at the scene lying on the ground outside his patrol car, unconscious and unresponsive. Patient was given three liters of IV fluid en route, a breathing tube, Sux, morphine, and Valium. CPR initiated en route after patient's blood pressure dropped to forty by Doppler and heart rate fell to forty-five."

A team swarmed around their patient and began a well-orchestrated performance. The pre-hospital team stepped back.

Maya walked outside and sat down on the bumper of the medic unit, put her head down, and started crying. In the fifteen years she had been a paramedic, nothing had fazed her... until now.

1

FLIGHT

SURPRISED BY HER breakdown after the police officer shooting, Maya realized she needed some time off. She had been burning bright for a long time. She loved her job as a paramedic and thrived on crisis. Volunteering for search and rescue with her dog, Kali, on top of her regular paramedic shifts, just added more stress. She prided herself on not letting the job get to her. She had double the burden to bear; besides being a paramedic, she was a woman working in a job that was traditionally the domain of men. That meant working extra hard, not letting her weakness show, and maintaining that wall to protect her from the constant criticism of her male counterparts. It was exhausting.

For Maya, getting away was finding adventure, solitude, and beauty in the outdoors. Recently, her friend Georgia and her husband Jack had bought a house in South Lake Tahoe, where they were planning on retiring in a few years. For now, she rented it out on Airbnb, mostly on weekends and holidays. The apartment was for friends. Georgia extended her an open-ended invitation to stay anytime in a loft apartment over the garage.

She'd gone to Lake Tahoe with Georgia in the past before they bought their house there. On those trips, they'd spent days hiking and mountain biking around the lake.

She packed her mountain bike and paddleboard, and along with her two dogs, headed south from her home in Seattle. Sometimes, her boyfriend, Nick, would accompany her on her getaways, but this time, she needed to sort things out on her own. He understood. Sometimes Maya would come home with that look that said, 'I've had a hard shift and I just need to be left alone.' He knew to just give her that space, and, eventually, she'd lighten up and reengage.

2

ACCLIMATION

IT HAD BEEN a week since Maya arrived in South Lake Tahoe. The first couple of days she had spent walking out in the meadow along the river. From Seattle, at sea level, she had driven to sixty-four hundred feet in the Sierra Nevada Mountains, so she needed to acclimate. The long walks settled her mind. The dogs ran out ahead, sniffing under logs, and looking into thickets for something to chase. Down at the river she threw sticks for Rio, who earned his name, Rio, Spanish for river, because he was a passionate water dog.

Three days after her arrival, she walked back from the meadow. The dogs, off leash, roamed near her. At the corner of the cul-de-sac, she saw a woman and a young man. They seemed to be arguing, but when she got closer they suddenly went quiet. She was going to just walk by, when the woman waved her over.

Maya called her dogs to her side and walked over to talk to them.

"Are you staying at Georgia and Jack's?"

"Yes, I'm a friend of Georgia's. I'm staying in the apartment above the garage. My name is Maya."

"Hi, I'm Kathy. This is my friend Xavier. He's up from the city."

"City?" Asked Maya.

"City, that is what we locals call San Francisco. Where are you from?"

"I'm from Seattle. Georgia and I are both from there."

Maya sized them up quickly. She immediately noticed the age difference. Kathy was probably in her 50s. She had a short natural haircut and greying hair. Her clothes were REI sensible. By contrast, Xavier, was more of a hipster. He had a man bun and a scraggly beard. His clothes were urban casual. Friend or... she thought.

"Oh, I've only met Georgia and Jack once. I was just telling Xavier, how nice it is to see the place in such great shape. They've really done a lot to improve the place. It was in such disrepair when they bought it."

Maya noticed that Xavier had an irritated look on his face as he watched Kathy talking to Maya.

"Georgia told me it was unfinished, and they did quite a bit of work on it. What a great place and so close to the lake."

Maya looked at Xavier. "Is that your Tesla?" Nodding at the white Tesla parked on the street in front of Kathy's house.

"He looked over at her. His eyes softened a bit as he answered. "It is. It's a Tesla S.

"I've had my eye on one of those. I managed to talk a friend of mine into letting my drive his. I was hooked.

"I've had it for about a year. No complaints here."

Kathy interjected. "Will you be staying long?."

"A few weeks."

"Well, that will be nice."

"Thank you. She felt an unease, like she was there to be a

distraction. "Well, I need to get these guys some food." Said Maya and looked down the dogs patiently waiting. "I'll see you around."

"Have a nice visit. It was nice to meet you." Said Kathy.

"Likewise. Nice to meet you too, Xavier."

As Maya left, she could see them heading for the house. They seemed to take up the argument where they left off.

Before she could get to the apartment, she was intercepted by the neighbor's dog who was more interested in her dogs than her. They happily engaged in some play jousting and butt-sniffing. The dog's owner came out and said a quiet hello and introduced himself as Brent. He, his wife and two kids lived in the house on the side of Maya's apartment. Rosie was the dog's name. She looked like a mix of terrier and brown lab. Maya told them she was Georgia's friend and was staying in the apartment above the garage for a few weeks.

"We had a bear break into my car last night. Make sure you lock your doors when you leave, and at night. They can smell a candy wrapper from a mile away. Oh, and make sure you lock your car doors. They have learned to open car doors. If you forget, you might wake up to find a large bear crap lying in your driver's seat." He laughed.

"Really?" she asked. "The bears break into houses here?"

"Yes, they do."

"Good advice," Maya said, and thanked him. She left Brent and Rosie and returned to the apartment. She looked at the house on the other side of Georgia's. It was impeccably clean. The sprinklers were drenching the flower garden in the front. The lawn was freshly mown. As Maya had learned, that was not a common occurrence in Tahoe since the Tahoe Regional Planning Agency encouraged homeowners to stick to native vegetation in their yard to lessen the demand for water and protect native plants. Low maintenance yards reduced the need for pesticides and fertilizers, which would eventually make their way to the Tahoe Basin watershed and then into Lake Tahoe.

Maya decided to touch base with her boyfriend and give him an update on her status. She picked up her phone and went to sit on the couch out on the deck. As she dialed, the warmth of the sun seeped into her mind.

"Hello," Nick answered.

"It's me."

"Of course, I saw your name pop up on my phone. How's it going down in Tahoe?"

"Great. I've settled into Georgia's little base camp. The dogs and I have been getting out for some easy adventures to acclimate to the elevation." Four ears perked up at the mention of dogs. "We spent the last three days walking along the upper Truckee River and Lake Baron, which we can get to right from the place. We hardly need to drive anywhere unless we need bigger mountains to climb."

"Well, you aren't missing anything here. It's been raining for the last three days. This is typical for June, but not for July. If it continues, I may have to join you in sunny California.

"Well, give me some time to decompress and maybe I'll be ready for you to fly down here. I was thinking it might be a great place for us to spend some time."

As she was talking, she watched as an official-looking vehicle pulled into the driveway.

"Hold on a minute, Nick. Somebody just pulled up." A woman got out of the vehicle wearing a dark blue uniform.

"Hey, Nick, I'll call you back. Maybe someone called the police and told them a woman and two dogs are robbing the place."

Maya hung up. The dogs started barking from the deck.

She corrected them and then put them inside the apartment and walked down to meet the woman.

"Hi, can I help you?"

"Hi, I'm Janet with El Dorado Animal Control. I had a complaint that your dogs were running loose and that they have been barking non-stop."

"Wow, well, we were walking in the meadow, but my dogs are very well trained. My female Mal is a trained search and rescue dog. As far as barking goes, honestly, they have been with me all the time. I'd know if they were barking non-stop. I'm sorry to hear someone has an issue with us being here."

"Well, we received a complaint and have to follow up. Are your dogs licensed here?"

"No," she said, "we live in Seattle. This is my friend's house. I'm staying here for a few weeks."

Janet looked at her suspiciously. "Well, if I have to come out again, I'll need to issue a warning citation. Please make sure your dogs are on leash and monitor the barking."

"Okay, I'm sorry you had to come out. Thank you, officer."

Janet walked back to her truck and sat for a minute with the engine running while she filled out paperwork on the criminal dogs. Then she pulled out of the driveway and left Maya alone. Maya looked out into the cul-de-sac, and the neighbors were nowhere to be seen. *Had they called them in? Brent didn't seem like the type and besides, his dog was off leash too. Maybe Kathy?*

She called Nick. "Hey, I just had an unnerving experience. The official vehicle was the dogcatcher. Someone called in a complaint about the dogs being off leash and barking. Wow, didn't expect that in Tahoe."

"Well, I guess you'll just have to keep them on leash until you get to the trails. People don't know the dogs. Yours are well trained compared to most."

"Yes, they occasionally bark at wildlife, but you know they mostly bark to let me know something is wrong or someone has arrived."

With that, they talked about the projects he was working on and about the possibility of him flying down to visit. After they ran out of things to say, they said goodbye.

Later that day, Georgia called to check in and see how Maya was doing.

"Maya, hey, how do you like the place? We just finished up furnishing the apartment."

"The apartment is great. Perfect, in fact."

"Are you feeling better now that you've had a few days to distance yourself?"

"Somewhat, but... I'm just not myself. I've never had a call upset me this much before. I'm having trouble sleeping and I'm having nightmares. When I first wake up, I feel like I'm still in the nightmare. It's intense. In the dream, the officer keeps asking me why I didn't save him. I just can't shake this unsettled feeling."

"I'm sure it will pass," said Georgia. "It was a pretty hard call. To execute a police officer for no other reason than some radicals decided they want to target police officers and emergency personnel in some ideological civil war. It's just crazy. I'm concerned that our jobs are going to get us shot just because we're wearing a uniform. I've never felt so vulnerable, even at the time of the gang wars in the nineties."

Georgia was a veteran Seattle firefighter. She'd been on the street for twenty-plus years. Seattle wasn't Los Angeles, but it was still a crazy place to work. To hear her concern meant that things were getting serious. Usually, they dispassionately commented that early in their careers, the biggest dangers were gangs, HIV, and drunk drivers. Today, Maya's concerns were becoming more alarming and harder to detach from.

There was a palpable fear of terrorist attacks, airborne pandemics, and mass shootings. She was feeling more exposed and that they were more at risk of things going sideways on a call.

"We'll get through this," Maya said. "You're so close to retirement. Besides, you're doing your last years at the 'vacation station' now. Do you even get up at night anymore?"

"Yes, but it's usually for an elderly person with chest pain. No gangs and so far no militias in Madison Park."

"Yes, unless you are talking about gangs of raccoons ransacking garbage cans for gourmet leftovers," Maya shot back.

They laughed.

"Hey, Georgia, I just wanted to let you know, I had a visit from the animal control today. Someone called in a complaint about my dogs being off leash and barking. You know them. They hardly bark at all, so I was pretty surprised. Especially since I just arrived. I'll make sure to keep them quiet. I don't want you to get a bad reputation with your new neighbors."

Georgia remained silent for a minute. "Hmm, I'm starting to wonder. One of our clients was barbecuing out on the deck in the evening a few weeks ago and they had a visit from the police, stating they had received a complaint that they were making too much noise. Our local manager followed up with the officer. Apparently, things are touchy in South Lake Tahoe right now because the locals aren't happy with all the new vacation rentals. The officer reminded him there is a curfew on noise at 10 p.m., but people can be cited any time of day if someone complains.

Georgia continued, "Maybe it's the same person who complained about the Airbnb noise. Let me know if anything else comes up. Neighbors! You would think just being in a place as beautiful as Tahoe would chill people out. I hope this doesn't continue. Nobody wants a nosey, complaining neighbor.

"Oh, and by the way, I have some Bay Area guests coming up tomorrow for the weekend."

After the call, Maya made dinner and settled into read an adventure novel. She loved traveling and reading a good book about a far-off, place.

3

ECHO LAKE

THE NEXT DAY, she decided to take the dogs on a more strenuous hike along the shoreline of Echo Lake at seventy-five hundred feet. It looked inviting from the photos she'd seen. She arrived at a small store, boat fueling station, and docks that marked the entrance to the lake. She left the parking area where residents of lakeside cabins and visitors parked. The trail crossed a concrete dam where the lake spilled out into a stream. The trail meandered along the contour of the granite cliffs and boulders that framed the sky. Below, pinemat manzanita clung to the steep slope down to the edge of the lake.

At this elevation, the gentle grade did little to help her lungs that were still trying to catch up with her legs. Even with the gentle terrain, at seventy-five hundred feet, breathing was harder.

At the top of Lower Echo Lake, she took a quick break. She still felt good, so she continued hiking up to the upper lake. The shoreline comprised sloping granite slabs with cabins anchored into the stone. The upper lake had small, tree-filled islands poking out of the lake's surface. When she arrived at the end of the lake, she stopped at a small dock with a wooden bench. Back in the trees, she found a booth with a phone in it. *It was an odd thing to find on a hike.* There were instructions for calling the water taxi. Apparently, a water taxi brought people up from the marina to the dock and back. The trail continued into the Desolation Wilderness. *I could spend a lifetime exploring here*, she thought to herself.

On the way back, just past the cabins, she found a route down to the lake. She and the dogs plunged into the cool mountain water and spent the rest of the afternoon lying on the granite rocks and swimming. Both dogs loved to swim and retrieve sticks in the water. Kali would bring the stick and place it in Maya's hand. Rio just wanted to play keep away. Kali's training was much more complete. She was always more focused and needed a job. Maya, sensing that, had trained her in scent detection, search and rescue, and Schutzhund protection dog training. They kept Maya entertained until the late afternoon sun nudged her out of her lakeside slumber.

4

THE AIRBNB GUESTS

WHEN MAYA ARRIVED BACK at the apartment, the guests hadn't arrived yet. She decided that tonight she'd check out some of the local nightlife. Stateline, on the border of California and Nevada, was tourist central, and she figured it would have a lot going on. After showering, she headed out. She brought the dogs with her so they wouldn't bark if Georgia's guests arrived before she returned.

She found a great restaurant in Stateline with outdoor seating and live music. A young blues band stroked some old classics to life. The warmth of the evening created a comfortable cloak around her as she relaxed and watched the hustle of tourists arriving for the weekend. She looked on as families and groups of young people walked along the streets in front of the restaurant.

People were laughing at the tables next to her. She suddenly felt awkward sitting alone, but that soon ended when a table of young Bay Area tech workers engaged her in conversation. They were up for the weekend to take a break from working and have some fun while having a going away party for one couple. She asked where the couple was going. They told her they were moving to Seattle in three weeks. When Maya told them she was from Seattle, the couple immediately perked up.

"You're from Seattle? We're looking forward to moving up there, but we're worried that we won't be able to find a place to live," the young Asian woman in the couple said. "We have temporary housing through our new employer, Amazon, but we have no idea where to look. Do you have any great neighborhoods you can recommend? We'll be working for the main Amazon office downtown."

Maya told them about the new apartments in the Denny redevelopment that would be within walking distance of their work. There are also some of the cool local neighborhoods like Queen Anne and Capitol Hill. "Rent's expensive, though. You can expect to pay at least twenty-five hundred for a small two-bedroom apartment, but probably more because the housing market is super competitive."

The couple laughed. "We are paying five thousand a month for a tiny three-bedroom in the Bay and we have roommates. Twenty-five hundred a month sounds like a bargain. Hopefully, we can afford a place of our own."

Maya had heard that before. Tech workers leaving the Bay Area for places where the cost of living was a little less. She knew firsthand, that locals could no longer afford to live in Seattle because of skyrocketing housing prices. 'Such is life.' The constant movement of people created tensions between locals and newcomers.

Maya, however, found the newcomers refreshing. She finished the evening by joining them for dancing. They found themselves at Montbleu for "80's Night". She watched as her new friends drank neon martinis and did drunken impressions of eighties stars like Cyndi Lauper and Michael Jackson.

Mostly, she felt too uptight and couldn't quite cut loose with the others, but she made sure she was entertaining and danced for a few of the better songs. She just wasn't herself and it showed up as a feeling of being weighed down by darkness while others went about their daily lives. At two in the morning, she said goodbye and headed back to the apartment. It felt great to have a night out with good company.

SHE RETURNED to the apartment to find an El Dorado County sheriff parked just outside the driveway. She pulled in and stepped out of her car. The sheriff was at the front door of the house, talking to the new guests.

Maya walked up to see what was going on.

"Hi, my name's Maya. I'm a friend of the owners. Is there a problem?"

Officer O'Brien introduced himself and replied, "We have received a complaint that there was an unauthorized vehicle parked in the cul-de-sac."

She looked out to the right of the driveway. There was a car parked in front of the next-door neighbor's house. There were two cars parked in the driveway.

The guest, a guy in his late thirties with a receding hairline, told the officer that their parents had parked on the street because they weren't sure where Maya would park. The owner told them only to park in front of the house or in the garage. They had only arrived an hour ago and once they finished unloading; they moved the car to the street.

Officer O'Brien explained, "Vacation renters are not allowed to park on the street per the El Dorado County vacation rental ordinance. Because this is a new rule. I'm just going to issue you a warning and ask you to move the car into the driveway."

"We're sorry. We just didn't know," the guest said.

Maya told them where she would park all weekend and told them to park in either of the two spots to the right, in front of the three-car garage.

The officer was empathetic to the disruption at two-thirty in the morning and wished them a good night's sleep. The son moved his parent's car into the driveway, and everyone said good night.

Maya pulled into the garage and let the dogs outside. It astounded her that anyone would call in an incorrectly parked car at two-thirty in the morning. She stood up on the deck and looked out into the cul-de-sac. There weren't any lights on in the surrounding houses. Was someone secretly peeking out their window, watching for Georgia's guests to make a mistake? Were they watching her now?

The dogs made their way back upstairs, just as a pack of coyotes started up a chorus in the distance. Maya listened to their song. Their yips and howls hauntingly echoed each other. The dogs briefly lifted their heads at the coyote song and then padded into the house. She shut and locked the door. *That'll keep the bears out.*

As she lay in bed, she replayed her day. It had been a good start. She drifted off to an uneventful sleep.

THE NEXT DAY, she formally met the family. They were from San José, California. The grandmother was celebrating her seventy-fifth birthday. The daughter, her husband, her brother, and two young kids came up to celebrate. They were happy to be up in the mountains and asked if she knew of any fun things to do.

Maya replied she was also a recent arrival, but that Stateline was a fun place to shop, eat out, and if they were interested, she saw they offered gondola rides up the mountain at Heavenly Resort.

Later, they all headed out. They waved as they left. She saw a woman standing out at the edge of her driveway, just behind a stand of aspens, as the guests left. She couldn't get a good look. The woman seemed to watch the guests leave. Was she the one who called the police last night?

When the family arrived back later in the afternoon, the quiet laughter and family banter drifted up to Maya's ears in the apartment. Maya, tired from the late night, had spent the afternoon reading her book and napping. It was a hot day, so she'd opened the windows to let a cooler breeze move through the living room.

She settled back into her book. She rarely took whole days off to do nothing. It was hard, but she really needed to learn to relax and not be so driven. Maybe if she'd learned to do that more often, she wouldn't have melted down after that call.

After she had dinner and was settling in to watch a movie, she heard a knock at the door. Rio and Kali sprang up and barked.

"Okay, you guys, sit," Maya commanded. They stopped barking and sat at attention, facing the door. She opened the door to find a little girl standing there with a plate filled with a piece of birthday cake.

"My mom wanted to offer you some of grandma's birthday cake. It's chocolate."

"How nice. I'd love some."

Behind the little girl, standing in the doorway to the house across the deck, was mom, Diane. Diane said that Emma insisted on making sure that Maya had some cake. "She was so concerned that you were all alone over there."

Maya looked at Emma. "Well, Emma, I'm not all alone. Rio and Kali are with me, and they're great company."

Emma looked tentatively at the dogs. "Can I pet them?"

"Well, sure, but you probably should give me the cake first or they may eat it before I get any."

They all laughed.

Maya took the cake and then released the dogs from their sit position. The dogs trotted out to say hi. "Gentle," she said. Both her dogs were big and Rio, being his exuberant self, might accidentally knock over the little girl as he gave her big, sloppy licks on the face.

Within minutes, both dogs were sucking up the pets from Emma. Soon Jake, the little boy, was also joining in. The dogs loved kids and true to form, Rio lathered big, sloppy licks onto Jake and Emma's faces as they giggled and turned away.

Diane thanked her for letting the kids pet the dogs.

"Say Happy Birthday to Grandma for me," said Maya.

What a nice family, Maya thought after they left.

At 8 p.m., she was just finishing up her movie and thinking about taking an evening walk. She put the dogs on their leashes. As she left the house, she heard the family laughing through the open windows and started down the driveway, just as another El Dorado County Sheriff's vehicle pulled up.

"Hey, weren't you just here?" Maya asked.

The officer got out of his vehicle. "No, I just came on duty. I'm Officer Grant. I saw that Officer O'Brien was here last night."

"Yes, he was," Maya replied. "I have to ask. Why are you here?"

"A noise complaint was called in at this address. They said there was a loud party here."

Maya looked at him incredulously. "I've been here all day. The only sounds I heard are the family next door laughing and having a birthday party for grandma. That was only when I stepped outside just now to take a walk."

"Are you the owner?"

"No, I'm a friend of the owner."

"Well," he said, "I have to address any complaint that comes in, but from what I can tell right now, there is no loud party. Still, I have to go up and contact the guests."

"Look, they're just a nice family celebrating the grandmother's seventy-fifth birthday. I have been here all night and haven't heard a thing. Couldn't you just leave them to enjoy their stay here? This is the second ridiculous complaint since they've arrived. I can vouch that they are not causing any problems."

Officer Grant thought for a moment. "I agree with you that there doesn't seem to be a problem. I'll document that I touched base with you and found that this was a false alarm. Why ruin someone's stay if I don't have reasonable cause to do so. Just don't tell my supervisor. I'm supposed to contact the guests on every call. These new ordinances and an enforcement emphasis are taking a lot of time. Have a good night." He returned to his car.

As Maya headed out for her evening walk, she could see him in the driver's seat, filling out paperwork. There were three houses with lights on in the cul-de-sac. She wondered if it was one of those three that had called the police, not once, but twice in one day.

5

ON THE TRAIL

THE OPEN FOREST flowed past Maya's eyes as she leaned into the wide arc of dirt trail. Her mind was focused, and her body was attuned to the movements of the mountain bike beneath her. She left behind the aftermath of feelings that lingered from the worst call of her paramedic career.

The smooth dirt transitioned into a technical granite rock garden. She focused on her line. On her mountain bike, she was immersed in the present.

She was on the Armstrong Pass trail outside of South Lake Tahoe. With her two dogs running along with her, they became a wild pack of three. Her white German Shepherd, Rio, tracked right behind her rear wheel. Her other dog Kali, a Belgian Malinois, ran up ahead to make sure the trail was clear of squirrels and other quick-moving critters.

Maya let off the brakes as the trail opened up, snaking back and forth over a wide ridgeline. She pressed the edge of her tires on the outside of the corners for traction and just let the bike and the terrain do the rest.

The trail turned and became straight and narrow. It

followed the side hill through towering ponderosa, lodgepole pines, and incense cedar. Below, she could hear flowing water. Sunlight broke through the trees, casting light on the forest floor. She figured she must be close to where the trail intersected Fountain Place Road because she was near the stream.

Kali dove left off the trail and bounded down the steep side hill. Another squirrel, Maya thought as her dog disappeared into a nest of streamside willows. She slammed on the brakes, skidding to a stop. Damn that dog! Now I'm going to have to rein her back in. As with all sudden exits into the wild, beyond the trail, her first fear was always that it wasn't a squirrel but a predator waiting to pounce on her unsuspecting city dog. She had heard that happened in Tahoe.

Suddenly, Kali started barking from the willows. Then she reappeared and ran right up to Maya and put her head against her leg. Kali trotted back toward the willow thicket. She paused, sat down, and looked back when Maya didn't follow her. Kali was letting her know she had found something like she was trained to do on search and rescue missions in the Pacific Northwest.

Maya's concern escalated a notch. She propped her mountain bike up against a tree, and with Rio at her heels, followed Kali down the steep slope of pine needles and dirt in between the trees. Kali disappeared back into the thicket and barking again. Maya noticed an area where the dirt was disrupted in large chunks, leading down to a place where the willows were bent back toward the creek. Lying tangled in the willows was a light blue mountain bike. The front wheel was bent at the base of a large willow.

Her heart fluttered.

Lying just downstream of the mountain bike was a small boy. He was face down, just at the surface of the moving water.

The current flowed around his submerged head and neck. The back of his helmet protruded out of the water.

Maya's training kicked into action. She quickly scanned the area for any danger and entered the shallow creek. When she reached the boy, she carefully touched his left arm. It was twisted at an angle from the middle of the arm above the elbow. Solid break. She held the boy's neck in line with his body and made her best effort to turn him over without twisting his arm further.

She rested his body on a larger rock. To her shock, she realized that the body wasn't that of a boy but of a small older woman. The woman's grey hair lying in wet strands across her face. Her eyes were open wide, dull, glazed, and lifeless. Her mouth twisted at a downward angle and slightly open.

Maya reached down to the side of the woman's neck to feel for a pulse. Nothing. She quickly pulled her cell phone out of her Camelbak. Even before looking at it, she knew she wouldn't have service. She checked it anyway. No bars. Rio whimpered. Maya turned her head and glimpsed something moving just out of her vision further up the trail. She turned her attention back to the woman. If something was out there, her dogs would alert her.

Her training taught her that a person was not dead until they were warm and dead.

In cold-water drownings, the patient isn't considered dead until they are rewarmed. People have survived for up to an hour in cold water because the diving reflex reduces the brain's need for oxygen. She knew it was probably a long shot, but she had to try.

She reached down, gently closing off the woman's nostrils with her left hand and blew in two breaths. A small amount of water flowed out of the woman's mouth and dribbled down the side of her cheek. Maya started chest compressions. With the first compressions, she felt the ribs crack under the pressure.

Rio, always the sensitive dog, continued to whimper in the background. Kali stood patiently in the water, watching.

She continued doing mouth-to-mouth and delivering chest compressions for what seemed like hours. She didn't want to give up. *What if I can resuscitate her?* She thought.

Finally, after forty minutes by her estimate, she checked for a pulse again and conceded that the woman was dead. There wasn't anything else she could do. She closed the woman's eyes, silently wishing her a good journey to her next life.

She left the body where it was. The police and medical examiner would probably want to do a scene investigation and an autopsy to establish time and cause of death.

Maya sat on the shoreline, scanning the area. Other than the broken branches on the way down to the creek and the broken tops of the folded over willow branches beyond the bike, there didn't seem to be much disturbance except for some indents in mud just to the other side of the creek near where she had found the woman's body.

She looked closer at the woman now that she was no longer focused on the CPR. Maya could see why she mistook her for a boy. She was thin and wiry, with no real definition to her figure. Probably in her sixties. Her hair was in a short ponytail beneath her helmet. The wispy wet strands that had been across her face had escaped her ponytail.

The woman's left arm was disfigured. She must have flown off her bike. If the impact didn't kill her, she might have drowned as she lay face down, helpless in the shallow current.

Maya also noted a small trickle of water-thinned blood oozing out from a puncture wound just below her right clavicle. The woman's muscles were still soft, and her body didn't have any pooling of blood where the body was lying at its lowest, which gave a clue about how long the woman had been lying there. That may have been because she was half submerged in cold water. She couldn't have been there too long.

With that, Maya decided to leave the woman and go for help. She stood up and gave the "follow" command to her dogs. They dropped in line behind her. She retraced her steps up through the willows past the woman's mountain bike, careful not to disturb the scene any more than they already had. Back at the trail, she checked her cell phone for signal. Of course, she didn't have any. In Tahoe, she was lucky if she had signal while standing in the middle of the tourist district. She got back on her bike and they slowly made their way up to where the trail met the top of Fountain Place Road. No reason to be in a hurry now. Dead was dead and nothing could change that after the fact.

6

IN SEARCH OF CELL RECEPTION

MAYA HAD to drive into the town of Meyers to get cell reception. By the time she found two bars on her phone, she was near the fire station, so she just pulled into the parking area and walked inside.

"Hi, my name is Maya. I'm a paramedic from Seattle. I want to report a body I discovered up on the Armstrong Pass trail today."

The receptionist looked surprised but immediately called in the fire chief. Maya described what she had found, what she did, and the outcome.

The chief thanked her, got on his radio and had dispatch call out the local fire crew, the police, and then told them to notify the Forest Service because it was on their land and part of their jurisdiction.

Maya rode up with the fire chief, feeling the camaraderie that comes with sharing the same profession. In moments like these, she found solace in someone who would understand. A fire/aid crew on the rescue rig and a local sheriff followed them up Fountain Place. As they drove up the road, she took more notice of the chief's tightly cropped greying hair and cleanly shaven face. He looked strong but had that slightly expanding waistline that said he was spending more time in meetings and pushing paper than adventuring in the Tahoe outdoors. She wondered if he was living in Tahoe for the life-style or the job.

As they turned onto Pioneer Trail, the chief, Paul Santizo, introduced himself. He had been with fire department in for twenty-five years. He lived in South Lake Tahoe with his wife and two grown boys. One of his boys worked for Carson City Fire Department and the other was studying business at San Diego State.

He lowered his window a little. I hope it isn't anyone we know. South Lake is a tight-knit community, but we have more tourists visiting every year. It's probably a tourist.

They turned onto Fountain Place and started the three-mile climb up the narrow road. A woman was walking her two small terrier dogs. The chief commented, "Coyote food, that is all those little dogs are up here. One of my neighbors recently had their small dog snatched off their back deck by a coyote. Gone before she could even react. They need to do something about the coyotes. They're getting more and more brazen."

Maya wondered what that something was, but all she said was that she was glad that her two dogs were large enough to, hopefully, fend for themselves.

Kali and Rio were back at the fire station, spending time with the volunteer crew hanging out at the station. Tahoe was a dog town, and everyone seemed to have one. The volunteers were all dog people and had said they were happy to watch her dogs while she went up to point out where she had found the woman.

They arrived up at the top of the road. So far, it looked like no one had come up there since she had left. She'd hate to see someone who wasn't used to seeing dead bodies find the woman down by the creek.

There were quick introductions. The officer introduced himself as Officer Andy O'Brien. Maya recognized him from the visit to investigate a noise complaint at Georgia's Airbnb last week.

The aid crew grabbed a Stokes litter and rescue ropes. The officer checked on the ETA of the medical examiner, who was dispatched at the same time. He had to come from Placerville, which was an hour away, so it might be awhile until he got there.

Then the two firefighters, the chief, the officer, and Maya, hiked down the trail. Maya retraced her route along the trail that paralleled the creek until she got to the place she had marked as the spot.

The police carefully flagged off the area that Maya indicated was the path most likely taken by the mountain bike as it exited the trail. It looked like she must have lost control and crashed.

O'Brien carefully made his way down to the woman first so he could note anything important. Looking at her, he exclaimed, "I know this woman. Where do I know her from?" His face turned serious. "Well, we're going to have a lot fewer complaints now."

The fire Lieutenant followed him, reached down and checked for a pulse, then confirmed the obvious. "Yep, she's dead all right. Time of of confirmation of death is 14:27."

O'Brien looked at Maya and said, "You found her face down?"

"Yes, just to the left of where she is lying now," Maya replied. She added, "She still felt warm, so I thought it was worth attempting CPR. I turned her over and did forty minutes before stopping."

"Wow, you're pretty dedicated," said Andy. "That's a long time for one person to do continuous CPR."

"I don't know how long she was there before I arrived," Maya replied. "She didn't have obvious lividity, but her pupils were dilated and fixed."

O'Brien said he was going to look around some more. He asked her to go back up to the trailhead and tie in with Officer Underwood.

Maya was relieved that she was finally off the hook. She was trying to get away from her job and here she was, shit magnet, even in the woods of Tahoe. The chief, who didn't really have any reason for staying, followed her up.

"I'll wait and give you a ride back to the station when you're finished. Nothing like being on duty even when you're on vacation," he said.

"Yep, we are never really off duty."

Officer Underwood was taping off the roadway.

He took her statement and her contact info. He gave her his card and told her they would contact her.

It was a quiet ride back to the station. Maya was feeling exhausted. She was ready to go back to her loft apartment, give her dogs big hugs, and settle down to drink some of the Tahoe Blue she had purchased the day before.

7

MOUNTAIN SOLACE

AFTER LEAVING THE FIRE STATION, Maya pulled into the driveway. She unloaded her bike, then parked in the garage. Kali and Rio followed her out the side door of the garage and into their own private dog yard. Rio went around and marked the aspens along the fence. Kali barked at some birds, sending them into the sky. Maya took a deep breath and called the dogs to follow her up the stairs into the apartment. She opened the blinds to look out the window at Mount Tallac. In the quiet living room, she finally had time to think.

She was feeling sorry for herself. She seriously needed a break from her job. That break did not need to include finding a dead body. She was tired of trying to make a difference. Her expertise was an insignificant blip in a sea of despair. She had watched young and old die because of gunfire or because of too many donuts. She'd seen the ugly way people can die and sometimes, the even uglier way they can live. She wasn't so sure that she wanted to suck it up anymore, especially after working so hard to save the police officer's life.

When they found out the police officer hadn't survived, it

had been devastating. The officer was well respected in the community. After work, he volunteered for an after-school program where kids could come to feel safe, play games, and take classes. He was a father with two young children, aged three and five.

She poured a tall glass of Tahoe Blue Vodka and her favorite mixer. Mostly, the glass was full of vodka. The slow burn warmed her insides and switched off her mind.

She sat down on the comfy couch. Kali came up to her and nestled her nose in Maya's free hand. She stroked her soft brown head. "Did you smell her, Kali?" Kali pushed her head in harder against Maya's hand.

Who was this woman? She was older. You'd think she would be smarter than to ride alone at that age. Maya surmised that riding alone with dogs when you are in your thirties is clearly okay. But when you get to your sixties, you have other things to worry about besides crashing your bike, like a heart attack or a stroke. Then again, it was Tahoe. She'd met seventy-year-olds that were more fit than a twenty-year-old college student.

Still, she wondered about what led that older woman to that moment when her life ended. Who was she? What had she done for a living? Did she have any children? Who would wonder where she was when she didn't come home? All thoughts she could follow up on tomorrow once the police and the medical examiner determined who she was. It would give her closure to at least know who this woman was.

She took another drink and turned on the T.V. Two hours and another couple of vodkas later, she was easing into a comfortable numbness that, hopefully, would take her through until morning.

She stood up and went to the window to look across at the moonlit view of Mount Tallac, beyond the river meadow. The light from the moon illuminated the last of the snow on the mountain. Then she noticed something creeping along the fence line that led out to Tahoe Conservancy land. She could barely make out the movement. A bear? Yet it was too slim for a Tahoe bear. It didn't look like an animal moving. It disappeared around the side of her garage toward the forest.

She decided to flush out the visitor and let her dogs out into the backyard. Two large barking dogs would promptly scare off whatever was there. She opened the door. The dogs sniffed, and then Kali took off like a rocket for the fence. She barked and gave out a low growl, an indicator she meant business. A form, a person, ran off into the forest and disappeared behind the trees. Kali continued to bark for a few minutes and then ran back up to Maya. Maybe it was someone looking to break into the garage. She was on the second story and had the dogs with her. She had a good sense about people, honed from fifteen years working on the streets. She'd keep an eye out for anyone who didn't look right.

They retreated into the apartment and then headed to bed. Sinking off into sleep, she felt safe with the dogs at the foot of her bed.

She awoke and bolted upright. Her heart was racing. There was the sound of gunfire and yelling. She could smell that sick-sweet smell of blood, and a feeling of helplessness over-whelmed her as she realized he was dead. The blood just kept flowing out of his wounds onto the floor of the medic unit, creating a moving pool that swished this way and that every time they took a corner. She frantically tried to mop it up and put it back in.

She awoke to the sound of Rio snoring. She felt disoriented until she realized she was emerging from a nightmare about her last call. She wrestled the panic that rose in her mind that told her this was different. The police officer was one of them. She just couldn't shake the feeling that if she had done just a little more, maybe she could have saved him. It was silly, of course, because they'd done everything humanly possible, and his wounds were too severe.

She looked at her iPhone. It was three in the morning. It seemed like it was always three when the new nightmare woke her up.

IN THE MORNING, she awoke to sun shining through the trees into her bedroom windows. Maya stretched her arms up, feeling the warmth radiate through the glass. It was such a pleasant change from her home in Seattle.

The dogs heard her move and jumped up to get their early morning pets. She got up and let the dogs out to pee. Below, she caught the quick movement of a coyote running across the street and into the meadow. The coyote likely heard the dogs and retreated to the meadow, leaving the dogs to their territory. Even though coyotes might pose a threat to her dogs, she loved the sound of their howls at night.

Today. she'd hit the trails on her mountain bike. Maya decided that today's ride needed to include wide-open views, untainted by yesterday's events. She decided she'd ride up the Tahoe Mountain and Angora Ridge Trails near Fallen Leaf Lake. Just as she finished up that thought her phone rang.

"Hello."

No one answered back.

"Hello?"

Again, no one replied.

She waited and then hung up. A few minutes later, the phone rang again. It was Officer O'Brien.

"Hello officer, what can I do for you?"

"I wanted to check in to see how you're doing," O'Brien

replied. "It isn't every day that you find a dead body while mountain biking."

"I'm doing well."

"I also wanted to ask if there's anything else you remember from yesterday. Did you run into anyone else on the trail? Did anything seem out of place?"

One thing that lingered in her mind was that just before she started CPR on the woman, she saw a movement on the other side of the creek. It barely registered in her mind because she was so focused on the woman. She mentioned it to O'Brien, conceding that it could have been one of her dogs.

"The medical examiner has some concerns that maybe this wasn't just an accident," O'Brien continued. "I can't tell you anything more, but if you remember anything else, let me know.

"Also, the firefighters asked if you wanted to join them for dinner at the station tomorrow night. Someone told them you were a paramedic up in Seattle. I had no idea that Seattle is famous for starting one of the first paramedic programs in the world."

"It was one of the places where it all started. I'm not quite in Seattle, but we're all part of the same team. Let them know I'd love to join them for dinner.

"Anyway, I have plans to go mountain biking today. Hopefully, I won't have to call you about finding another dead body." Maya laughed nervously at her own gallows humor and also hoped it was true.

"Yes," O'Brien replied. "Let's hope so, or we might wonder if you're killing mountain bikers."

"Yes, that's me, from life saver to murderer. Am I supposed to joke about things like that with a police officer?" she asked. "Joking aside, I really would like a nice uneventful afternoon!"

• • •

SHE LOADED up her bike and the dogs and headed out towards Fallen Leaf Lake. It was already looking like a warm day. Good thing they were starting early; the dogs would appreciate the cooler temperatures.

She parked at the pullout just at the end of the Angora Ridge trail on Tahoe Mountain Road. A couple of other cars were parked there too. She leashed her dogs for the short ride up the road to the start of her ride.

When she arrived at the trail, she unleashed her dogs. Then she pedaled up the trail. It felt good to move. Kali was scouting out ahead, and Rio was again tracking on her rear wheel.

She turned on to the upper Valley View Trail. In 2007, the Angora fire erupted in the valley and climbed up the ridge, burning houses along its path. She could see remnants of the burn in the dark trunks of fire-scarred pines sticking up like lonely reminders of the larger forest that used to fill the ridge.

They tracked down the ridge between giant granite boulders and dropped into unburned forest before crossing Tahoe Mountain Road and climbing up Forest Mountain Road to the Mule Deer Connector Trail. From there, it was a steady climb through low thickets of white thorn and manzanita that filled the blanks left in the landscape by the fire. The sun was fully on them as they climbed.

They arrived at the road that was the dividing line between burned and unburned forest. Now she dropped into the unburned forest on the lower Angora Ridge Trail. As she rode the trail, she found it hugged the outer edge of the ridge above Fallen Leaf Lake. It revealed the lake and the surrounding ridges between breaks in the forest cover.

She enjoyed the view of Fallen Leaf Lake and the backdrop of Desolation Wilderness, with Mount Tallac standing watch on the lake's opposite shoreline. Farther to the east, the spine of the mountain sloped downward to a thin bridge of land that separated Fallen Leaf Lake from Lake Tahoe.

As she continued, the dogs ran on and off the trail, exploring the forest on either side. Her phone rang. She ignored it and focused on navigating through the rocks as she descended the narrow trail.

The last of the trail turned sharply and dropped through a tight rock garden, slowing her as she arrived back at her SUV.

She climbed into the driver's seat, feeling satisfied. She had finally gotten her escape on a beautiful, uninterrupted ride.

BACK AT THE HOUSE, there were three cars parked in the cul-de-sac. At the house, on the right, stood three people. They looked up as she drove in and stared at her as she passed. She wondered what was going on.

When she entered the apartment, her cell phone rang. She answered it. "Hello, Maya here."

"Maya, hi, this is Chief Santizo. I tried to call you earlier. I wanted to let you know that we've identified the woman you found yesterday. She didn't have any identification on her, so it took a while to track her down. Looks like she was a part-time resident here. She and her husband live in Meyers. I wanted to let you know more about the situation.

"Seems that the medical examiner determined the bicycle crash wasn't the cause of death. I can't tell you anything more than that. You'll be receiving a follow up call from the sheriff's office. They are going to want to interview you further because now this has become a murder investigation."

She sat down on the couch. Murder. Was she now in danger when she went out by herself to explore the trails? The questions loomed large in her mind as she got off the phone. A moment of panic welled up. She had joked with the police officer about being a murderer. Not good now that they determined that the woman was murdered.

She just couldn't believe that she had found herself leaping from one murder in Seattle to another murder in Tahoe.

Jesus, I can't get away from this crap, she thought. She poured herself a glass of vodka and pushed her thoughts aside as she took another drink.

8

MOUNTAIN MURDER

TWO DAYS after finding the dead woman, Maya's phone rang in the morning, and she saw the Tahoe area code. It was Officer O'Brien.

"Is this about the woman's death not being an accident?"

"Yes, it appears it was not an accident, but murder," Officer O'Brien replied. "That's why I am following up with you. Can you come in at two this afternoon to be interviewed again? We'll need to go over everything in more detail."

He gave her the address of the local office. Now that it was a murder investigation, everything would be taken much more seriously. Each piece of information would be recorded, dissected, and looked at. She wondered if she was now a suspect. Her guess was that at that point, everyone was.

After getting off the phone with him, she took a walk down to Tahoe Paradise Park with the dogs before the interview. Afterward, she'd go have dinner with the local firefighters. They could talk shop and compare stories. She bet they had seen some crazy things because of the transient nature of their tourist clients.

She walked out into the cul-de-sac. Brent and his family were outside in the backyard as the kids played in a plastic blue kiddie pool. Rosie the dog played with the kids by jumping in and out of the pool.

As she crossed the cul-de-sac, a woman came out of the house on the other side of the family house. She was tall and willowy thin with a look of casual confidence. She was walking out to a Ford Explorer. She waved hello. Maya waved back.

"Hey," she said. "Are you staying in the apartment over the garage?"

"Yes, my name's Maya. I'm a friend of Georgia and Jack, the owners."

"Oh, that's great. I've only met them twice. They seem like a friendly couple.

They're from Seattle, right?"

"Yes," Maya said. "I'm also from Seattle. I'm down here for a few weeks on vacation." She lied. Too much information would probably end the conversation.

"I'm Marla. I live here with my son, Danny. Nice to meet you."

Maya noticed her looking across the street at the house to the right of Georgia's house. She looked back. "Did you hear? Don's wife died two days ago. I heard it was a tragic accident. She crashed while riding her mountain bike. It is in the local paper, but I didn't know it was Karen until I saw him yesterday with Kathy and some of their friends. They told me they're staying with him while he figures out what to do next. I feel sorry for Don, but honestly, I can't say that I, or anyone else in the neighborhood, will miss that awful woman."

Maya was stunned. The woman she had found lived next door to where she was staying. Her mind reeled, but she quickly reined in her thoughts. Now that she knew that it might have been a murder and not just a mountain bike crash, she responded as if she hadn't found the woman. She just wanted to be left alone and not end up part of the rumor mill. "That's terrible. What happened?"

"Like I said, I heard she crashed while riding her mountain bike. She loved to mountain bike. Sounds like she headed out on her own the other day."

"I'm curious. You said that no one in the neighborhood would miss her. Why?"

"Well, she was always calling the police or animal control or code enforcement on everyone. Before my ex-husband left, Don threatened to fight him in the street when they got in a disagreement because Karen wanted us to move the logs from a tree we had cut down out of our front yard. It was an eyesore, she said." Marla rolled her eyes. "Everyone has a story about her. Maybe we'll have a party to celebrate." She stopped and suddenly became quiet.

"Wow." Maya replied. Obviously, this woman didn't like the deceased. Now that she knew a little more, maybe that visit from animal control and then the officers had something to do with the dead woman.

"Marla, the other night I was looking out the window and saw someone walking slowly down the trail between the houses. When I opened the door to let the dogs out into the yard, they ran off. Have there been any recent break-ins?"

"Not that I'm aware of. Many people use that trail as a shortcut to the local Lake Baron. You shouldn't have any issues with these two dogs. They look like they could take on an intruder."

"That makes sense. I didn't realize it was a trail that people used. Good to know, so I'm not surprised when I see someone walking there. But you're right, the dogs, this is Rio and this one is Kali, are quite the intimidating pair!"

The dogs wagged their tails. Marla reached down and gave

them pats on the head. "Welcome to Tahoe, dogs!" Then she turned back to Maya. "Well, I have to go pick up my son from school. Nice meeting you."

Maya left the cul-de-sac and headed out to the meadow. She walked along the trail meandering between green sage, bright yellow woolly mule's ears and lodgepole pine trees. She turned down a short trail to the Upper Truckee River.

Down at the river she ran into two older men, each with their own dog. One had a short Basset Hound mix. The dog's belly barely cleared the ground. The other man had a small Collie. Hardly the typical adventure dogs you'd expect to see in Tahoe. Both men looked to be in their seventies. She wondered if they'd lived here for years or were they retirees living the mountain life?

Maya's dogs went up to the new dogs and they started sniffing each other's butts. Kali started barking with her play bark. Rio acknowledged their presence and then dove to the river's edge. This was water time, which was much more important than meeting a couple of neighborhood dogs.

Maya picked up a stick and threw it out into the lazy current for Rio to swim to. As she did, the men switched their attention back to their conversation. It turned out their topic was the dead woman.

"Apparently, her and her husband saw some firewood that George cut up from a tree that fell down in the meadow," the Basset owner said. "He left to go get his trailer so he could load the wood and take it home. She and her husband came up and started loading the wood into their truck. Fred, you know Fred, came out and told them that George cut up the wood and was going to be back to load it. Her husband, Don and she started arguing with him. How it was on public land, and it was anyone's wood. They were already here and ready to take it. Fred apparently told her it wasn't very neighborly to take it from George. She yelled at him to mind his own business. He called her a bitch. Then Don comes up to him and says, 'Let's take this to the street.' Fred, jeez, he didn't want to get into a fight with an old man. Besides, it wasn't his wood. He backed off. Can you believe that? Those two were quite a pair!"

"Well, said the Collie dog owner. In the old days, we'd just have had it out in the street. They've been a pain in this neighborhood for years. Maybe now that she's dead, we'll have some peace. I'll never forget the Corteze's dog."

"What about their dog?"

The Bassett owner started telling what seemed like an old, worn out story. "Apparently, the dog was barking out in the yard when the Cortezes were at work. Crazy Karen kept calling the dog pound. When they didn't address it to her satisfaction, she let the dog out of their yard and then called the animal control to come get a 'loose' dog in the neighborhood. The Cortezes had to go retrieve their dog from the animal shelter and pay a fine. They didn't realize the dog had been intentionally let out of their yard.

Two weeks later, the dog was found dead in the meadow, partially eaten by coyotes."

"So, she let the dog out and the coyotes got it?"

"Well, some people believe she intentionally poisoned the dog and then dumped it in the woods. Later, someone else found a couple of dead coyotes not too far from where they found the dog," the Collie owner explained.

"The Cortez's sold their house after that and moved out of Tahoe. Who knows if it's true? I wouldn't put it past her."

At that point, Maya threw the stick again for Rio. Kali was now the point dog, bringing the stick back for her to toss again.

"Hi," she said to the two men. "I overheard you talking about the woman who just died. Sounds like she was quite a piece of work. I'm staying at a friend's house just next door to where she lived."

"Well, aren't you lucky. If she were still alive, she'd probably have harassed you too!" said the Collie owner.

"Well, maybe she did start... before she died. I had a visit from animal control and my friend's guests had two complaints called in to the police.

"That was probably her. Everyone hated her. It's a long list. That husband of hers, nice guy, but he always jumped in to defend her when she was going after someone. She and her husband harassed the retired sheriff that lives right behind where you are staying."

"Wow, you guys are the second encounter I've had with a neighbor who hated her. I just talked to Marla, who lived next to her." Maya commented.

The Bassett owner rambled on. "Jesus, I forgot about that. We would see her ride her bicycle into our cul-de-sac. She looked like the withered old, Wicked Witch of the West riding in on her broom, only it was a beach cruiser. She'd go up to their door and start yelling at them to shut their dogs up. I heard him yell at her to get the hell off his property.

"I talked to him after she left. He was so concerned that she might poison their dogs. They put up security cameras after they saw Karen and her husband agitating the dogs through the fence and then calling animal control, yelling into the phone, "See, we told you they were barking!" The sheriff and his wife were so shaken up. They hardly come here anymore. Can you believe that? He's a retired sheriff. They were afraid for their dogs. They never left them in the yard unattended. Who knows how far she would go?"

A sinking feeling settled into Maya's gut. Had she been sleeping right next to a dog killer? Her dogs were her life. Anything that harmed them would get the full brunt of her wrath. She shuddered. She just couldn't get away from terrible people. Well, at least, she hated to think this, but she was glad the woman was gone. To think she attempted to save someone's life that may have been responsible for killing someone's dog was a horrible feeling. Gossip was gossip, but she couldn't help but feel that maybe she had dodged a bullet, not once but twice now.

She called in her dogs and continued down the trail. She needed time to think. Revelations like these led to other thoughts, like her job.

Often, she felt that what she was doing was intervening to save a life that would eventually lead to someone else's death. How many times had she pulled off saving a gangbanger only to see the retaliation shooting by his buddies later?

Then there were the drunk drivers who somehow managed to be the only ones to survive after causing a car crash. She'd save them, they'd do their time, and if the story had a happy ending, they wouldn't drink again. If it didn't, they might end up killing someone else.

Those were the thoughts that led to job burnout. The heroics were easy. Saving the life of an innocent child or resuscitating someone's grandmother or wife. Those were the good saves. But underneath all that was an underbelly of society that sometimes imploded within their communities. At other times, they crossed the centerline and intersected with people whose only crime was being in the wrong place at the wrong time.

How close had she come to being part of someone else's crazy? A line from a hit T.V. Show, 'Orange is the New Black,' crossed her mind. 'You can't fix crazy!' Yes, she thought, you can only run like hell away from it!

She cleared her mind as she walked, then ran, and upon reaching the lake, she jumped in, and, with her dogs, swam the entire length of the small neighborhood lake. The dogs were happy to be swimming in the water next to her. She focused on her breath and swam as hard as she could. At one point, Kali exited the water and ran along the shallows, following her. The lake was narrow and long. It was a manmade lake by the look of it. A wide path ran along one side. Maya arrived at the other end, out of breath and tired.

She lay there on the sand and she looked up at the high alpine blue sky. Next thing she knew, Rio laid a big, wet, sloppy tongue across her face. "eww," she yelped and sat up. "You crazy dog. I love you." With that, she got up and they walked back along the wide path, then through the sage and yellow wildflowers.

Maybe some of what she had heard today would be worth mentioning in her interview.

9

INTERROGATION

SHE WALKED into the El Dorado Sheriff's office and checked in at the front window, letting them know she was here for an interview with Officer O'Brien.

They led her back into a small room off to the side of a hallway and closed the door. She felt like she was in an episode of 'Law and Order'. Sitting in an interrogation room, waiting for the good cop and bad cop to come in and get the interrogation underway.

Officer O'Brien, another officer, and an assistant entered the small room. They introduced themselves. The other officer was Detective Dan D'Silva. He looked more like a professor than a police officer. He had long greying hair, steely blue eyes, and he wore corduroy. His pants were wrinkled, like he'd just tossed them on after getting out of bed. *Who wears corduroy jackets anymore?* The assistant's name was Susan. She had a digital recorder and a notepad.

"Maya, we will record this conversation, so if you could state your name, date of birth, address of record, and phone number first. Then we'll get started."

"Okay," Maya replied. She stated the information clearly for the record. She knew some of the process. As a paramedic, she attended several depositions and had to testify in a few trials. She thought about the shaken baby trial in which she had to testify a few years back and the trial for a drug dealer who had died in police custody because he swallowed his drugs. They had burst in his stomach.

The trials were the aftermath that she was asked to relive in order to find the truth. Besides the lifesaving efforts, her job was to document the patient and scene to leave a record of what had happened. If something resulted in a trial or deposition, she was called in to support her documentation and answer questions about any details considered relevant to the case.

This time it was a little different. She was potentially a suspect in that murder; however, the process would be similar. This did, however, add a level of fear for her. Anything she did and said could be used against her.

D'Silva was the interviewer. "Can you lead us through the details of what happened that led up to finding the deceased? Be as specific as possible."

She recounted what she had been doing prior to going for the ride and then what time she started on her mountain bike ride and when she had found the woman. She described what happened. Then she detailed what she did after she determined that the woman was dead and where she went afterward.

Then he said, "I want to ask a few questions related to the scene first. Did you see anyone near where you found the woman?"

"No," said Maya. "However, I saw movement out of the corner of my eye just before I started CPR, but I was distracted, and it was fleeting. I don't know what it was."

"Did anyone else walk, ride, or come down the trail while you were there?"

"No, not that I'm aware of. I was pretty busy trying to resuscitate the woman."

"Was there anything else about the scene that might be of interest to this investigation?"

"No," said Maya.

"Now I just have a few additional questions I want to ask you, and then we'll be done."

"Sure," she replied.

"Had you ever met the deceased prior to finding her?"

"No, I had not met her." Maya felt nervous. Although she knew she was innocent and most likely not a strong suspect, she felt as if anything she said could be used against her. She wondered if she should get a lawyer, just in case.

"Did you know she was the neighbor right next to where you are staying?"

"No, at the time, no, I was not aware. I just found out this morning after talking to one of the other neighbors."

"Were you aware that a few days prior to you finding her, she had called County Animal Control on you?"

Bingo, her mystery caller had been confirmed! "I didn't know that. I don't live here, so I had no way of knowing," she carefully replied.

"Is there anything else you would like to add to your statement?"

Maya thought about it. "Yes. This may not be relevant, but in the last few days, I have encountered three different neighbors who told me about incidents where the deceased had harassed them or others. I know this is just second-hand info, but she, it sounds like, was not well liked by her neighbors. Three neighbors I encountered relayed some concerning stories about her and her husband's behavior. You might want to look at more than just the obvious suspects.

"Given what I've heard, she had quite a few enemies. If three people were that unhappy with her, how many more are there out there who feel the same... and would they be angry enough to murder her?"

They looked at each other and back at her. "Interesting," said D'Silva. She gave them a brief rundown of what she had heard and the names she remembered hearing.

"Maya, will you be here for a while in case we need to ask you back in?"

"Yes, well, I'll be here for another couple of weeks. Then I have to return to Seattle."

"We will definitely touch base with you before you leave. Just so you know, right now, we don't consider you a suspect. We just need to make sure we are thorough and get all the facts," said Officer O'Brien.

"Thanks. That makes me feel a little better. Even not being a suspect doesn't make this process any less intimidating. I've been through several depositions for cases related to my work."

"We understand," said Officer O'Brien. "Hey, enjoy your time here in Tahoe. Don't let this overshadow your stay."

She left the station. Between the interview and some professional banter, it was now 4 p.m. She needed to get back, feed the dogs, and head out to dinner at the local fire station. She'd asked to bring something. They said since she was the first paramedic tourist, who was involved in a local murder investigation, she had the honor of bringing cake and ice cream. She chuckled to herself. It had been a long time since she had had any firsts in the fire station. Whenever a new rookie experiences their first structure fire, car crash, or unusual call, it was their responsibility to bring enough cake and ice cream to the table for everyone in the firehouse. She thought. "I guess I'm a rookie sitting on the other side of the scene before everyone arrives."

10

THE FIRE HOUSE

AFTER MAYA MADE a stop at the local Holiday Market for cake and ice cream, she parked at the front entrance and rang the doorbell of the fire station. Silence. The main office was closed for the day, so she waited. A few moments later, a firefighter answered the door.

"Hi, you must be Maya."

The guy who answered was a young firefighter, who looked like he was in his middle twenties. He must be their rookie, sent to answer the door. Maya loved seeing the next generation entering the doors of the firehouse. All eager and excited for everything that came along.

"Yes, I'm Maya, and you are?"

"Todd Blackmore, nice to meet you. This is where the pencil pushers hang out during office hours. Follow me through this maze of offices to our quarters."

She followed. They walked through a door and across the engine bay. The station was a newer one. She noticed a brush rig, a small pumper truck, a classic engine, and next was the aid

/rescue vehicle. At the back of the station, along another row of doors, was an antique fire truck. The polished chrome horn gleaming next to the polished red of the truck. Sitting in the driver's seat was a large Smokey the Bear, an iconic symbol of fire safety for the Forest Service. He was wearing a fire department bunker coat and a red structural fire helmet.

Everything was spotless. The rigs, the polished concrete floors. The firefighters' bunker gear hung in orderly rows along the wall.

California firefighters, these professional firefighter teams, always had to be on their 'A game'. Fire was synonymous with California. The men and women who fought fire in California were aggressive. They had to be. They had to stop fires before they burned out of control. Once they lost the frontline, all bets were off.

Two firefighters were in the kitchen, cooking up the night's meal. Some of the best meals she had ever eaten were in the firehouse. From the aroma wafting from the grill, she knew she wouldn't be disappointed.

There were four firefighters, plus Todd, when she arrived. Chief Santizo was also there. "I heard you were coming to dinner," he said. "We get lots of visitors, but not too many are involved in such a crazy scenario."

"It's good to see you again as your guest instead of on the scene of a dead body," Maya said. "I can't say my plan while on vacation was to find a dead woman. I didn't let that upset my plans to go mountain biking again. Today, I rode Angora Ridge."

He laughed. "There's never a dull moment during tourist season in this town. We get some crazy calls, but I'm sure it isn't any different for you in the city."

The chief introduced her to the rest of the fire crew. "This is Ben O'Malley. He's the lieutenant on the engine crew." Ben was a stocky guy who looked like he could swing an axe or a large chainsaw with one arm. O'Malley, Irish, of course. The Irish were the traditional cops and firefighters, although that was changing.

"This is Steve Pagliani, who you've already met. He's our lead on the aid car tonight."

"You already met Todd. He is our newest rookie. Just graduated from the academy six months ago. If he is lucky, he'll make it through probation and join the full-time ranks of firefighter / EMT."

"If he just works on his cooking, he might just make it through probation," O'Malley ribbed him. Everyone laughed. The chief filled in the missing information. "Yes, some of these young guys grew up on organic beans and tofu. We have to retrain them to cook like real men. Give me a rare steak cooked over a grill with baked potatoes and sour cream. None of this fake vegan meat and quinoa. We'll get him trained soon enough!"

Todd looked down and smiled. "Yes, but I'll be carrying you out of the fire scene when you have a heart attack after a dinner like that."

Maya could already tell they really liked him. He could get away with throwing the jokes right back at them.

The other two firefighters, the cooks, were Chris Jackman and Tyler Anderson. Chris was a fit, man in his thirties with sandy blond hair that was a little longer than normal for the fire department. He sported some great Celtic design tattoos on his arms. Tyler was also on the aid / rescue truck on the call. He was your typical geeky firefighter. She could tell, just from looking at him, that he was the kind of guy who never broke the rules, always did the job, but was wound a bit too tight for her liking. Guys like him were always the ones who complained whenever you missed dotting your Is or crossing your Ts.

"Dinner for the night," Chris said, "is grilled BBQ chicken burgers with grilled sweet potatoes braised in olive oil and sea salt, and salad."

Not bad, since she expected that after the meat and potatoes remark, they'd be having steak.

Ben went outside to the grill. He returned with a pile of grilled chicken and slices of sweet potato. They sat down at the table, and everyone ate first. Talk would come later. If you didn't eat when you had the chance, you might miss out if the alarm bells went off. After a few hurried bites, the conversation picked up. The chief brought up the woman. "Well, it's interesting that the woman you found didn't die from a mountain bike crash. The sheriff is saying it was murder. That wasn't quite what I expected. Although later, after I found out who she was, I have to say, I'm not surprised."

"She was the crazy woman we had to ban from the fire station during the Angora fire in 2007," Ben chimed in. "She ran into the local lumber store and started protesting that the fire department wasn't doing anything to stop the fire and that they needed to do their job. The owners asked her to leave. People yelled at her to get out. She refused, so they had to call the police to escort her out the door. She was hysterical."

"Afterward, she started showing up at the fire station and harassing our office staff, calling them names, and demanding that they do something," Steve added. "They felt threatened and had to call the police to have her removed. They did a 5150 involuntary psych commitment. We never heard from her again after that, but she was apparently still in the area. I hope she got some help during her commitment."

Maya recounted her brief experience of staying next to her house. "I heard from some of her neighbors that she might have killed a neighbor's dog. If my firefighter friend, Georgia, had known that, she never would have bought the house next door. She loves dogs and anyone that harms a dog is the worst kind of human in both our minds.

"I am glad I never met her. It just makes me shudder to think that my dogs were not safe around her. She was probably the one that called the animal control on them right after I arrived."

"I don't think anyone is going to miss her. I can't fathom living next to such a terrible neighbor," Chief Santizo said.

"This dinner is amazing," Maya commented. "When I smelled this delicious chicken, I realized how hungry I was. Thanks for inviting me!"

Todd leaned in and asked, "So, what's it like being a paramedic in Seattle?"

Maya thought about it. "Well," she said. "I work south of Seattle, so it's a little different. I can't compare it to anywhere else, since it is the only place I've worked as a paramedic. It has been amazing. I work in an area that has a very diverse population. Our response area covers rural and urban areas. I've responded to a gunshot on the street and then turned around and responded to a guy who was thrown off his horse out in his pasture. In more remote areas, we use helicopters to transport trauma patients to the major trauma center in Seattle. We've landed helicopters on our local highways to pick up patients and fly them out."

"So I've heard that you can do field crics. Is that true?" Todd asked.

"Yes, we do. So far, I've done three in my career. I'll tell you they are my least favorite procedure. If you're in that deep, it usually means you have a pretty sick patient. I had a young man shoot himself in the mouth with a 22-gauge shotgun. It was enough to do some damage but not kill him. We also ran into a problem when we went to put a breathing tube down his throat. His airway was already deformed from a prior suicide attempt with a gun. We couldn't get the tube down his trachea, so we ended up having to make an incision in his neck to do a cric. That wasn't easy because his airway was already deformed. I really wanted to give him some advice. If he was going to do this a third time, he might want to consider a larger caliber gun. All he did was make more of a mess of his life."

Maya shook her head.

"I don't really like being in the position of having to do that kind of last-ditch procedure, but when you need it to save a life, you really need it!"

Todd leaned forward and asked, "So, what is the worst call you've ever been on since you started working as a paramedic?"

She dreaded that question. Everyone always asked that. He was so new and was still trying to get some experience. To him, she thought, I probably seem like an old, seasoned veteran who has seen it all. She paused before answering.

"Todd, I've seen a lot. However," she paused again, "I'd have to say that my last call was the worst call I've ever been on."

She hadn't intended to talk about it, but somehow, at that moment, it all came out. She recounted it very matter-of-factly but also stressed that it had really spun her out, and that's how she found herself in Tahoe taking a breather. "It must be what it feels like, somewhat, to be a field medic in the army in a wartime situation. We were literally pinned down and unable to leave the scene with the police officer dying right before our eyes." She went silent.

"Wow, you were on that call?" the chief said. "We all read about it and heard about it on the news. I'm all for gun rights but targeting police officers and EMS personnel. That doesn't make any sense."

"What makes sense anymore?" she said. "I thought, at first, it was a gang execution. We've had a police officer executed by a well-known member of a gang in that same area. Initially, we thought it was one gunman who had taken down the officer. Our understanding was the shooter had fled the scene, and we were just coming in to treat the officer. Then it all went sideways. There was gunfire from two directions. No clear idea of who was doing the shooting. No way to exit without exposing our firefighters. A medic unit is not good enough cover for automatic weapons. Finally, we took advantage of a lull and got ourselves out of there. Barely!"

She suddenly went silent and felt very uncomfortable. It felt like she may have said too much. She had no idea how on edge she was until that moment. Maybe it was the dog killer who had been right next door to her. She didn't know.

"Hey, guys. I'm sorry to dump that on you. I've been a bit on edge after the shooting at work and then finding that dead woman. My stress level has been pretty off the charts." She looked around the table with a grim smile.

"Hey, we've all been there at one time or another," the chief said. "This job is one of the best in the world, but there is the other side, which is the incredible stress, the horrible things we see and experience. Give yourself some credit. You and your team took care of the officer, kept your heads down, and it sounds like you strategically planned your escape so that you could give everyone the best chance of survival. Sounds like a solid performance.

"Chief, thanks for being supportive. It's so great to see more of us really talking about the realities of the job and the impact that it has on us. When I started, that wasn't the case."

Well, you know, us California firefighters are sensitive." He winked, and they all laughed.

"Hey, it's time to lighten things up with dessert," said Ben.

Tyler walked over to the kitchen and grabbed bowls and spoons.

Maya jumped up and retrieved her ice cream from the freezer and the cake from the counter.

"I hope you guys like chocolate because I bought Cherry Chocolate Moose Tracks and chocolate cake.

11

PADDLEBOARDING ON LAKE TAHOE

SHE FELT lighthearted after spending time with the local firefighters and enjoying a firehouse dinner. Even though it was a little unnerving to have shared so much about her experience, she felt better. The world didn't end. She didn't break down and cry again. Maybe that was a good sign.

Today she'd leave her dogs at home and spend some time alone on the lake or alone with hundreds of other tourists. She hoped that leaving at 8 a.m. she would beat the crowds and have a calm lake. The weather was supposed to be in the eighties. She was looking forward to a perfect day on the lake.

Since it was early, she could pull right into the parking area next to Baldwin Beach. She pulled out her inflatable paddleboard and walked across the golden sand to the water's edge. When she was traveling without set plans, she liked to bring the inflatable paddleboard. It gave her the freedom to come to a developed park like Baldwin, or she could hike to a mountain lake or run a class II section of river. It expanded her adventure options.

She rolled out the paddleboard and inflated it. Another woman pulled up with a paddleboard atop a small hybrid car. The length of the board dwarfed the compact car. She recognized the woman. It was Kathy that she had met the other day. Maya turned back to blowing up her board. She felt something touch her ankle and turned to find a small tan mop of a dog inquisitively sniffing her ankle. Kathy immediately yelled toward her. "Don't pet him, he bites. People make him nervous." Maya quietly ignored the dog. Hopefully, by not moving, she wouldn't alarm the ankle biter, and it would just move on.

"I'm sorry. I didn't know he had hopped out behind me." Kathy walked over and scooped up her moving mop. She took him back to her car. "He's a rescue and is afraid of people."

As Maya watched as Kathy unstrapped her board and attempted to lift it off the top. It was obvious she was struggling with the awkward length of the board. Maya walked over and offered to help her.

Kathy appreciated the help. "I usually paddleboard with one of my friends. Today, I'm on my own."

"Is your friend still visiting? Asked Maya.

A fleeting look of discomfort flashed across Kathy's face. "No, he left right after you met him. He had to get back to the city."

"Oh, too bad. He's missing out. Have you paddleboarded here before?" Maya asked.

"Yes, a few times, but like I said, I usually go with a friend."

They carried Kathy's board over near hers.

"From here you can paddle all the way out to Emerald Bay. It's definitely a workout, but so beautiful."

"I've never been here before. I'm just up for exploring the lake. This looked like a good place to start."

"Well, I'm not the best paddleboarder, but I know the area. Would you like to join me? I'm planning on paddling to Fannette Island in Emerald Bay. The round trip is about seven miles."

"Sure, that would be great," Maya said.

Looking at her, she doubted that she was a speed demon. She seemed like the kind of person who would stop and enjoy the views.

"I take my little doggy with me. He loves the water. He'll just sit on my paddleboard the whole time.

"Do you live here, in Tahoe, full time?"

"No, I'm still working and live outside of Santa Rosa. I run the philanthropy program for a tech company. I mostly work remotely. I come up here and stay whenever I get the chance. Lately, I've spent more time up here because I had to evacuate because of another wildfire. Luckily, this is the one place that isn't inundated with smoke."

"Is your house threatened?"

"No, not yet. The fire is a few miles away, but they evacuated everyone because these fires can expand so quickly."

"That's good!"

"True," said Kathy. She retrieved her mop of a dog from her car. "This is Buddy, because he's my buddy."

I wonder if she is married. Maya thought. From just a general observation, Kathy seemed like one of those single women who have a dog for a companion.

They pushed off on to the water. Maya followed behind Kathy and her Buddy. Buddy sat just in front of Kathy's feet after she stood up. He looked pretty at ease as he looked out at their route like a motley bow sprite. His light tan hair was a mix of wiry tufts and coiled curls. He was definitely a mutt, a rescue mutt who bites. Maya felt like Kathy had taken on quite a project with her little dog. Some people were just that way. They could accept edgy animals or people in their life. Their sense of self came from rescuing and supporting those in need.

Maya realized she was being judgmental and knew it was in her nature to try and read people. In her job as a paramedic, she learned more about a person from their environment, how they lived, and their surroundings than she did from what they said. Often, she saw them, as she put it 'in their underwear'. It is hard for someone to put on a facade when they are critically ill or injured. However, on the other extreme were the system abusers, people who called seeking narcotics or attention. Their motives were for reasons other than a genuine emergency. She had to be able to read a con when she saw it. Usually, something in their demeanor gave them away. She'd only been fooled a few times.

Kathy kept a nice, leisurely pace. Maya mindlessly followed. Following freed her up to enjoy the journey. Some beautiful homes lined the shoreline, with docks reaching out into the water.

They made their way along the point of land, between Baldwin Beach and Emerald Bay, that was part of Eagle Falls Campground. Kathy kept her updated on where they were. When they reached Eagle Point at the entrance to Emerald Bay, they pulled over to some exposed rocks and took a quick break.

Maya sat down on her paddleboard and held onto the rock as the water gently swayed in and out against the rocky beach. Kathy stroked Buddy's head as he lay down on the board. She then opened her dry bag and pulled out some treats.

"Lucky dog!" Maya exclaimed.

"He really is," Kathy said. "I've had him for five years. Before that, someone had locked him in a cage most of his life.

At first, every time I'd reach down to pet him, he would flinch like he was waiting for me to hit him. I just can't imagine what he must have gone through. Anyway, he has a better life now. Do you take your dogs paddleboarding with you?"

"Yes, but they're both much bigger than Buddy, so I usually only take one with me. Mostly the smaller female, but today I took some time for myself."

"Oh, I hope I didn't spoil your alone time."

"No, it's actually very nice to have company and a tour guide at that. I just wanted to shed some responsibility. I've been going out with them a lot lately. It's good for them to have a day off from me too," she joked.

"This is such a beautiful route. I love these giant rocks. They are like small islands surrounded by this incredible blue water. And it's so clear. I can see below the surface to the bottom."

They sat back on their boards and looked out to the east. The sky was clear blue and cloudless. The sun had risen and with it the summer heat. Just a gentle breeze created enough movement to cool them off while they sat there.

"Are you ready to go?" Kathy said.

"Absolutely."

They pushed off from the rock and paddled, standing on their knees until they were clear of the rocks. Then they stood back up. Buddy sat back up at Kathy's feet.

Within minutes, they were turning into Emerald Bay. The narrower entrance opened into the larger bay. The two of them hugged the left shoreline to give a wide berth to the few motor-boats that were making their way into the bay. The wakes that caught up with Maya and Kathy were mild. Maya had been paddleboarding long enough to know how to steady herself as the gentle rollers passed under her board. Kathy did the same. Maya noted Kathy looked comfortable on her board.

Although they had entered the bay, Fannette Island was closer to the other end of the bay. It was almost as far to the island as it was from Baldwin Beach to Eagle Point. She was going to feel it in her arms tomorrow.

Kathy called back as they were paddling near the shoreline. "There is a trail that goes around Emerald Bay, the Rubicon Trail."

Maya peered into the forest along the shoreline to see if she could detect the trail. She could only see the forest of pines and occasional rock outcroppings. There were so many places to explore. She could feel her mind starting to unwind. She knew she was feeling better when her sense of adventure overpowered the heavy thoughts that lingered from her job... or finding a dead body.

They landed on Fannette Island, also known as Tea Island. They tied their paddleboards up along the south side of the island below a small rocky trail. Maya held the boards while Kathy made her way up on a rock. Then she reached back down and scooped up Buddy. They grabbed their dry bags and headed up the short trail to the island's 'Tea House'.

Kathy gave her a little history about the island. "The Tea House used to be a privately owned retreat for a woman named Mrs. Knight. She enjoyed drinking tea while enjoying a three-hundred-and-sixty-degree view of Emerald Bay."

For now, they had the place to themselves. She could imagine, just for a moment, that it was their private retreat. They sat down in the stone framed window that looked through to Emerald Bay and beyond to the main lake. Maya didn't have tea, but she had some pure Tahoe water and a peanut butter and jelly sandwich to enjoy.

Kathy pulled out a Tupperware with a green salad and some string cheese. She then reached back in and pulled out a bag of hard crunchy dog treats for Buddy. He was given his food and then she reached in again and pulled out a hydro flask. She pulled out a cup. "Do you want some tea? It isn't hot, as I imagine Mrs. Knight's tea was, but it is still tea to drink at the teahouse."

Maya laughed. "Certainly, I can't pass up the opportunity to drink tea in a Teahouse. Can you imagine spending evenings out here and having the place all to yourself because you own it?"

"Yes, but that is a bit above my bank account. I love my quiet mountain house. I've owned my little house for five years. It's so peaceful. Buddy and I love spending time there."

Maya thought this might be a good time to push for more information on Kathy's relationship with the infamous Karen. "Kathy, did you know the woman that lived in the house across from you, the one who recently died?"

Kathy paused. "Yes, Karen was a good friend of mine. I wasn't going to talk about it because, well, I didn't want to ruin a beautiful day. I can't believe she is gone. She and Don were so nice. They take care of my house for me when I'm gone. Without them, I don't know how I could take care of my place when I'm not there."

Maybe that's the difference, Maya thought. Kathy doesn't actually live there permanently, so she depends on them to take care of her place.

"Did you know her before you moved there?"

Kathy quickly replied, "No, I met them after I moved in. I was so fortunate to have found such great neighbors and friends."

Maya was surprised. All she had heard until now was what a horrible woman Karen was. Now, here was someone who considered her a friend, or at least, a useful neighbor.

"How is her husband doing?"

"I can only imagine what Don is going through. They were

together for years. They lived in Berkeley until last year when they retired. She was a real estate agent and property manager there. Don helped her manage the properties. Now they split their time between here and Hawaii. They had everything planned for their retirement. They were so excited to finally cut their ties with the Bay Area and split their time between Tahoe and Hawaii. Now, sadly, everything has changed."

She added, "He's waiting for them to release her body from the medical examiner. I guess she didn't want a funeral, just a cremation and to have her ashes spread in Lake Tahoe. She loved the quiet mountain life here. At least she died doing what she loved. She loved to mountain bike. I guess she crashed her mountain bike, and someone found her."

"Oh." Maya didn't comment further. No need to bring up the fact that she was the one who found her. Better to be a fly on the wall and learn more about Karen. The more she learned, the more she disliked her. Yet here was a different perspective. I guess maybe she wasn't so mean and controlling with everyone she interacted with.

"What was Karen like? I only ask that because, well, it's a shock to find you are vacationing next to someone who has just died. I didn't see her at all after I arrived. At least, I don't think I did."

Kathy had a fleeting look of suspicion, but then it quickly transitioned into a look of thoughtfulness. "Karen was an intense woman. She and Don were avid mountain bikers and paddleboarders. She was a perfectionist. If you haven't noticed, their house and yard are immaculate. She kept her grass perfectly mowed and her flowers carefully tended to. Honestly, I felt that mowing your lawn twice a week was a little over the top. Personally, I like native wildflowers and grasses in my yard. It's better for the environment.

"We were great friends. I knew she could be difficult for

some people to deal with, but the only issue I had with her is she kept turning my sprinklers on to water my lawn after the Angora fire. She was terrified of fire and wanted everyone to have a green lawn. The water utility showed up and gave me a citation for watering on the wrong day. I simply told her that if she did it again, she would have to pay the fine. After that, she stopped.

"We shared a lot of the same interests, like gardening and hiking. I miss her immensely, even though I only saw them in the summer here in Tahoe. In the winter, they were in Hawaii, and I hardly ever come to Tahoe in the winter.

"I'm sure you will miss her. I know it's hard losing someone close to you. As you said, at least she died doing something she loved. We should all be so lucky." Maya watched as Kathy gave Buddy the last of her string cheese as a treat. He daintily took it from her fingers. Maya thought about all the ways she had seen people die. The lucky ones went quick in their sleep or simply collapsed and died. The unlucky ones, well, there were so many horrible ways to die that she didn't want to think about it.

"Thank you for being so thoughtful," Kathy said. "Yes, she was lucky, I guess. She was a healthy woman. She would have probably lived to be a hundred and five if she hadn't had the accident."

A hundred and five, Maya thought. *I bet there were many people who would have dreaded that idea!*

"Well, should we head back? I don't know about you, but this will have been a big day on the water for me," said Kathy.

"Yes, I'll be tired too."

They wrapped up lunch and hiked back to the paddle-boards. Kathy carried Buddy back onto the board. They launched just as a motorboat full of teenagers motored up. The energy changed as the group of six jumped into the water and swam from the boat onto the island. The three boys were obviously showing off for the young girls. It was just a fun day on the water of Lake Tahoe for them.

I remember when life was so playful and easy, Maya thought. Laughter was harder to find in the last couple of weeks.

THEIR RETURN WAS ROUGHER. It was later and now the chop from the afternoon wind and boats on the water made standing a little more challenging. Maya lost her footing twice and went for a swim. The sudden plunge into the lake was a welcome feeling as the cool blue water enveloped her and cooled her sunbaked body. The second time she fell off the board, she took the opportunity to float on her back, looking up at the blue sky, and listening to the muffled sounds of waves and distant motors bounce off her ears as the water swirled around her partially submerged face. Then she popped back up on the board. Kathy looked back at her. Then continued. She and Buddy stood solidly on their board.

A little head wind had kicked up, which added to the work of paddling back to Baldwin Beach. Maya tended to dig in at times like these. She'd put her head down and just press on. It was that tenacity that had gotten her noticed when she applied for her paramedic job. Faced with post-college graduation, she had been uncertain about what career she wanted to pursue. She had a graphic arts degree but had worked as a volunteer firefighter while in college. Jobs in graphic design didn't seem too promising. Her volunteer job was exciting and felt more important. She was doing something to make the world a better place.

After graduation, she moved up to Seattle and started working for a private ambulance company as an Emergency Medical Technician. There she saw the underbelly of the world and rode that edge of adrenaline that comes with having to make life and death decisions on the fly. After a year, she realized she wanted to be a paramedic. She wanted to test herself against the world in which life and death are merely a tipping point along an edge that in a moment can shift one way or the other. She wanted to know, at the end of the day, that she had done something that mattered. Saving a life or the simple gesture of comforting someone on the worst day of his or her life mattered!

When she tested for her current paramedic position, she had to do a practical skills test that comprised overseeing a mock medical emergency. They gave the scenario to her as she walked through a door. She had to react and make decisions based on the information they gave her. She did her best.

Afterward, she heard that the seasoned veteran medic testing her said that she was the only one that day who got it right. Another said that when they saw her testing, her ability to focus purely on what she was doing impressed them.

She aced the physical testing and passed the written exam. She was accepted into one of the most prestigious medic programs in the world. Her success convinced her she'd found her calling. Now, years later, she was digging her paddle into the lake current with her head down, running from post-traumatic stress and wondering if she had made the right decision.

Kathy was alongside her now, chatting to her. Maya was deep in thought. "I'm sorry, Kathy. Can you repeat that?"

"I'm planning on hiking in a couple of days. Would you like to join me?"

Maya thought about it. "I'd love to, but I plan on going for a mountain bike ride tomorrow, and I may be ready for a break after today and tomorrow."

"I imagine so", said Kathy. They finished out the last mile in silence. Rolling up on shore, they found the parking lot full and the beach filled with sunbathers. Getting past them was a little tricky. Maya stayed with the boards while Kathy took Buddy to her car. Then they both carried an end of each board to their cars, one at a time, weaving around towels, beach umbrellas, flip-flops, and people.

After loading their paddleboards, Kathy said, "Well, I hope I see you again soon."

"See ya, neighbor."

Maya thought about the day. Having someone who knew the lake and could take her on a tour of Emerald Bay was a welcome addition to the day's adventure. She thought about Kathy's friendship with Karen. At least some people had liked Karen. She wondered what it took to be on Karen's friend list versus enemy list. She guessed she'd never know, now that Karen was dead.

Maya turned into the cul-de-sac. She saw Don, Karen's husband, in his driveway. He was a tall, imposing man with wide shoulders and long, fit legs. She noticed he still had a full head of hair, although it was grey now. He was probably a blond in his early years. He had a small soul patch on his chin. An old guy with a soul patch, so California, she thought to herself. She imagined he might have been a California surfer dude. She could tell from his build and how fit he was that he was a good-looking man in his day. Maybe even a strong, violent one when matched with the stories the other old men had talked about. Now he just looked like a defeated and tired old man in his suburban mountain yard.

His shoulders were bent forward as he was sweeping his driveway with a push broom. Head down, he moved slowly, pushing debris off to a corner. He was surely in shock, slow and automated like his body was moving, but his mind was somewhere else. Forward, back, forward, back. She felt like she should say something about his loss but decided against it. She didn't even know him other than what others had told her. Hopefully, he didn't know that she'd found his wife. Better just to leave him to his friends and family. It was just... at that moment, he seemed so alone.

He looked up at her, and for a moment, it seemed as if he recognized her. Maybe he had seen her coming and going the past few days. It seemed as if the comings and goings were the major highlight of their life in this small cul-de-sac. Given their history with neighbors and complaining, she was sure not much went unnoticed by them.

She pulled into the garage. Worn out from a long day on the water. However, she would have to appease her dogs by taking them out for a short walk in the meadow.

She walked up the stairs to the apartment. There, taped to the door, was a written notice from El Dorado County Animal Control. On it was a warning for a second notice of nuisance barking. 'What the hell?' she murmured to herself. 'I thought the person who harassed the neighbors was dead.' She looked over to where her husband was sweeping... and he was gone. Well, this would continue to make her stay difficult. She took stock of the complaint, leveled it with what she knew about her dogs and realized that there was no way they were 'nuisance barking' unless someone was at the door or in the yard egging them on.

A deep feeling of defeat settled over her. Why were some people so awful? It just seemed that some people were so petty. Couldn't people just mind their own lives and leave others alone? Why did they seem driven to share their unhappiness with those around them?

She swept her negative thoughts away knowing that she was only here for a short time. The most that animal control might do is fine her. In the meantime, she'd make sure she didn't leave her dogs unattended in the yard and make sure there wasn't any suspicious activity or additions to the dog yard. Even though Karen was dead, maybe her husband was equally part of their sinister plot to police the neighborhood. Didn't Kathy say they were in property management in the Bay Area? Had they been the self-appointed HOA supervisors of the neighborhood?

12

THE FAMILY

MAYA LEASHED the dogs for the walk and headed out, locking the door behind her. As she left the driveway, Don pulled out in his truck, waved. Well, that was odd, she thought. He probably just called the authorities on her dogs, and now he was waving.

She noticed Kathy wasn't back yet as she passed by her house. It was a neat, small brown rambler with a few large pine trees in the front yard. Nothing really personal distinguished it from any other home. It was very tidy and, as Kathy said, the yard was a mix of native grasses and wildflowers.

Once they were in the meadow, Maya let the dogs off leash. They bounded in different directions. Kali took off, running at top speed, blowing off some pent-up energy. Rio walked from spot to spot, inspecting the scents. Many had been there before him, and he was identifying each one of them: Coyote, Collie, Husky, Beagle.

She led the way toward the river spot where she could let Rio swim after sticks. The evening was warm. The light softened around the edges as the sun made its way down towards the southern edge of Mount Tallac. This was Maya's favorite time of day when the day was almost over and the softer light highlighted the landscapes, casting them in gold.

Languid currents of the Upper Truckee River swirled beside willows and rocks. The granite rock glowed golden orange just under the river's surface. It was just before nightfall, so the forest critters were waking up for the night's forage. If she was lucky, she might catch an osprey circling overhead or a coyote along the far river's edge.

At the river, Rio waited for her to get her act together and launch some sticks for him to retrieve. After she felt they were sufficiently appeased, they made their way back. On the main trail, she saw two young men and two small children.

"Hi," she said.

"Hi back," said the small boy.

"Back at you, hi," she replied.

They all laughed. The taller man, who wore a more serious look on his face, smiled, and the other man warmed right up. "You must be Maya. Georgia said you were coming to stay. We live in the house on the corner of the cul-de-sac. If we hadn't been so busy with the kids, we'd have already been over to say hi way before now. However, now that we have you in our sights, my name is Deni. This big hunk here is Mark. These are our kids, Alex and Olivia."

"We are planning on making dinner. We were just going back to get it started. Would you join us? Isn't it a beautiful night?" Deni asked.

The dogs had discovered the two kids and Rio was planting big wet nose kisses on Alex's face. Kali pushed her nose into Olivia's hand, demanding pets. Maya laughed. "Sure, why not. I'd love to join you."

"Good, then it's settled. Dinner is at seven-thirty."

They walked back together along the trail.

Deni engaged Maya in conversations. "Mark is an emergency department physician at Barton Hospital, and I am a stay-at-home dad, slash, professional wedding photographer. Alex is four and Olivia is six.

"You probably didn't meet the crazy lady next door to you." Asked Mark.

"No, I didn't," Maya said.

Lucky you! She died in a mountain biking accident. Did you know that?"

"Yes."? Maya said and stopped there. *News travels fast*, thought Maya.

From the minute we moved in, she started complaining about the kids making noise. She'd yell at them and then march over to the door to let us know how unhappy she was that her 'quiet Tahoe life' was being ruined by our poorly controlled children, who were just being normal, playful kids. We nicknamed her Mrs. Kravitz. You know, the nosey neighbor from the old series, Bewitched?"

"No, I'm not familiar with that show, but nosey sounded about right. I've heard a lot about her from other neighbors since I arrived."

It's horrible to say this," Mark whispered, so the kids wouldn't hear, "Now that she's dead, maybe we can relax and enjoy living in our house!"

"Don, her husband, will hopefully be more reasonable without her around. He always backed her up, but if you got him alone, he seemed like a nice guy. Too bad he was married to that bitch. Whoops, sorry, didn't mean to say that in front of the kids. Well, enough about that." Deni shrugged.

As they came to the main street, Maya put her dogs back on leash. They continued past Mark and Deni's house. She said she'd be back at seven-thirty and thanked them for the invite. The kids waved as they disappeared into their house.

She couldn't imagine having children and living next to someone like Karen. Sometimes that oath she took as a medic meant she had to save even the bad people. That was the job. She had treated a known child molester for chest pains, resuscitated bad guys who were killing each other in the streets, and cared for criminals shot by police officers.

Thinking about the horrible people she'd saved set her off. Inside the apartment, she was overwhelmed by the sound of gunfire. She found herself outside the medic unit with nowhere to duck. Panic rose inside of her. The sweet metallic smell of blood overwhelmed her as tension coursed through body.

Quickly she peeled off her clothes and jumped into the shower. She cranked up the hot water and felt the water pelt against her head and shoulders and then slide down her back and chest, the heat almost searing her skin. She closed her eyes and let the sensation of the water bring her back to the present. She returned to the safety of the present as she focused on washing her hair and body.

SHE FED the dogs and then headed across the cul-de-sac to Mark and Deni's house. When she passed by Don and Karen's house, it was quiet and dark inside. As she walked up the driveway to Mark and Deni's, she saw an assortment of wildflowers. Bright red Indian paintbrush, purple lupine, small white flax ground cover. They even had a small cluster of mariposa lilies that grew in the meadow across the street. All along the base of the house were flowers in various stages: purple coneflowers, Shasta daisies, and pink cosmos.

Next to the door was a sign that said, 'A House is not a Home without Paw Prints'.

The door flew open, and there was Alex's elfish face. "Hi, Maya!" he exclaimed. Behind him, Deni was coming to the door. He reached out and gave her a big, unexpected hug. "Come on in, you," he said.

Maya was so surprised. His warm greeting relaxed her. She smiled back and immediately felt welcome inside their home. Alex was tugging on her shorts. "Maya, Maya, would you like to see my new truck?" He held up a bright red fire truck.

"Yes," said Maya. "That's a ladder truck. Do you know what they do?"

"Yes," he said. "They put out fires!"

"Yes, they do. The ladder is to help them put out fires on very tall buildings, like the ones in big cities."

"Oh, like where we used to live," he said and put the truck down on the floor and zoomed it around. "Zoom, zoom,"

Deni waved her into the kitchen. "Mark, is outside cooking us up some amazing burgers.

Deni was cutting up some tomatoes and onion. Olivia was sitting at the kitchen table, coloring what looked like a bear.

"Hey Deni, I had another notice from animal control when I came home tonight. Did my dogs bark while I was gone?"

"Oh no," Deni said. "We didn't hear your dogs at all. It was probably Don. Oh well, there goes my theory that now that Karen is dead, we'll have some peace! Karen and Don were always yelling at us when we had our dog, Dante. He would bark a couple of times to be let back in the house and next thing I knew; we'd hear one of them yelling at the dog to shut up."

"I saw your sweet sign outside. Where is Dante now?"

Deni lowered his voice. "He died a couple of months ago. One evening, he started acting strange. Then he vomited up some blood, so we took him to the emergency vet in Carson. They think he must have had a tumor that erupted in his stomach. We had to put him down. So sad, he was only seven, but he was a big mastiff. They don't live very long, anyway. We just haven't had the desire to get another dog. It was hard enough just dealing with Karen and Don going after the kids. Add the dog in the mix, and we seemed under constant attack by them. Isn't it crazy how the real disruption in the neighborhood is them, but somehow in their mind it is everyone else. Maybe now that she is dead, he'll sell the house and leave! We can only hope!"

She replied, "Sometimes the only way people can deal with their feeling of powerlessness is to complain and try to make other people as unhappy as they are. I hope, for your sake, that he moves as well!"

She thought about mentioning what she had heard from the dog owners down at the river. She shuddered to think that their family dog might have been a victim of poisoning too.

Olivia, hearing "dog," piped up, "I want a puppy!"

"Yes Liv, we'll get one someday," Deni replied. "It's time to put your coloring away. We need to set the table for dinner. Maya, do you want to assist Olivia with setting the table?" He winked at Maya and directed her to the cupboards to the right of the sink.

Maya was comfortable here. They made her feel like she had always been a friend and she liked that. There wasn't any awkwardness that she sometimes felt when she met new people. They felt almost like family.

Alex was the star of the family. He was curious, asking, "Where are your doggies?"

"They are sleeping at home. You wore them out earlier." She smiled. "They love you guys. I could tell. They don't immediately come up and give big slobbery kisses to just anyone."

Alex chuckled. "Yew, my face is covered in dog drool. I love Rio!"

After they finished up eating, Deni and Maya went and sat in the living room. A large screen T.V. adorned one wall. The couch was a 'man cave' couch. She sank into its big and incredibly comfortable cushions.

Deni filled her in on a little more history of how they ended up in Tahoe. Mark was a competition snowboarder when he was young. He blew out his knee just as he almost qualified for the Nationals. Faced with a serious injury, he redirected efforts to medical school instead. He was accepted at the UCFS Medical School in San Francisco, where he studied to become an emergency department physician. There he met Deni, who was a jazz dancer and freelance photographer. They fell in love and, being in California; they were able to get married. After, they moved to Los Angeles, where Mark worked as a physician in the emergency department at L.A. County Hospital and Deni was able to pursue his photography career and do dance.

"When we decided to adopt children, we realized we wanted to leave L.A. for a better place to raise kids near the great outdoors. Mark had lived in Tahoe when he was training for the Nationals. It seemed like a great place to return to with their young family. He applied for the job as a physician at Barton and here we are." Deni explained.

"The kids love it here. Two winters ago, we enrolled them in snowboard school. In the summer, they are learning to paddleboard, swim, and taking youth art classes. They go to the local elementary.

"We've started walking them to school and back. I'm trying to get rid of the weight that I put on. Raising them when they are super little is so exhausting. I'm just getting back to feeling like I have enough energy to work out now that they are both in school. It's crazy how much time and energy they take from you. It is worth it, though. We have never been happier."

Maya broached the subject with care. "So, how is it living in Tahoe as a gay couple? I'm sure L.A. is easy, but how is this small town?"

"Honestly? It's been great. Mark, working at Barton and being involved in the community, has really introduced us to the best in this community. We have gay and straight friends. We really feel accepted. Of course, we were nervous about what we would find. But Tahoe is a tourist community with lots of different people coming to work and visit here. So it has been everything we had hoped it would be. I mean, it isn't as exciting as L.A., but we wanted a slower lifestyle with room to raise children."

I can see that. So far, people here are friendly."

Deni then leaned in. "We love everything about this community except our neighbors. Make that one neighbor now. Everyone we have met has been welcoming and friendly, except for Karen and Don. I started to tell you about them on our walk home, but there is more, much more. From the day we moved in, they started harassing us. We didn't know if it was because we were gay or whether they were like that with everyone. First, they called the police because we parked our travel trailer on the street while we were getting moved in. The police showed up. That is how I met our other neighbor, Marla. We explained the situation. I told the officer we were moving in and had it parked there temporarily. Marla informed him that our new neighbor was always calling the police on everyone. We had no idea that we were moving next to such a nasty couple. The police officer told us we were parked legally. So we left it there. Four days later, she called the police again. When the police informed her it was legal for us to park it there, she screamed at them to just have it towed. After that, they apparently told her if she continued to call, they would cite her for false police reporting. It seems she called it in as an abandoned vehicle." He rolled his eyes.

"That is insane!" Maya said. "I have heard nothing but terrible things about her from you and others. I just keep thinking about how I gave her mouth-to-mouth…" she trailed off and paused.

Deni suddenly got a look of understanding. "Were you the one who found her? Oh my god. What happened?"

"As much as I'd like to tell you, I can't. It's an ongoing police investigation. Sorry."

"Police investigation? I thought she just crashed her mountain bike. How interesting. I hope at some point you can tell me more. Just know that very few, if anyone, will miss her. After she couldn't get our trailer towed, she'd wait until we were gone and then call animal control and tell them our dog was barking uncontrollably. We finally had to put cameras up that recorded video with audio, so we had a record. Imagine having to put cameras up to protect yourself from a neighbor? It is insane." His face turned dark. "We stopped letting the kids play in the cul-de-sac because when they did, they yelled at them. We became afraid for their safety.

"The last straw for us was a year ago. We had signed up to be foster parents. As you probably guessed, Olivia and Alex are not our children by birth. We are also foster parents. We got a call out of the blue asking us if we could foster a newborn baby. They told us the mother had mental health issues and had fled the hospital after she had the baby. While they were trying to locate her, they needed someone to foster the baby immediately. How could we say no? They brought the baby over that afternoon. So, we went from a family with two kids to a family of three. The little boy was so beautiful. He was underweight and wouldn't eat. Our job was to get him to eat, hold him, and make him feel safe. He immediately improved. He started eating and putting on weight.

"They finally located the mom and had her admitted for a mental health hold. She was suicidal and had postpartum depression. Anyway, the Child Services caseworker would pick the baby up every day and take him to visit with mom in the afternoon. Then she would return him later in the day and we would take over.

"Everything was going great until one evening. We got a call from the caseworker. She said as she was leaving, this woman waved her down around the corner and started telling her what terrible parents we were and how they should take the baby away. Luckily, the caseworker knew us very well and told the lady, Karen, to mind her own business. We were horrified. She just went too far. She not only put the foster baby at risk, but the agency could have come in and taken all three kids until there was an investigation, and we were deemed safe.

"After that incident, we went to court and were awarded a restraining order. She and Don could no longer harass us and they were barred from our property. We had just had it. She really crossed a line!"

Maya was horrified. "What could drive someone to be so cruel?"

Matt, Alex, and Olivia came into the living room. "Dishes are done," said Mark. Olivia and Alex scooted onto the couch. Olivia sat on Deni's lap and Alex slid in between Deni and Maya.

"I want to play a game!" Alex said. "Maya, do you want to play Monopoly with us?"

"That is Monopoly Junior," Mark stated.

"I've never played Monopoly Junior before. I'd love to."

Maya spent the rest of the evening with them playing a hilarious game of Monopoly Junior with two enthusiastic kids and her new friends, Deni and Mark. She completely forgot about everything she came here to forget. For a few hours, she was immersed in something so simple as a fun game with this family. It made her want to rethink her decision to forgo children and a family. But then again, she had the benefit of enjoying their company without the responsibility of changing diapers, driving them to school, or living through their terrible twos. Maybe she'd just settle for being an aunt to her brother's kids or an adventure aunt to her friend's kids.

Finally, she said good night and headed back to the apartment.

13

THE RENTERS

AS MUCH AS she wanted to relax and focus on going on outdoor adventures, somehow, the specter of the dead woman kept interrupting her solitude and peace. As she was leaving with her dogs to go mountain biking the next morning, she encountered Brent's wife. The young blonde woman was heading to Lake Baron with her two young children. Rio and Kali immediately introduced themselves to the kids. The kids were not afraid at all. The woman introduced herself as Heidi. "Deni told me you had dinner with them last night. You're friends with Georgia?" she inquired. "We've seen your dogs over there. Rosie, our dog, has been very curious about the new neighbors."

"Yes," she replied. "Georgia and I are friends."

Heidi immediately brought up Karen. "So you are the one who found her?" she said innocently. "Deni told me, but he wouldn't give me any more details."

"Well, I can't comment either way, as it's an ongoing police investigation. So let's just leave it at that."

"Well, Deni said he told you we all hated her. She was

awful. My husband and I rented from them. We were so happy to find a good house in this area. Unfortunately, having them as landlords was a nightmare. She seemed visibly distressed. We are finally moving in a week.

She was beginning to feel like the neighborhood counselor. It seemed that everyone had some burden related to this woman that they wanted to share. She knew that her demeanor naturally drew people to her. They invariably knew that she was someone they could trust.

14

A CLEAR DESCENT

MAYA MADE a last minute decision to try a new trail from Spooner Summit. She picked the trail because it started at the top of Spooner Summit and descended for over fifteen miles to the Carson Valley in Nevada. She called the Tahoe Shuttle Company that morning to inquire about a mountain bike shuttle. Since it was a weekday, they were happy to pick her up from the bottom of the trail and shuttle her up to the top.

Now she was on her way to enjoy another amazing ride in Lake Tahoe and the neighboring Carson Valley. This is more like it, she thought. Out on the trail, she was free.

She left her car at a parking area surrounded by sagebrush. The van shuttle driver put her bike on the rack. Rio and Kali were allowed to go in the shuttle. She jumped in toward the back and had the dogs lay down at her feet. There were two other riders, both men, doing the shuttle. She introduced herself and her dogs.

One of the men replied, "I'm Geoff and this is Stefan." Stefan said hello. They were about her age and looked very fit.

Both were tall, very good looking and had the build of road cyclists. Maya asked where they were from.

"We are from Hamburg, Germany. Are you from here, in Tahoe?" Stefan asked.

Maya replied that she was from Seattle and just visiting too.

The driver introduced himself. "I'm Dave, I'll be your driver for the day. I overheard that you two are from Germany, and you're from Seattle. Welcome. It's true, people come here from all over the world to ride mountain bikes. You'll love this ride. The singletrack is fast and flowy, but don't get too comfortable. There are some good rock gardens and drops that sneak up on you. And the views are awesome! At the top you're in forest. As you descend, you'll exit into this desert landscape along that ridgeline up there." He pointed up at the open treeless hills above where they were parked."

"Who are the two furry adventurers?" Dave inquired.

Maya introduced Rio and Kali while making sure they stayed put. "They are my mountain bike buddies for the day. This will work them, for sure."

Dave pulled out with everyone onboard. It wasn't a long drive, shorter than the actual mountain bike ride. At the trailhead, Dave unloaded the bikes from the roof rack. Maya handed him a tip. She was thankful she was able to book the shuttle at such short notice.

The Germans had invited her to ride with them but she explained that they would probably lose her on the downhill. Her dogs were fast but the heat would slow them down.

They left her as she unleashed the dogs and put the leashes in her pack. "Run," she commanded. Then they were off. The first section was a short gradual climb up smooth singletrack lined with bright green aspens. The dogs, eager to shake off some energy, shot ahead, apparently trying to catch their new

German friends. After failing to find them, they settled back into their normal routine with Kali tracking ahead. Rio took up his position in the rear, near her back tire.

They crested the short climb as they transitioned into dense mountain forest. Light filtered through the tree limbs and a mountain breeze took the edge off the summer heat.

The trail hugged the edge along the ridge that twisted inward, then crossed onto another arm of the ridge, before passing through a shallow boulder garden. She breathed and focused on her line around the smaller rocks emerging from the ground. Some, she rode over, and others she effortlessly picked her way around. She'd been mountain biking for years. The bike was now just an extension of her body. A slight shift in weight to the right, and she missed a sharp-edged rock. A shift back to the left, and she found a clear path through larger boulders. She loved mountain biking. It was like running a river of dirt.

The rhythm along the fast-flowing singletrack captured her attention. As they descended, the trees became smaller and the vistas started to open up. The trail came around a corner below a giant boulder. She stopped and scrambled to the top of the rocks. Below her, the Carson Valley spread out beyond the forest.

Kali climbed up the rocks and sat next to her, perched on the knobby edge. Her Malinois was a climber. Maya had watched her scale ten-foot rock walls along a river gorge in the Pacific Northwest. Her nails were as hard as titanium and worked as claws when she climbed. She could descend just as easily. Rio sat below, guarding her bike and whining because he couldn't make the leap up the steep rock.

They continued. The smell of sage and dust was thick in the air. Out in the full sun, the heat rose from below and above.

Maya slowed the pace to let the dogs adjust to the temperature change.

On another rock outcrop, she stopped and enjoyed the unobstructed view. Now she could not only see across the valley but also the parking area where her SUV was parked. She wasn't in any hurry to end the ride, so the dogs found shade behind the rocks, and she sat out in the full sun just feeling it radiate into her muscles and her bones.

As she enjoyed her perch, another mountain biker slowed, then stopped where she was. Kali and Rio sprang up and stood between her and the new arrival. A man. She suddenly realized it was Don, the neighbor. She was surprised to see him. Hadn't his wife just died? She was starting to feel a bit unnerved. Rio and Kali must have felt her alarm because Kali let out a low growl and both stood their ground. Don immediately backed up and looked nervous himself. *As he should be*, Maya thought.

"Are you Don, the neighbor that lives next to Georgia in South Lake Tahoe?" she asked outright.

"Yes," he said. "How do you know me?"

That caught her a bit off guard. Obviously, she had driven by him on her way in and out. He had to have seen her. He had called the dogcatcher on the very dogs that were standing between her and him right now. At that point, she just decided to bait him. "Oh, I was visiting Deni and Mark the other day. You were out working in the yard. They told me your name. My friend Georgia lives on the other side of you, so your face and name stuck in my mind."

She saw something flash across his face, recognition that she had just lied to him. Then his face became neutral, and he turned on the charm. "Oh, yes Deni and Mark. What great guys! They've lived next to us for a couple of years. We've really enjoyed having them as neighbors. Georgia, too, but we hardly ever see her and her husband. How do you know them?"

Inside her, alarm bells were going off. He said *we've*, not I've. He is lying too, she thought to herself. From what Deni and Mark had told her, the couple had hated them. What was going on here? Was he following her? As her feelings of alarm rose, so did her sense of calm and purpose. Her mind was used to holding alarm and at the same time figuring out a course of action. She called the dogs back to her and had them sit, which they did but they didn't take their eyes off him for a minute. She felt safe. Unless he had a gun, she figured her dogs could take him out before he knew what had happened.

"Georgia and I work together," she replied. "We all know each other from working in the medical field." She lied. She figured that he wouldn't know that being an emergency department doctor in South Lake Tahoe wasn't a general connection for a firefighter and a paramedic from a completely different state and town. Then she threw out the bait to see if he'd cop to recognizing her. "I've been staying at Georgia's house the past couple of weeks, too. I was sorry to hear about your wife. Didn't she die mountain biking on a trail in South Lake Tahoe?"

His eyes grew dark for a minute. "Oh, I didn't know someone was staying at Georgia's house. I've been a little lost since she died." He looked downward and when he looked up she could see what looked like genuine grief.

"We were together for twenty years. I'm lost without her." Then he suddenly broke down and started to cry. Maya was so taken aback that she just sat there.

He got off his bike and collapsed into a sitting position just off the trail. This tall muscular man looked like a sad child with his broad shoulders sinking forward and his head bent to hide the tears that streamed down his face. Great heaving sobs erupted from his mouth.

Then he surprised her with a confession. "I'm so sorry," he said. "I called the dog pound on your dogs. I was so broken up

93

and I think I was just reacting to your dogs barking constantly as I was sitting there all alone in the house, without her. I didn't realize that you knew Georgia. I just thought you were another vacation renter. We hated those strangers coming into our cul-de-sac. I just wanted some peace and quiet. You know Karen and I moved to Tahoe after years in the Bay Area. Karen was looking forward to her quiet Tahoe mountain life."

She sat speechless. Here he was confessing to calling animal control and at the same time trying to make her feel guilty because, supposedly, her dogs were barking non-stop. She absolutely knew that was a lie. Her dogs didn't nuisance bark. She knew it for a fact. She decided to put on her caring face and consoled him.

"Don, it's okay. I know it's hard to lose someone who meant everything to you. Don't worry about the visit from animal control. I can understand you are not feeling like yourself right now." She said it with more feeling than she actually felt. With all she had learned about them, she had a sneaking suspicion that she was being played, for what, she didn't know.

She kept her distance. They made small talk while he collected himself. She didn't pry for more information. She didn't really want to know anything more about him, Karen, or this whole crazy mess. She decided that she was done. She was going to pack up and leave. She was simply not going to get the emotional break that she needed while stuck in a cul-de-sac with murder and malice hanging like a Seattle rainstorm overhead.

When he seemed like he was composed, she asked if he was okay. When he replied that he was, she made her escape. She offered an excuse. She was supposed to meet a friend in town and was already running late. She hoped that he understood and that he would be okay on his own.

He looked at her with sad, pathetic eyes. "Yes, I'll be okay.

I'm so sorry. I didn't know I was going to fall apart. Go ahead, I'll be fine on my own." A painful expression briefly crossed his face as he seemed to realize how alone he was.

With that, Maya grabbed her bike and hopped on. She and the dogs took off as fast as she could.

15

REVERBERATION

RIO AND KALI were fast asleep on their dog beds. Both were exhausted after their fifteen-mile trail run. Rio was quietly snoring. Kali's legs were still running in her sleep.

For dinner, she made herself a large salad topped with feta and wild smoked salmon. She added some peasant bread and a glass of white wine as the finishing touches. She'd settle into a couch coma in no time.

She sat down and turned on the television. Just as she was about to dig into the salad, her phone rang. The fork hung at her lips as if the alarm bells at work had just gone off. She saw it was her coworker, Jeff, calling. She immediately answered it. "Hello."

"Hey, Maya, it's Jeff. How are you doing?"

Maya thought about that for a moment. "Well, I'm doing better. I've been mountain biking and hiking down here in Tahoe with my dogs."

"Great. I wanted to check in and make sure you were doing okay. Sorry I didn't call you sooner, but I wanted to give you a little time before I called. I know that call hit you pretty hard. It's been tough for me, too."

"Thanks Jeff."

"The other reason I called is to give you an update on the specifics of what happened to us. They arrested six men in connection with the police officer's murder. It turns out we were being ambushed and the police officer was the bait.

"A few members of a right-wing militia group out of Eastern Washington decided it was time to start a war. The guys the officer pulled over along Pacific Highway were the ones that shot a black kid walking down the highway a few days before. They pulled over, shot the kid in the head, and drove off. Dave and Colin responded to that call. Initially, the police thought it was a gang shooting, but a camera near the scene showed two white men intercepting the kid at one in the morning. They executed him!"

"This is disturbing on so many levels! I've been making a point of trying not to think about that call or watching the news. I'm glad I'm hearing it from you. You said they were an organized group?"

"Excellent decision about checking out from the prime-time media circus this has created! The group released a manifesto outlining their reason for targets for execution. For the group, it wasn't enough to shoot black people. They see the emergency responders as enemies because they save black people or any people of any color. They used the officer as bait to lure in firefighters and other emergency personnel to teach them a lesson. Like somehow they believe we need to stop saving people they don't approve of. It is some pretty messed up grievances.

"We'll probably be going to court on this one," she replied. "If they plead 'not guilty,' there will probably be hours of depositions and testimony."

"Just how I wanted to spend my time off duty," Jeff said. They have made national and international headlines. Again, elected officials are calling for these right-wing fringe groups to be labeled as domestic terrorists. It is completely out of control and we're caught in the middle. Something has got to give. They can't just keep giving these guys a pass because they are supposedly 'true American patriots'. There isn't anything patriotic about gunning down your own countrymen!"

Maya's mind felt numb. She really didn't want to think about this right now. She needed time to process the experience, not relive it again and again. That's why she hadn't checked her Facebook account or turned on the news.

"People are just becoming unhinged," she said. "Everyone is just angry at anything they believe threatens their way of life."

Then she changed the subject. "You'll never guess what has happened while I've been down here..." She told him the story of finding the dead woman and then finding out more about her and realizing that she was a neighborhood terrorist. "Can you believe it? I tried to save a woman who harasses families and hates dogs! And that is putting it mildly."

"Wow, she sounds like she was a piece of work. You are a shit magnet even off duty!"

"You know it," she replied. "Anyway, I'm thinking about leaving Georgia's place in a couple of days."

Jeff agreed maybe it might be a good idea to find a mellower place to escape to.

"Jeff, thanks for checking in on me. We all have that one call with our name on it that just shakes our foundation. I'll be fine. I just need some time."

"We all have our hard times," Jeff replied. "It's good for me to talk about it too. If you feel like you aren't working through it or things get worse, think about giving our psychologist a call.

Schedule an appointment for when you get back. There is no shame in getting help, but you know that. You are the first to tell our people that. Just take your own advice."

"Jeff, I will. Thank you."

Maya hung up the phone, and instead of dealing with it, she drank herself to sleep with a bottle of Chardonnay.

16

SEEKING SAFETY

THE NEXT DAY she slept in until 11 a.m. She woke up with a terrible headache and chastised herself for drinking an entire bottle of wine the night before. She had slept through the night without nightmares, but the price she paid wasn't quite worth it.

She decided she'd take the day off and just lounge around the apartment and catch up on some rest. She didn't feel like venturing out anyway. It seemed like every time she did; she ran into another neighbor with another story about the dead woman. Now she had Don to deal with. She dreaded running into him.

She made some coffee and pulled out her laptop to search for an alternate place to stay while she was here. She loved the place and the fact that it was Georgia's, but it just wasn't the place for her, given all that had happened.

It was the height of summer, so there wasn't much available. She found a mountain cabin that backed up to Forest Service land near the top of Kingsbury in Nevada. They wanted five hundred dollars a night. A small price to pay for some peace, she thought. At least it had a hot tub. She sent off an inquiry about renting it starting the next day. Then she called Georgia.

Georgia answered on the first ring. "Hey you, how's it going?"

"Well, it's not going too great," Maya replied. "It's been pretty crazy.

"What's going on now? More dead bodies?"

"No, no more dead bodies, just crazy neighbors and lots of drama. I keep running into your neighbors who hated Karen. On top of that, I ran into her husband, Don, yesterday on Clear Creek trail. He just happened to be mountain biking down the same trail. Kind of creepy!"

She told Georgia about the encounter and the feeling of unease she felt in his presence. "It's all too much, especially because I'm feeling pretty emotionally raw from what happened at work. I think I'm going to get an Airbnb up in Kingsbury."

"Geez, Maya, I agree with you. I'd feel much better if you went somewhere else too. Besides, you need to feel safe and it just doesn't seem too safe there right now. I sure hope we didn't make a mistake buying that house. We just loved the location, but if he is going to stick around, I'm not sure it will be the right place for us. I guess we can only hope he'll move now that she is dead or else... die.

"Georgia, how cold hearted! Wishing someone dead," Maya said.

"Hey, I'm not wishing anyone dead. I just want the process of nature to happen faster. From what you've told me, it points a finger and explains the frivolous complaints we've had about clients since we started doing the vacation rental."

"Also, Georgia, just so you know. The woman's mountain bike accident has now become a murder investigation. Seems that maybe someone couldn't wait for the natural process to occur. Just another reason for me to get some distance from here.

"Jesus, Maya, what have you landed in the middle of? I thought I was offering a peaceful getaway. Now I've landed you right in the middle of a murder investigation and twisted neighbor drama. You definitely need to find another place to stay. Have you found a place already?"

"I just made an inquiry. Let me check and see if they've gotten back to me yet." Maya looked in her e-mail and sure enough, there was a reply.

"Okay, she says the place will be available, but she just got a booking for the weekend. She said she could book me for Monday, with a 4 p.m. check-in. So, four days away. I can do that. I'll just stay busy and stay away as much as possible until then."

Maya replied to the host while she was still on the phone with Georgia.

"Please be safe. If you just can't stay through the weekend, just leave and find a hotel. It isn't worth staying a few extra days if you can't relax. Keep me posted on how things are going. Have you thought about inviting Nick down for some company?"

"I've thought about it. He said he can come down in a week. I just want a few more days to myself. You know I like my independence."

"Yes, we both do. Jack is off on a male bonding trip, riding motorcycles through Montana and Colorado right now. I'm on my own. It's nice to have the house to myself for a while. Just Chloe and I."

"She is such an awesome dog! Give Chloe a hug for me!"

"I will," said Georgia.

She spent the day relaxing, reading her book, and catching up on e-mails to friends at home. Then she watched a movie with a dog on either side of her, snuggled in on the couch.

17

PACK OF THREE

HANGOVER FREE, she awoke to the sun coming through the window.

She decided to explore locally. Washoe meadow was just across the river from the house. She put the dogs on a leash as she left the driveway.

As she entered the meadow she saw a coyote exit a stand of trees. It paused, just standing at the edge of forest, watching them. Maya made sure the dogs were at her side and had them sit. They watched the coyote watching them. Both dogs were curious and she could feel the tension as they waited for her to give the command that would cut them loose to go investigate this new arrival. "Stay," she whispered. The coyote then dashed back into the forest. Both dogs whimpered with anticipation, but she didn't release them.

A few moments later, she heard high-pitched yips and howls that echoed through the trees. The dogs hunkered down next to her. They seemed to sense something that she couldn't read. The yips and howls continued. Maya wondered if this coyote was calling its pack because intruders had entered the area, or was it trying to lure her dogs in so they could all attack them?

She decided they would move on and let the coyote have his meadow back. She commanded again, "with me." Rio and Kali followed Maya, with Kali in front and Rio behind. Kali's nose lifted as she registered a scent in the air. Both dogs were alert as they continued to walk.

The trail looped to the outer edge of the park and traversed along some boulders. Maya and the dogs hopped up the boulders. They scrambled up more boulders and came up to a ten-foot wall. Maya thought she'd give Kali a challenge. She gave the command "climb." Kali surveyed her options and with one movement leapt from the ground; caught the rough surface of the wall and climbed vertically up the wall. At the top, she wagged her tail and did her dog equivalent of a smile. Maya praised her. "Good climb." Rio, not as young as Kali, whimpered as Maya climbed the wall behind Kali.. He ran back and forth and then followed her hand as she motioned up a lower ledge and then traversed the gentler slope up to where they were standing. They relaxed, perched atop their lookout.

She could hear the rush of early incoming traffic as Bay Area residents escaped to the mountains for summer vacation. She'd been amazed the weekend before how the energy changed with the influx of so many weekend tourists. She wondered how many people came for a longer time and how many came for that short break between their work week.

One reason that Georgia and Jack had bought their house here in South Lake was because they could rent it out as a vacation rental when they weren't using it. They would retire soon and wanted to have a home base that offered them the opportunity to do everything they loved and a place where they could launch from for bigger adventures, both local and international.

From Maya's perspective, it seemed like the perfect plan, unless...

She thought of Karen. From what Maya had learned, she knew Karen had had a run-in with just about every neighbor near her. Kathy had said something about them moving to Tahoe for a quiet mountain life in their cul-de-sac after years in the Bay Area.

That struck her as very presumptive. Their cul-de-sac? Maybe that's why they thought they were in charge of keeping everyone in line. From what she had seen, most of the houses that she passed actually had people living in them versus other tourist areas that seemed like empty ghost towns except during tourist season. How could she expect that the neighborhood would be quiet and peaceful all the time? People had lives. Dogs barked, children played, people had parties, and babies cried. Just how far had she gone to keep the quiet in the cul-de-sac and beyond? It seemed she wasn't above screaming at little children and calling the police the minute anyone at Georgia's house laughed too loud. Was she mad enough to poison dogs? Did she?

Was she dead because she ran into the wrong person and they had decided they'd had enough? What was Don's role in their relationship? Was he a participant or a victim himself? Maybe she'd give Officer O'Brien a call and fill him in on more of what she had learned about Karen. Shaking off those thoughts, she made her way back.

As she turned to enter the cul-de-sac. Kathy waved at her from her front yard. Maya hesitated, but Kathy had been enjoyable to paddleboard with. Just because she was associated with Karen and Don, didn't mean that Maya had to put her at arm's length. She could be friendly until she moved on to her new Airbnb.

"Hi, Kathy."

Kathy walked up to her and started telling her Don had to go in for a second interview with the police today.

Maya's muscles tensed. She couldn't wait to leave this drama behind.

Kathy continued. "Why are they dragging that poor man through another interview? I honestly can't believe it. Do they think he is a suspect? Don would never do anything to hurt Karen. I just know that they'll realize that he wouldn't kill Karen. Don't you think?"

Maya stared at Kathy. "Kathy, I don't know Don. I have no idea whether or not they will think he did it."

"Well, it's just that you..." She stopped herself. "You met Don on the trail the other day. He told me he ran into you. He said he broke down in front of you and you were kind enough to console him and help him regain his composure. I'm sure you must have seen how much pain he is in."

Bingo. Now she had a hunch about Don's motive the other day. Maybe if he created a story that he had broken down in front of her because he was devastated by his wife's death that would make his denial more plausible. Abusers (or in this case, a murderer) seemed to think that if they cried and acted vulnerable that it somehow negated the fact that they'd just lashed out violently against someone they were supposed to love.

It was more than likely that Don was the one who killed Karen. Someone familiar with the victim more often than not, perpetrated murder. She had been on so many domestic violence scenes over the years. Husbands were usually the perpetrators. She'd seen women shot, stabbed, and beaten. Some had died, and others had not.

Did Don know Maya was the one who had found Karen? No one officially knew she was the one that found Karen, but this was a small town and there were no secrets in small towns.

She had made the mistake of almost telling Deni, who told Heidi.

"Yes, Don ran into me on the trail as I was taking a break," Maya replied. "He seemed upset, but that still doesn't mean I know whether he was capable of killing his wife.

"It's just that, well, I know him so well. It's hard for me to believe he might be capable of murder," Kathy said.

Maya caught something in Kathy's eye.

"Kathy, I'm sure that the detectives will eventually find out who murdered her. Although I think they are going to have to wade through a long list of suspects. From what I've learned from other neighbors, people here hated her. She was harassing almost everyone."

Kathy looked down. "Yes, I know, but she really wasn't that bad. It's just that a lot of people here are, well, slackers. They don't have good manners and she thought they should be more respectful." She looked over at Mark and Deni's house. "Those two just let their kids run around without supervision and they play out in the street until dark. We're older. We go to bed early, which is hard to do when you've got a bunch of screaming kids running recklessly around."

Maya was seeing a change in Kathy. Maybe Karen was the more visible complainer. She made a mental note to herself, do not become a curmudgeon in her old age!

"Kathy, it has been good to touch base with you. I'd love to catch up with you later, after we've had something to eat and rest."

Kathy stepped back and apologized for keeping her. "You could come for dinner at my place later. I'll make extra," she said.

Maya agreed. She could use some company, and maybe she'd learn more about Kathy's relationship with Don.

Buddy hid behind Kathy's legs, his eyes glued to her. She

felt on edge a little. She had never had a dog not like her. She also felt like if she made one wrong move, Buddy might take out her ankle. Even her big dogs avoided little Buddy.

MAYA ARRIVED for dinner at Kathy's. "Make yourself comfortable. I'm just finishing up with dinner. We'll eat as soon as I wrap up making the salad."

Maya looked around. It was a small but tastefully and recently remodeled house. The hardwood floors were spotless. A comfortable couch sat below the living room window. The artwork and photographs were more decorative than a display of fine art. There was a black and white print by Ansel Adams along the far wall. Small paintings of mountain wildflowers led down the hallway. A photo of Buddy hung on the wall between the door and the kitchen. The décor was Mission style. Lots of stained wood, without the tacky feel of the rough-cut mountain pine look that seemed to define the mountain house décor in Tahoe. She also didn't see any kitschy bear statues anywhere. There was a wooden relief map of Lake Tahoe on the wall to the right of the kitchen. That was really the only thing that identified this as a Tahoe house. Kathy definitely had good taste, simple, comfortable, and not flashy.

"Kathy, you have a beautiful little house. It looks like you remodeled it recently?"

"Yes, I had it remodeled about three years ago. Actually, it was Don that remodeled it for me. He did everything while I was gone. He does excellent work. He also built the porch and back deck too. I don't know what I would do if I didn't have them to help me out. Trying to find a reliable contractor in this area is next to impossible and they are so expensive if you do find a good one. It's a tourist market. Anyway, it took a while, but Don did an excellent job." She looked around the room in admiration.

"Wow, he did do a great job. Is he a carpenter?"

"Yes, he said that he worked for a while doing high-end remodels when the tech boom hit SF in the nineties. When Karen and Don worked together, he worked as a handyman on the properties they managed. I think Don will be lost without Karen. She was the driving force in their relationship. He just kind of went along with what she wanted. She could be very demanding and driven."

"But you said you don't think he could have murdered her? Yet it sounds like she could have been difficult to live with."

"Yes, but they seemed to have a good balance. As I said, he just went with the flow. I've never seen him get angry in the entire time I've known him. Sometimes she'd yell at him and it just seemed to roll off of him. He was just used to her mood swings.

"Both of them were so good to me and he was so helpful. Anytime I had something break, he'd be over to fix it."

Maya compared that with what she had heard from the other neighbors. When put together, these accounts created a contrasting picture. Clearly, to Kathy, Don could do no wrong. Yet a neighbor said Don threatened people with physical violence.

"So, is there any indication of when they will release Karen's body? Is Don going to have a funeral? You said that she wanted her ashes spread on Lake Tahoe, correct?"

"Yes, they are just about to release the body. They did an autopsy. Don probably won't have a big event. They have a few local friends."

Maya changed the subject. "Kathy, do you have any family in the area? Are you married or divorced? I hope you don't mind me asking. I'm just curious."

"Oh, I've never been married. Just never met the right man. My parents are dead and I had one sister who died ten years ago of breast cancer. She had a daughter, my niece. My niece also died five years ago. So, no, I don't have any family... except Buddy." She looked down at him. A look of real sorrow clouded her face. "My niece was such a beautiful girl. I became like a mother to her after my sister died. Xavier, who you met was her boyfriend. He comes up and visits me every so often. Are you married?"

No, I'm not married yet. I have a boyfriend. We've been together for four years, so it's almost like being married. We live together."

"What does your boyfriend do?"

"Nick works in cyber security. He's the guy that company executives hire to monitor and protect their reputations online."

"That sounds like an interesting job. What companies does he work for?"

"Mostly high-tech company executives that need to make sure their reputation and online presence are managed. His company works for small to mid-sized tech companies. Most of his company's clients are in the Seattle area, but they also work for some companies located down here in Silicon Valley, as well as some international companies.

"He is trying to clear up his meeting schedule so that he can come down. He hasn't taken a vacation for quite a while, so I'll be happy if he follows through and comes down here for a few days.

"Are you interested in going hiking tomorrow? I just don't know where yet."

"I'd love to, but I told Don I'd be around in case they release Karen's body and we can move forward with planning Karen's cremation and the spreading of her ashes. He is really lost and needs my help to make decisions."

"That's so nice of you to help him with the details."

"Well, I want to. I honestly really miss her. She was my friend and Don means a lot to me too."

"I understand. Do you think Don will stay here now that she has died?"

"You know. I have no idea. I don't think he has thought that far ahead yet. Who knows? He loves Hawaii more than here. This was always more of her favorite place than his. I think he really loves island life and the water."

"Well, who knows? Maybe I'll buy their house. It's right next to my best friend and I know most of the neighbors now," said Maya.

"Well, if he sells the place, I'll let him know you may be interested."

Maya left feeling like she had learned a little more about Karen, Don, and Kathy. She also understood why Kathy would think so highly of the couple. It sounded like they were instrumental in helping her remodel her house and took care of things when she was gone. So, it sounded like if you didn't actually live next to her; she was fine. If you weren't there, you couldn't be noisy.

18

THE LOCAL CONNECTION

THE NEXT MORNING as Maya was leaving to go hiking, she saw Kathy heading over to Don's house. She wondered if they were going to release his wife's body. Time to plan a funeral, of sorts.

THAT EVENING she decided to get dinner in town at Lake Tahoe Aleworx. She parked and brought her dogs with her. She sat at a table where she could people watch. The waitress took her order.

She gazed out at the people just starting to trickle in. It was still early. The waiter brought her beer and a bowl of water for her dogs.

As she watched people coming in she recognized Todd Blackmore with his girlfriend or wife? He noticed her too. She waved. He walked over to her table.

"Hey, Maya, right?" he asked.

"Yes," Maya replied.

"Hey, this is my girlfriend, Brandi. We're just getting something to eat before heading to Stateline for an outdoor concert at Harrah's. Can we join you?"

"Hi, Brandi, nice to meet you," said Maya. "Yes, please do. I'd love company. My boyfriend, Nick, is coming down soon, but for now I'm on my own." She said this for Brandi's information. It could be disconcerting to go out with your boyfriend and then suddenly find yourself joining another woman for dinner.

"Awesome," Todd said.

Brandi sat down next to Maya. Todd grabbed a chair from another table before sitting down across from Maya. The waiter, seeing that two people were joining Maya, came over and brought them menus and took their drink orders.

As they looked through the menu, Brandi asked Maya a few questions. "So, you're visiting? Where are you from?"

"I'm down for a few weeks on vacation. I'm from Seattle. In fact, the owner of the house that I am staying at is a friend of mine. She's a Seattle Firefighter," Maya added. "Todd, you should meet her when she comes down."

Todd looked up. "That would be great. In fact, I wanted to ask you more about working as a paramedic. I've been thinking about going to paramedic school."

"Me too. I'm studying to be a nurse in Reno," Brandi interjected. "I love emergency medicine, and I'm considering an emergency department job at Barton when I finish school. I'm also interested in looking into becoming a paramedic / flight nurse."

"I'm happy to answer your questions."

The waiter returned to their table with the couple's beer.

"So, what made you become a paramedic and not a firefighter or both?" he asked.

Maya thought about it. "Well, I loved wildland firefighting, but structural firefighting just didn't appeal to me. I hate confined spaces and wearing a bunch of equipment to go into a burning building where I can't see to put out a fire. I'm an outdoor kind of gal.

"The paramedic job was more interesting. I enjoy helping people. Plus, you see a lot more on a day-to-day basis when you do pre-hospital medicine. Working up north is amazing. I love the level of independence to make decisions.

Todd sat listening intently. So did Brandi. Todd knew about the bad call, but she hadn't gone into how she felt she'd lost her edge and how she was feeling that she didn't want to go back to work at the end of her time off.

"How is it being a woman working as a paramedic?" Brandi asked.

"Well, I can't really say what it would be like anywhere else than where I currently work. I imagine it is different depending on where you work and the underlying culture. Where I work, well let's just say it is getting better. With young men like Todd coming on board, I've seen a big shift in attitude. Todd, I'm assuming that your mom worked?"

"I get what you're saying," Todd replied. "Yes, my mom worked for a software company in the early days. She worked her way up in the company, but she faced a lot of bias and road-blocks. I think, knowing her, the fact that I knew she was competent, and a strong woman made me realize the challenges that women can face. She also made sure to teach me to always treat women with respect. I have no doubt that you, Brandi, or any other woman can do a great job in any profession that you choose."

Right answer, Todd, Maya thought. "That's what I'm talking about. You have grown up knowing women who have worked in high-performing jobs. It just seems normal to you, whereas in the early days, women faced challenges on so many fronts. One of the original female paramedics not only had the challenge of being the first woman, but she also had the firefighter's wives go after her. They were afraid of a woman working alongside their husbands and sleeping in the same bunkroom as them.

Luckily that is behind us. Now most fire stations give everyone their own small room and the women have separate bathrooms. The good news is you no longer have to sleep next to someone who snores!" They all laughed. "So, we've brought some good changes to the firehouse."

"So do you know anything about being a flight nurse / paramedic?" Brandi asked.

"Only that it looks exciting. We use them in the remote areas of our district or during gridlock traffic in our urban areas. We have a great system up in Washington. The service flies helicopters all over the region for emergency transport and they also have a fixed wing division that does inter-facility transfers from as far away as Montana and Alaska."

"Wow, so do they just transport, or do they also do prehospital care?"

"In our areas and the more urban areas, they mainly transport because we've done most of the initial triage and treatment before they arrive. However, in rural areas where they are mostly dealing with volunteer fire departments and less experienced emergency medicine providers, they may be the first ones to arrive with advanced lifesaving skills. In that case, they would do advanced paramedic / emergency nurse care like administering drugs or placing a breathing tube."

Brandi commented. "That sounds pretty challenging to do flight medicine in rural areas. I'm interested in having a look at working in that kind of system."

"I'd get some good solid ER experience under your belt and critical care in a cardiac or intensive care unit. You'll be out there on your own with another nurse or paramedic depending on where you work. You'll want all the experience you can get. Trust me, when I entered the paramedic program in Seattle, I was a test case. There were two of us who had less than three years of experience as Emergency Medical Technicians prior to applying to paramedic training. They wanted to see if they could train inexperienced EMTs as paramedics. That way they could mold them right from the start.

"It was tough. I had some experience, but really felt that I lacked confidence that comes from gaining more experience. I also had a steeper learning curve. I didn't have previous experience as a paramedic to fall back on and I hadn't seen enough patients, as an EMT to draw on. So, my advice is to get lots of experience under the supervision of people who have more experience. That way you can learn without the profound responsibility that comes with positions where there are only two of you. Either as a paramedic on a two-person medic unit or as part of a two-person flight nurse team."

"Thanks for the advice. I'm sure you've seen a lot over the years," said Brandi.

"Those are also notes to my younger self. I was so passionate and gung-ho that I charged right in without really thinking it through. I thought I was invincible. Now I know better. Now I'm a more cautious version of Wonder Woman." They laughed.

Todd chimed in. "I read the article in the South Tahoe Now with an update about the woman you found. I haven't heard anything about whether they caught the killer.

"Crazy, we have quite a few murders in South Lake Tahoe for such a small town, but very few of them happen on the trails of Lake Tahoe. They probably held off letting the media know until they were sure. That isn't good advertising to promote tourism. I'm not too worried, though, it was probably someone who knew her."

"It has been interesting staying right next to where she lived," Maya said. "Her husband is a strange one. I thought once she died that I'd quit getting visits from animal control, but I came home the other night to another notice. Also, he just happened to be on the same mountain bike trail as I was. I was stopped at the overlook on the Clear Creek trail when he just came riding up.

"We were talking and he suddenly started crying and admitted to calling animal control on me because my dogs were barking. Now I'm just trying to avoid him until I move to another place on Kingsbury."

Todd looked at her with concern. "You know, you should get out of there. We knew there was something wrong with her, but it might not just be her. Maybe her husband is just as crazy as she was.

"I am moving, but I can't get another place until Monday."

"If you want to get away from there tomorrow you should take a day trip over to the South Fork of the American River. It's beautiful and it's a popular whitewater boating river. The whole area is interesting. There is Placerville also known as Hangtown and Coloma where gold was first discovered in California. It's really hot there in the summer, but you and your dogs can go down to the river. That way you could get away from the drama and see another area close by."

The waiter brought Todd and Brandi's dinner. While they were eating, Maya caught Todd and Brandi's attention. Don had just walked through the door with another man. She nodded in Don's direction. "That's him, Don. Interesting that once again he shows up at the same place as me. It just keeps getting weirder! It feels like it is more than a coincidence."

Todd nodded. "Hard to tell. This is a popular place with locals, but yes, it could be weird. Does he know you found his wife?"

"I'm not sure. I let it slip out to a neighbor and he told another neighbor, so he probably does know. But why would he follow me down the trail and not just ask me?"

"Maybe he wants to, but just can't get the courage to come and ask or... maybe he killed her, and he thinks you know. No matter what, I think you need to be careful, and you need to get out of there. I'm going to give you my number and if you have any concerns or need my help, call me!"

"Okay, I will. Both of you, if you ever want to come and visit our flight nurse program up in Seattle, just let me know. You could also come ride on the paramedic unit with me when I'm at work." Maya loved to support the next generation, especially other women who wanted to pursue emergency medicine. She didn't have the support of other women when she started. She wanted to make sure that young women coming in now had the support they needed to make it in these emotionally, mentally, and physically demanding job environments.

As they paid and left, she could feel Don's eyes on her. When they walked out, Todd leaned in and said, "He was watching you as we left. You need to be careful. Like I said before, if you need help, call me."

Maya shuddered. This was getting too real.

19

THE BREAK-IN

MAYA RETURNED HOME. As she reached the top of the stairs, she saw that her door was open. Her muscles tensed up. She could swear she had locked it when she left. "Is someone in there?" she called out.

Before she could stop Rio and Kali, they rushed in, their noses hitting the ground as they tried to identify any new smells in the apartment. Maya turned on the hall light and her iPhone flashlight and tentatively followed them in.

They ran to something lying on the floor near the dining table. Kali got there first. Maya could just make out that Kali was eating something before Rio pushed her out of the way and finished the feast of... an animal? She ran over and pushed them out of the way. All she could make out was some greasy residue and small pinkish moist flakes, like smoked salmon. She had smoked salmon in the fridge. The fridge door was open. A jar of peanut butter was broken below the fridge.

She looked inside and saw the fridge was in disarray. The salmon was missing.

She relaxed a little. Well, she had heard that Tahoe bears

were excellent at B & E, but now she has seen it firsthand. She switched on the kitchen light and saw that one of the dining room chairs was knocked over as well. Now that the lights were on she saw white paw prints leading from the pantry. Inside, a cache of staples: flour, sugar, beans, noodles, pasta sauce, and Clif Bars were strewn about. Pasta sauce was mixed in with the flour. Wrappers were torn open and Clif Bar remnants were mixed in with the rest of the mess. She closed the door to keep the dogs out.

The dogs were still sniffing around the chair. She then checked her bedroom and bathroom. All clear. She walked out onto the deck and stared out to the front yard, clear. Then she went down to the backyard. She walked the perimeter of the apartment and the main house. Everything was quiet. The doors to the main house were closed. She checked them to make sure that they were locked. All snug and secure. She returned to the apartment, relieved that her criminal bear was no longer at the scene of the crime.

She grabbed some paper towels and a wet rag to mop up the salmon remains. She set to work cleaning up the pantry. After two hours of pulling everything out, cleaning, and then replacing the undamaged supplies, she finally finished. She must have left the door unlocked and the bear just walked in and helped himself. She wouldn't forget to lock the door again. *A fed bear is a dead bear.* She didn't want to contribute to the death of a bear because of her forgetfulness.

20

GOLD COUNTRY

BEFORE BEAUTIFUL OCEAN beaches and Hollywood, California was famous for the gold rush. She found out that Coloma, where gold was discovered, was now the center of whitewater river rafting on the South Fork of the American River.

Taking Todd's advice, Maya decided to explore beyond Tahoe and visit Coloma. She also made an inquiry about a cabin at the American River Resort. Now she wouldn't have to stay at Georgia's house. She'd stay in Coloma.

She packed up her paddleboard and with her dogs drove out of the Tahoe basin, heading west towards San Francisco.

Traffic was already flowing in from the west as tourists came in from the Bay Area for a weekend. The highway climbed along the granite cliffs above the Christmas Valley. As she climbed, she could see the lake in her rear-view mirror.

Turning her attention forward, she passed by Echo Summit. Then the road twisted along the edge of giant granite mountains past Horsetail Falls, still flowing from a carved granite valley high in the Desolation Wilderness.

She passed the town of Strawberry before the road followed the curves of the South Fork of the American River from its origin high in the Sierras. Tight current coursed over boulders and dropped over ledges as it made its way from the steep mountains to the foothills towards the Sacramento Valley.

As she traveled further down the highway, the forest feathered up along the valley sides. Rocks poked out from the trees reminding her she was still driving through the rugged Sierras. As the river valley widened, the road, became four lanes, arriving in 'Old Hangtown', Placerville, and the center of Gold Country justice. She turned left and drove through the downtown. The street was crowded with tourists. At Town Centre, a bell tower divided two streets.

It was an interesting town built on an old west theme and gold. Brick buildings and old west facades in bright colors gave the impression of its place in history. A manikin hanging from a rope on the side of the building marked the Hangman's tree, a historic spot.

At the end of town, she crossed Highway 50 and connected to Highway 49. The golden chain that linked the historic gold mining communities along the foothills of the Sierras. As she drove down the highway, it twisted one way and then the other. She gained glimpses of tawny grass covered hilltops through oak trees that framed the roadway. The dogs braced themselves with their heads out the windows. Like surfers, they adjusted as she turned one way and then the other. Their noses lifted, catching all the new scents along the way.

She descended toward the river and entered the historic town of Coloma. She saw a café on the side of the roadway as she slowed. It seemed like a good place for her first stop.

The Argonaut Cafe was in a rustic, old west building with a covered porch and a tin roof. Small tables were nestled along the porch. One table was open, so she hooked the dogs up to the railing securing her spot outside and headed in to see what food they offered. The cafe advertised from farm to table.

From her corner table, she watched as people made their way along the historic roadway. Next door was the old post office. Across the street a museum. Cars with whitewater kayaks on top passed by. A whitewater tour van towing a trailer with whitewater boats was heading out the way she had come in.

It was hot. It was still early but she could feel the change in temperature. She figured it had to be at least twenty degrees hotter than Tahoe. She'd definitely spend time in the river.

After finishing her lunch, she left the cafe and decided to walk along the roadway. Just beyond the cafe she passed an old wooden building with an outside area that was advertising 'Gold Panning'. Inside were a couple of families swirling out their dreams of finding gold at the bottom of their pans. Beyond was a road that led to a one-lane bridge over the river. She made her way to the bridge and then watched as single cars traded turns going across. She found a gap in cars and walked out across the bridge. The river flowed beneath her. Willows undulated with the current along the river's edge. On the other side of the river, tawny grass-covered hills framed the river valley.

A car approached from the other side, so she turned around to go back the way she had come. As she did, she saw a white Tesla turn around and then turn right onto Highway 49. She felt a sense of déjà vu. White Tesla. Of course, Kathy's friend had a white Tesla. She was in California, home to Tesla, and she was near the Bay Area, where lots of tech workers could afford the price tag of a Tesla, something she couldn't even consider as a single, professional paramedic.

She turned right herself and explored. The Gold Town

Grange was on the corner. Beyond the grange, she found a trail into the Marshall Gold Park. She followed it through a grassy field with stands of oak trees and old wooden buildings. She turned down a trail to the river's edge. She could see groups of rafts floating by. One group was shooting water guns at another group.

She skirted around the parking area and found herself at Sutter's Mill, a large historic display. Apparently, while they were milling logs they discovered flakes of gold in the water being diverted for the mill. That find led to the gold rush in 1849. She perused the history. It was interesting, how one seemingly inconsequential event could change the course of history or someone's life. She hung on that thought for a moment and felt herself spinning toward her dark place. Kali nuzzled her hand and brought her back to the present.

They walked down to the river and found a large memorial built out of river stone at the water's edge. The words Sutter's Mill were created with smaller, lighter stone.

Rio tugged her to the left and down to the water's edge. His look telling her he wanted to swim. Maya let the dogs get a drink, but they'd have to wait until later for a swim. The water was swift and running through stands of willows just down-stream along the edge.

A swim sounded good right about now. Sweat was dripping down her back. The sun was beating down on her forehead. She'd melt before long.

They continued along the river trail and found themselves at the whitewater launch. There was a group of kayakers peeling off their river gear. Their kayaks were lined up drying on the grass. She approached a woman in the group and asked her about kayaking the river. The group had just done a run called 'Chili Bar' that was located upstream. Next to the group was an incoming rafting group. Another group was unloading rafts from trailers. That group looked older. Grey hair under sun hats gave them away.

She dropped to the far side and found some random sticks to throw for Rio. She struck up a conversation with an older man that was inflating his boat next to them. She shared that she and her boyfriend were a whitewater guides and that they had rafted the Grand Canyon a few years ago. "It was the biggest whitewater I've ever experienced," she said.

The man, Gary, said he had also rafted the Canyon. "I've been rafting for nearly thirty years. My wife and I have rafted almost every river in California. This is our favorite for a quick day trip. It's so close to our home outside of San Francisco. We spend a lot of time up here in the summer rafting. We also volunteer as guides for an organization called Environmental Traveling Companions. We take people with disabilities down the river."

"Wow, you guys have done a lot of rafting. I'll have to tell my boyfriend about this river."

Rio started whining. Maya threw another stick. Kali deposited the previous one at her feet. She asked Gary if he would mind if she took a photo of him and his boat to text to her boyfriend. "Sure." Maya took the photo and then texted it to Nick. "The South Fork America River. Lot of fun to raft. Maybe go while you are here?"

Nick texted back, "Does that mean you want me to come down?"

Maya replied, "Yes, soon!"

Maya thanked Gary. Then she decided it was time to go swimming. She led the dogs over to the slow water farther upstream of the rafters. She sat her stuff down, and with the dogs still on leash, waded into the water. A shock ran through her system. She hadn't expected the water to be so freezing cold. The contrast between the scorching heat from the sun and the icy cold water sent shivers up her body. She had two choices. Inch her way in slowly or just take the plunge and get it over with. She chose the latter.

She unclipped the dogs and threw the leashes on shore and then dove into the frigid water. She felt that momentary stun as the cold penetrated every pore in her body. She swam quickly out into the slow moving water, using the heat of her movement to help her acclimate. Rio and Kali followed her like baby ducklings. Rio's big paws acted like paddles as he powered through the water. Kali's dainty feet just barely kept her afloat. They were so different. Maya swam strongly upstream against the lazy current. Her body was slowly warming, or she was becoming numb. She wasn't sure which. She kept up the pace until she felt comfortable enough just treading in place. The dogs swam in circles around her. She lay back and looked up into the sky until Rio bumped into her shoulder. She turned over and dunked him under. He came up and shook his head. Water flew everywhere as his ears caught the surface of the water.

"Okay, okay," Maya chided, "I'll get moving again." They slowly swam downstream. They'd stay in as long as she could feel her toes. She laughed.

They finally exited the water and lay on the rocky beach until they were dry enough but still cooled off. Then they walked across the road to the other side of the park and followed a trail up through a display of Native American bark teepee structures and up past a large granite boulder that was a Native American grinding stone. Smooth circular depressions stood out on the flat granite surface. The trail continued upward and entered oak forest. The shade provided a slight relief from the heat, but sweat quickly started dripping off her again. They found themselves atop a small knoll with a statue, the James Marshall monument. James Marshall was the one who discovered the gold, she read. It said, 'the figure of Marshall atop the monument is pointing to the place of discovery on the South Fork of the American River.' Then, as a footnote, she discovered that while he was the one who discovered the gold, he didn't get rich and died a poor man.

She decided it was time to find a place to wait out the heat. They hiked back to her SUV. She turned on the engine and cranked on the air conditioner. Within minutes, they were cooling off. She brought up Google maps on her phone and looked for a place to enjoy the river. She left Coloma and made her way up Highway 49 to a park called Dave Moore Nature Area. It was a short hike, but she knew that sometimes it was just the extra bit of effort that weeded out a lot of people.

The park was named after a park employee who had developed Multiple Sclerosis. As a tribute to him, they made a disabled-accessible river trail. They made their way down to the river quickly to get to the cool water. The river curved to the left and large boulders poked through the water. Below the boulders were some eddies that created calm water. It looked like a perfect spot to sit out the day. Maya found a place under the cover of an oak tree.

The dogs ran around and greeted two other groups. There was a Hispanic family with two little girls in their matching pink life jackets. Mom and dad sat in their short lawn chairs at the water's edge, their feet sitting in the cold river water. Rio and Kali immediately made friends with the little girls, who then went in search of sticks to throw for them. Maya cautioned them to only throw sticks into the slow water. Her dogs weren't ready to swim class III whitewater because they didn't bring their life jackets. The girls giggled at the thought of the dogs wearing life jackets.

The other group was a mixed group of twenty-somethings. There were three guys and two girls. They had the classic

Styrofoam beer cooler. The focus of their energy was on getting a suntan and drinking whatever was in their cooler.

Her mind shot back to all those summer days when they responded to the occasional drunk person who had fallen and hit their head while hanging out in the local Green River Gorge where she worked. Inevitably the alcohol contributed to drownings, trauma, and at times, violence along the river as people flocked to the river's edge on the hot days of summer. She and her coworkers referred to this as job security. There wouldn't ever be a lack of people doing stupid things that led to bad outcomes.

As the summer heat ramped up, so did their calls. Their job was to pick up the pieces and try to save people, often from themselves. She thought about how much she had become jaded since she started working as a young, idealistic Emergency Medical Technician years ago. Now people had become defined by what medical illnesses they might have or what decision would lead them to some traumatic emergency. She could predict what type of calls happened during certain times of year. Summers were for trauma.

She anticipated problems. Her profession presented a skewed picture of the world. It was a world where danger could be anywhere. It could be in something as seemingly benign as a bee sting or the slight feeling of indigestion or a patch of ice on a winter road.

She heard one of the little girls scream. She looked up to see Mom running over to scoop up her youngest. Rio was slinking away looking chastised. Dad was walking toward him with a menacing look on his face. Maya jumped up to intervene. The man started yelling at her that her dog had knocked over his daughter. Maya looked at the little one. Her nose was bloody, and she was crying uncontrollably. She stood between the man and Rio. She calmly looked him in the eye and said with a steadfast tone, "I'm sure it was an accident. He is a big dog, and he gets exuberant when he is playing. I'm a paramedic. If you can back off from my dog, I'll come over and look at her to see what we can do. I just need you to realize that I have my dogs under solid voice command, so they aren't a threat to you or your family. Please let me help!"

The man hesitated in his forward motion and stopped. The little girl was still crying. Maya directed the dogs over near her towel and told them to lie down and stay. The man watched as she did this and looked relieved to see her dogs obey her commands.

"Okay," he said, "just keep that dog away from us! I'm going to be watching and if..."

"You can do that, but I assure you it won't be necessary," she said calmly.

The dogs stayed put. Maya now concerned herself with the little girl. She walked up to Mom and the little girl. Squatting down, she introduced herself and asked the girl if it was okay to look at her nose. The little girl, crying a little less, renewed her intensity. Maya could feel the father's tension behind her, even though she couldn't see him. Mom clutched her daughter tightly, trying to console her.

Maya did a long distance examination. Yes, the little girl had a bloody nose, but looking at it, it appeared that most, if not all, of the bleeding was from a superficial scrape where the bottom of her nose had impacted the rock. Maya asked the mother if she could apply pressure on the scrape at the base of her nose. Then she explained to her that so far, from what she could see, the bleeding was coming from a scrape rather than from inside the nose. She explained that facial wounds bleed profusely because the blood vessels are close to the surface. While they look terrible, they are often more minor than they look. She said the most important thing they could do was to get that bleeding under control and when she calmed down, take a closer look.

"Elena," the mother said. "Elena is her name."

Maya noted that they were making progress. "When Elena calms down, we can make sure that everything else is okay."

Now the father was sitting down on a rock. He was watching Maya and then shifting his eyes to watch her dogs. That's okay, she thought, dads are protective. She just needed to make sure to keep everyone's emotions in check.

Mom took a tissue and put pressure on the bottom of Elena's nose. Elena had her arms wrapped around her mother and the side of her head buried in her chest. The cries were subsiding, and her eyes were getting heavy. Good sign. Kids tended to fall asleep after the emotion subsided. Maya just needed to evaluate her to make sure that she didn't have anything more serious than a nosebleed. After a while, the little girl was calm. Maya asked Mom if she could take a closer look. They removed the tissue and the bleeding had stopped. The blood was caked around her little nostrils, but it was on the outside of her nose and not the inside. Maya noted that she didn't have any deformity in her nose or anywhere on her face. Her skin color was good, and her pupils were equal and reactive to light.

Then Maya asked if either of them saw exactly what happened. Both said that they had been focused on other things when they heard her cry out. Dad looked up to see the little girl rolling away from the rock, and start crying uncontrollably. Rio was standing across from her on the other side of the rock. Maya slowly got up and walked over to the rock. There, lying wedged between the rock and the rock behind it, was her little plastic sandal. She reached down and retrieved it.

"It looks like her sandal got caught in between the rocks. She probably couldn't get it out and fell forward. I think she'll be fine from what I can tell. After she calms down a little more, I'll just do a quick head to toe survey to make sure we didn't miss anything." She included the parents to give them the control they needed to feel like they were part of the solution with her. Then she started some small talk to get everyone relaxed.

"By the way, my name is Maya. I'm a paramedic from Seattle. I've taken care of a lot of kids over the years. What is your other daughter's name?"

"My name is Margarite. Her name is Ale," Mom replied. Ale's watchful, dark eyes were focused on her sister as she stood next to her mom.

"And your name?" Maya smiled and directed her gaze at Dad.

"I am José," he said.

Maya could see he had calmed down. "Do you guys live in the area?" she asked.

"We live down in El Dorado Hills," José answered. "It's about twenty miles from here."

"So, you guys probably come down to the river to get away from the summer heat?" she asked.

"Yes, I grew up in Los Angeles, but the heat still gets to me. It's easier to handle when you are close to the ocean. We've lived up here for five years now. Moved up here right before Ale was born. We love it here, but the summers are hot, and we don't have a swimming pool."

"Well, this isn't a bad place to spend your time. What a beautiful location."

Elena was now fiddling with the clip on her life jacket. "Momma, I'm hot, off," she said, as she squirmed away from her mom.

Margarite, smiled. "Well, it looks like we are pretty well back to normal. I think she'll be fine."

Maya smiled. "I think so too. I really think it looks worse than it is. Just keep an eye on her. If she complains of head pain, gets unusually sleepy, or starts to bleed out of her nose, take her in. Better to be safe."

"Yes, I'm sorry I got so angry," José chimed in. "At first, I thought your dog had bitten her. So many people come here with their dogs and don't have control of them. We always worry. I can see by the fact that both dogs are still right where you commanded them to be that you aren't one of those."

"I completely understand. I would never let my dogs off leash around kids if I was concerned that they might bite them. Rio's biggest fault is he is such a big guy that he might accidentally knock a smaller child over. However, he is a big love bug." Maya got up and walked back over to where they were sitting and scratched Rio's ears.

"Tell you what. Just for the sake of your peace of mind, I'll keep them by my side. We'll go swimming again, when I swim with them, they stick to me like glue."

José agreed that he would feel better for now if she kept them close. Maya understood. They talked a little longer about Elena and Ale. Both were young. Ale was starting first grade the next year and Elena was starting kindergarten. Maya relaxed, knowing that she had managed not only to defuse the situation and take care of the little girl, but she had made a connection with the family. She was relieved that the situation didn't escalate where Rio was accused of something he didn't do. That could have potentially led to having law enforcement and animal control involved... and potentially lawyers. Most situations could be resolved if people just stayed calm and communicated. When people acted on their strong emotions, that was when trouble came to visit. She'd seen it too many times.

After she left, she felt the fatigue and tension well up inside her. It was like every emergency, even something as simple as a bloody nose, exhausted her. It was like she had a reserve tank that was getting emptier, and it was harder to refill; the main tank was already bone dry. She felt emotionally and physically fatigued and on edge like she couldn't turn it off. Jumpiness and a sense of danger crept up in her mind again. It wasn't as much a real thing, as an emotional sensation that screamed at her, danger, run! As she headed back toward Coloma, she decided to stop in at Marco's Cafe and get something to eat.

21

MARCO'S CAFE

AFTER MAYA LEFT THE BEACH, she drove to the American River Resort and checked in to her cabin. She had lucked out again and found an amazing place to stay. Maybe things were looking up. The cabin was on the edge of the river, just upstream of a rapid called Troublemaker. Her deck was perched next to a rocky shoreline before it dropped off into the currents of the river and then the green tongue slithered down and met the roaring sound of Troublemaker, a whitewater rapid that probably lived up to its name.

It was going to be a great night. She could feel it. A little rocky start at the beach, but it should be smooth sailing from now on. She headed for Marco's Cafe, a local favorite hangout. Todd had suggested that as a great place to have dinner and check out the local scene. Also, they had outdoor seating so she could bring her dogs in out of the heat.

The cafe was located just beyond the intersection of Highway 49 and Garden Valley Road. A few miles from where she spent the day. It was a small wooden building nestled under large shade trees. The parking area was nearly full as she pulled in. It looked like it was a popular spot along the highway.

She walked around to an entrance to the outdoor seating area, with Rio and Kali, and asked a server if she could sit outside with them.

"Absolutely, but I'd order first at the counter around the front."

Maya went around to the front. There was a short line of people waiting to order. She checked out the menu and ordered a potato pesto pizza, a salad, and a beer with an interesting name and an even more interesting description: Monkey Nutz Coconut Porter. Described as 'Coconut and chocolate dominate this smooth silky porter.' This should be interesting, she thought. She loved trying out the latest brews from local breweries.

She took her beer and picked a table along the wood fence under a large shade tree. The dogs could lie down comfortably under the table. The place was filing up with people. A band was setting up under a white tent along the back. Their banner read, 'Little Hurricane.' She liked the name.

She sat down, taking a drink of her Monkey Nutz. It did have a smooth, chocolaty coconut flavor. Thick and rich as it found its way down her throat, the dryness of the air slipping away with each sip.

A couple of tables of people looked like young river guides who had just finished up a day on the river. They were wearing their river sandals, shorts, and sun hats. A young woman and man in their group were speaking Spanish. A young blond man was laughing and greeting other friends as they arrived at the table with their beers in hand. Another table to the left of the stage was a group of old timers. Four tanned older men and two women sat comfortably together.

A flamboyant character was animatedly explaining something to them. He had an accent that Maya couldn't quite place. He had long greying hair pulled back in a ponytail. He had one of those giant walrus mustaches and bushy eyebrows. He was built like an aging fortress, but his movements seemed to belie his age. His barrel chest filled out a white Grand Canyon T-shirt. His shorts were long and baggy. He sported a pair of vintage river sandals, circa 1990s.

She listened vicariously as he was telling his story of a flip on a river called the Tuolumne. His friends listened intently, nodded with enthusiasm and laughing as he motioned and described the boat becoming airborne and everyone falling out. There were laughs of familiarity, as if it was a story they already knew well. He glanced in her direction. Catching her eye, he winked and turned back to finish the story. He had noticed she was also listening intently. She felt a sudden rush of embarrassment as she realized they saw that she was eavesdropping. The hazards of sitting in a bar all by yourself, she thought, and reached down to scratch Rio's head. Well, not quite alone.

She moved her attention to the rest of the people in the cafe. It was a mixed crowd of younger people, families, and the happy hour crowd in their late forties and fifties. A family, complete with grandma and grandpa were celebrating what looked to be an eight-year-old's birthday. They all wore party hats and one kid occasionally let out a squeak on his curly noisemaker.

The server came over and asked Maya if her dogs wanted something to drink. Maya said yes and thanked her for thinking of them. The waitress disappeared and returned a few minutes later with a blue bowl of water for the dogs. They each got up and she could hear the loud slurps as they sucked up the water from the dish.

She took another drink of her beer. The storyteller was getting up from the table. As he passed by, he paused and asked her where she was from. Maya said she was visiting from Seattle, via South Lake Tahoe. He smiled. "Well, you look so lonesome sitting there on your own. You're welcome to join us. We have quite a group congregating here for dinner," he said. "Besides, my friends are sick of my old stories. They have heard them a million times."

Maya said she'd love to join them. He hustled her and her dogs over to their table. "Hey guys, this is... what is your name?"

"Maya, my name is Maya. This is Rio and this is Kali. My adventure dogs," she said.

"Welcome, Maya," said one woman. "I'm Anna. "

The storyteller introduced himself. "I'm Jay. I'll be back. I'm off in search of more beer. Maya, can I get you anything?"

"No, I'm good right now, but thanks."

"I'm Elaine," said the other woman sitting across from Anna.

The men introduced themselves. "I'm Juan. I'm visiting from Rome." She noted he looked Italian and still had a silky head of wavy dark hair with a touch of grey.

Steve introduced himself. He looked a little older, probably around seventy; his hair was shorter and tucked under a safari style green hat. He wore a Friends of the River T-shirt. "I'm from Coloma. My wife Anna and I have lived here since 2010.

Joe introduced himself and said he was here from San Francisco with his wife, Elaine.

Maya sat down and put the dogs to the inside of the table near the fence. She sat next to Anna and Elaine. She asked what had brought them to Marco's Cafe.

"Oh, we come here every year," Anna replied. "We have a cabin along the river and spend our time rafting the river during the days and then coming to Marco's on Saturday nights for music. Tonight, we are also celebrating my son's birthday and going to hear live music at the Grange."

As she said that, four, young men in their thirties walked up. Anna jumped up and quickly hugged one of the men. The young man had a similar smile and she guessed that was Anna's son. She was a petite woman with blonde hair and a big smile. Her son's smile seemed just as big. He had shorter, blond hair under a blue baseball cap with his sunglasses sitting over the brim. He wore a black T-shirt and cut-off blue jean shorts. He looked to be in his early thirties. Maya's age. Anna introduced Maya.

"Jaden, these are our new friends, Maya and her two dogs, Rio and Kali."

Jaden held out his hand. Maya commented how impressed she was that Anna already had their names down. Jaden introduced Maya to his three friends, Connor, Burt, and Reyd.

The four young men slipped into seats at the opposite end of the table. Reyd jumped up and went to order for the group. Jaden looked down the length of the table at Maya. He had piercing blue eyes highlighted by his blond hair. She smiled. Jaden commented, "So, who roped you into sitting with these old farts?"

"You know Jay," Anna chimed in. "He is always picking up stray young women with their dogs." Everyone laughed, including Maya.

"To my benefit. Besides, I was eavesdropping while he was telling that interesting story about... flipping on the Tuolumne."

"Awe, yes, Jay and his stories. We've all heard that one a hundred times," Joe said dramatically. "It gets wilder and more embellished every time he tells it. I was on that run. Yes, he flipped and got washed along the bottom of the river for a while, but he makes it sound like he was running the river at ten thousand cubic feet per second. It was only five thousand cfs."

Jay came rambling back balancing three pitchers of Pilsner ale between his overstretched fingers. He slid into his seat and placed the pitchers evenly on the table. Not a drop of beer was lost as he settled in. "We have ourselves some more beer. Drink up mates!"

Ahh, he's an kiwi, Maya thought. Of course, he was, and quite a character too.

"Well, has everyone introduced themselves to Maya? Jaden, you've arrived. Have you met Maya too?" Jay winked at Jaden.

Now Maya knew why she had so casually been recruited to join them. She was their ace to keep the young men interested in hanging out with the parents and friends.

Was Jay playing matchmaker? It was too early to tell if that might be a good thing.

"Maya are you a boater?" asked Jay.

"Yes, actually I am. I've been kayaking and rafting since I was in college. I worked as a river guide for a couple of summers while I was in college. I've worked as a member of a swift water search and rescue team out of King County near Seattle. I don't respond for swift water rescues much anymore since I trained Kali to be a search dog. Now I'm mostly doing backcountry and trail rescue."

"Do you do that for a living?" Anna asked.

"No, actually I work as a paramedic near Seattle. Search and rescue is just a side thing I do, since I already have the skills as a paramedic and a lot of outdoor experience."

Reyd returned with a tray of bottled bear for the new arrivals. Jaden, Connor, and Burt grabbed their beer. "I've ordered a plate of Nachos," said Reyd.

"You know I used to run a swift water class on the Rangitata River in New Zealand," Jay said. "Best dam river for training."

He started telling them how he and his buddies ran the Rangitata during the biggest flood year in New Zealand's history. His friends again listened as he told his tale of near death as the river seethed over the gorge banks and giant whirlpools appearing to suck the tubes of their fourteen-foot rafts as they spun through the narrowest section. "Matt, he swam. The river opened wide and sucked in his top tube. The next thing we knew, he had just disappeared into a dark, swirling whirlpool. My bow paddler was keeping an eye on where he went in as we passed. He said he swore he could see Matt's face looking up at him from deep in the maw of water.

"I was just trying to keep us from getting thrown up against the gorge walls like a ping-pong ball. Suddenly, we saw Matt pop up like a rubber ducky downstream, his face pointing upward toward the sky. Then all we saw was flailing arms as he made a mad dash toward George's boat. He literally leapt into George's boat without even touching the raft. His eyes wild and crazy scared. He yelled, "Mate, I saw the gates of hell down there. I saw the devil himself, reaching up to grab me and drag me down into the dark abyss. I punched him and told him, another day. I'm not ready to die. I gotta finish this river run!"

"Naw man," I yelled, "that was just Luke looking down at you from above."

We made it down that river, but it was the hairiest run I've ever done through that Gorge. We flipped five of the ten boats that day." He waited for effect.

"Ya, and I bet you did it with a blindfold on!" Joe piped in.

They all laughed, and Juan jabbed Jay in the ribs. "Wow, last time you told that story there were only four of you and a dog. Didn't the dog save you?"

"No that was another trip but, the dog, he just kept swimming and made his way to the shore and climbed up on the rocks. He refused to get back in. Just flat out refused."

"I don't blame him," said Maya. "Dogs are smart. They know when they are in over their heads, so to speak."

Elaine looked at Maya and asked, "So, tell us about your side job doing search and rescue. We've heard Jay's stories over and over. What's the craziest search and rescue mission you've been on with... Kali?"

Maya thought about it. "Well, the craziest one I've ever been on was a rescue where Kali was the star. She accomplished it almost on her own. We were sent out to find a hiker and her dogs. One of her dogs had shown up at the trailhead and alerted a couple that had just arrived at the parking lot. They thought it was odd that the dog was all alone. They tried to coax it over to them, but it just kept walking toward the trail, turning around and waiting for them.

"Finally, they followed the dog down the trail. Then the dog took off through the brush down along the base of a cliff. The cliff paralleled the trail where it narrowed. The man marked the trail and attempted to go in a ways. He turned back because the terrain was very steep and rock started to give way under his feet. He decided not to follow the dog any further. The dog came back and sat right at the trail and barked. They heard another bark further up the trail. They walked up to where the trail ran along a cliff. Below the cliff was the river. Halfway down the cliff, he could just make out a Border Collie standing on a cliff ledge barking too. He couldn't see anyone with the dog, so he figured maybe the dog had fallen and was caught on the ledge. Of course, they also wondered if the dog's owner maybe somewhere down below as well. The woman volunteered to go back and call 911.

"By the time we arrived it was late in the afternoon. Kali and I went out with the first group to do a search before it got dark. When we reached the dog sitting along the trail, he got animated and started barking vigorously and turning toward a route downward. Kali dove in and followed the dog as he made his way under thick brush and rocky ledges. I wasn't as able to crawl under the brush, but I managed to weave my way around.

"I could hear the others going up the trail with the man to see if they could find another route down to the other dog. When they were in the parking lot, they noticed that there was only one other car. It was a blue Subaru with blankets down over the back seats. It looked like whoever had the car also had dogs. They figured they might find whoever owned the car if they could get down near the other dog.

"Anyway, Kali was following the other dog when they came to another ledge above the river. Off to the side along the trail, a cliff face rose to where the dog on the cliff ledge was located. Below, in the narrow canyon, was a young woman sitting on a rock in the middle of fast-moving current that tumbled down into a series of whitewater drops below her. It was lower water, so probably a Class IV with Class V consequences."

They all nodded, realizing that her rescue story was turning into a river rescue.

"The woman was holding on to a nubbin of rock to give her a feeling of being attached to the rock. She had been yelling for help, but the roar of the water drowned out the sound of her voice. The first dog had led the couple to where they could get closer to her. The other dog had followed her over the cliff after she fell. He was stuck on the ledge above her.

"At this lower ledge, I couldn't go any farther. I could see her, but I couldn't reach her. She was only about ten feet below us, but she was separated from the shore by the water that met the cliff wall. No way to get to her. I radioed back to the team leader that we had located a woman and her dogs. We would need to set up a high angle rescue across the river because it was too narrow to get a helicopter in and there wasn't any shoreline to speak of. We'd have to come in from above and pluck her off the rock.

"By this time, it was starting to get dark. We were running out of daylight. The darkness was going to make the operation much more challenging. I looked for a way to get her out quicker. The gorge was only about ten feet wide. Further downstream, there was a narrow tree trunk anchored across the river. It looked like it was wedged between two rocks on our side and on the other side it was laying solidly across a ledge. From that ledge there was a series of rocks protruding from the cliff that formed a very sketchy route up to the cliff above where the woman was. The ledge on that side of the river was closer to her and there was another tree that could be used as a rope anchor.

"I called back and requested they send Kali's and my life jackets up with the next person, along with my helmet for a rope rescue over water. Then I pulled out my fifty-foot line and started to think about how I could at least get something warm down to her. She looked blue. I was afraid that she wouldn't make it until we could get out there to rescue her. The canyon was shaded, and she was half in the water wearing running shorts and a T-shirt."

Maya paused. "Do you guys want me to continue? It turned into kind of a long story."

"Yes, go ahead. We love to hear these kinds of exciting stories; besides, we need to hear some new ones," Jaden said. "Jay has worn us out telling the same tales over and over."

Jay rolled his eyes, but he, too, wanted Maya to continue.

Maya hoped that she hadn't alienated the young men with her tales of daring rescues. Too many times, when a guy found out what she did for a living, he suddenly became intimidated by her. She wasn't a damsel in distress kind of gal and that scared a lot of guys.

"Well, I'll get to the main act," she said. "So, I realized that if I could get the rope down to the girl, I could at least slide my jacket with a thin merino wool hat and gloves in the pockets down to her. That might buy us a little more time until we could set up a rope rescue. I also thought if I could cross the river on the log, I could climb up the rock to the ledge lower down, but above her location.

"When Roy showed up with my gear, I sprang into action. I told him what I was going to do. He immediately said no, I couldn't do that. We needed to wait until everyone showed up and then set up a proper rescue operation. I ignored him. I knew it was risky, but I felt comfortable with my ability to discern whether or not I could pull it off. I'd deal with the fallout later, unless, of course, I didn't survive my calculated risk.

"Kali and I carefully climbed down to where the log crossed the river. I looked it over carefully. It wasn't rotten and the trunk seemed intact. I tested it by slowly adding my weight to it. It seemed to hold. It was only about fourteen feet from end to end across the river. I put our life jackets on. We'd cross the log and then make our way up to the ledge. From there, we'd be available to catch the rescue line when the others got it set up and then anchor it to the tree. While they were working to set up, I could lower my jacket down to the woman.

"Kali jumped up onto the log and before I could even think twice, she fearlessly walked across and waited for me. I made my way across a little more slowly. Trying to cross a log as water is rushing by below is unnerving. As I stepped, I felt the log bow under my weight. Not enough to break, but for a moment, I thought I was going to lose my balance, but I kept it and made my way slowly across. On the other side, I pointed to the rocks that made their way up to the ledge above us. Kali literally took two leaps and scaled the ten-foot wall. I started to make my first step and realized that the rock was wet and slippery. As I tried to step up, my foot slipped sideways, and I almost fell into the river. I realized that scaling that wall was not going to happen. It was covered with a slick layer that I couldn't get a purchase on.

"What came next was invention. I tossed the rope up to Kali and she grabbed it in her mouth. Then I gave her the command, directing her toward the tree. The next command was to 'go around', which meant that she was to go around the obstacle, this being the tree. She did. Then I motioned for her to bring the rope back down to me. She easily scaled the steps back to me.

"Without a thought, I took off my life jacket, and hooked it to the rope using the rescue loops around the waist and securing it to the rope end with a figure eight and a carabineer. Then I commanded Kali to 'go find'. She leapt back up the cliff to the ledge and walked to the edge. I let the slack out of the rope and then when she was ready, I said, 'jump'. Kali leapt off the ledge and landed on the rock in the middle of the river on the narrow space between the woman and the fast-moving water. She wagged her tail and licked the woman's face. I motioned to the woman to get the life jacket on and cinch down the straps so that it was secure. This was difficult, given that the river drowned out the sound and the woman was uncoordinated because she was so cold. The terror in her eyes was palpable. She carefully got her right arm through the arm of the life jacket and worked to get her left arm in. She then cinched up the straps, so they were tight. She pulled out the hat and gloves and put them on. Then she grabbed onto Kali for support.

"I made a calculated risk. If we could get her to stand up,

we might be able to pull her up the cliff on the side for support and keep her from going into the river. It was risky. If we didn't pull fast enough, she could get caught by the current and dragged downstream and underwater.

"Roy chimed in on the radio. 'Have Kali bring the rope back across. We can use the tree to set up a pulley system and then have the woman clip in using the carabineer.'

"I realized that was a much better choice and a better guarantee of success. I motioned to the woman to unhook the rope from her life jacket and keep the carabineer. Then give the rope to Kali. Luckily, she followed the commands. She put the rope in Kali's mouth.

Now the question was, could Kali get back to one side of the river or the other? I commanded Kali 'jump'. Kali looked up at the way she had come down. She hesitated. It was quite a jump from the rock up to the top of the ledge. I watched as her body became taut and she crouched before leaping straight up and out, clearing the edge of the ledge and landing just on the edge. One foot slipped, and just for a second, I thought she was going to slide backwards, but she dug her nails into the rock and held her ground. Suddenly, her whole body shuddered. I think she realized how close she had come to not making it. Then her tail wagged, and she looked at me with her expression that says, 'See, Mom, I did it.'

"I'll take some more beer now," Maya said. She completely had their attention. No one was fidgeting or looking bored.

"Absolutely. I'll pour, go on," said Jay.

"So, Kali scrambled down to me bringing the rope with her. We made our way back across the log and tied in with the rest of our group. We anchored both ends of my rope on a pulley system farther up the hillside on another tree. Then we sent out a line attached to the main line. It was long enough for the woman to attach her carabineer to the hook on her life jacket and then to the line. Once she was attached, we had her test it to make sure it was secure enough to take her weight. Then we threw her another rope that we could use to help pull her up and out of the gorge to our side of the river. We pulled the main rope taut, which lifted her up off the rock. Then we slowly had her pull herself across, arm after arm, as we pulled upward, lifting her up while she moved across and above the river. Finally, she was able to place her butt on the ledge. Roy and Kent reached over and pulled her up farther onto the ledge to safety. The first thing the woman did was drop down and give Kali a huge hug, and then her next question was, 'Where are my dogs?'"

"Wow, that is intense. What a story! So, what had happened to her and her dogs?" asked Connor.

It turns out she was out for a trail run with her two Border Collies. One of her dogs, the one caught on the ledge below the trail, saw a rattlesnake and jumped on it to protect the woman and in the process slid over the ledge with the rattler. Luckily, the rattlesnake tumbled farther down into the river. The girl, in an attempt to rescue her dog, tried to climb down the ledge and had slid over some scree and plummeted into the river just above the rock. Luckily, she was able to grab hold of the rock and yard herself onto it before being propelled down the white-water drops below the rock. But she was stuck.

"The other dog kept trying to get to her, but she yelled at it to get back. We think, when the dog couldn't get to his owner, he went back to the trailhead to get help. You know, kind of like Lassie leading rescuers to Timmy who fell in the well."

They nodded and laughed at the reference.

"She was so lucky. She knew it too. She was so apprecia-tive. Later in the summer, we ended up going on to 'Northwest Back Roads' to do a reunion and a reenactment. It was a signifi-cant rescue. I was able to touch base with her again. It really felt good to have rescued someone who survived and then reconnect with her later.

We hiked out after dark. The other rescuers were able to rappel down, put a harness on her other dog, and lift him up to safety. Good thing both her dogs were pretty trusting, or who knows if we could have gotten her dog off the ledge. Anyway, I love to tell that story because Kali was the hero, and it had a happy ending."

"Bravo, bravo," said Jay. "That's the best story I've heard this year."

"It sounds like you live a pretty exciting life," said Anna. "You, Kali, are quite the dog." She looked down at Kali, now lifting her head after hearing her name. Rio whimpered. "Oh, I'm sure you are too," Anna reassured Rio that he was also a star.

"It has its interesting moments," said Maya. *If you only knew.* "Never a dull moment! I feel like I've taken too much of your time. Where were we? Oh yes, more beer."

She took a long draft of the ale that Jay had brought to the table.

They made small talk after that. Jaden was turning thirty-three. He was on his way to Norway the next day with his three friends. They were doing a diving trip in the frigid waters of the fjords. It turned out that they were all quite the travelers and explorers. She liked them. They lived life and didn't let it pass them by. She needed to spend more time with people like this.

The band started to warm up. They listened to a couple of the opening songs. Good band, she thought. Then Jay invited her to join them at the Grange. "These guys are good, but the Island of Black and White are the best local band around. We'll be dancing up a storm until we drop. Join us. They'll have great beer there as well."

Maya drained the last of her beer and asked for a to-go container for her pizza. With all the talking she had been doing, she had completely forgotten to eat. She'd just take it with her and eat it later. She remembered where the Grange was because she'd walked by it earlier in the day. She told them she'd meet them there. It was almost dark as she pulled out of the parking lot and made her way down the road back to the old historic part of town.

When she arrived, she saw that the road near the Grange was lined with cars on both sides. Realizing it wasn't too far from the American River Resort, she decided to park at her cabin, feed the dogs, and leave the dogs there and walk back. The dogs quickly settled in. They were tired from the long day of excitement and activity.

22

ISLAND OF BLACK AND WHITE

SHE MADE her way to the front of the Grange. A couple of young people stood below the weak light under the western awning, smoking cigarettes. The place was packed. There were old hippies, young adults, kids, and families. Maya looked over and saw Jay and Jaden buying beer tickets. She paid her ten dollars and then caught up with them.

Maya looked over and saw the rest of the group sitting at a table next to a wooden bench against the wall.

"We have friends in the band." Jay winked. "They saved us the table."

They walked back across to the table where everyone was sitting. People were already jumping onto the dance floor as the band introduced their next song.

"We're Island of Black and White. We got a little known song for you right now about the weather." Anna, Juan, and Elaine sang along with the lyrics. The sound was upbeat and with a little edge of country.

Maya sat down with the younger men on one side and Jay and Elaine on the other. She felt like she had just been included in a big family reunion. It seemed like everyone knew everyone.

She watched as a group of kids skidded in their socks across one side of the dance floor. Across the room, she could see a few old timers sitting in their chairs at the edge of the dance floor, the matriarchs and patriarchs of the community, she guessed.

The band transitioned into their next song. The dance floor filled up. Jaden grabbed Maya and they entered the dance floor. It took her a minute to lose her stiffness and find her rhythm. She could tell Jaden was comfortable dancing.

Maya could feel the music taking over and she lost her senses to the summer heat and the way the blues always made her feel like she was just an extension of the music. Her hips swayed. Jaden noticed. He was a good dancer, not one of those stiff and self-conscious guys on the dance floor.

The next song was upbeat swing, and it turned out, Jaden could swing. So could she. She found herself laughing as she twirled into his arms and then back out. They were the center of attention on the floor. They gave the crowd a show and then bowed out as another couple took over.

Jaden and Maya continued to dance and dance. It seemed like an hour before they finally surrendered and went back to the table. By this time, Maya was starving. She still hadn't eaten her pizza. She opened the box and dug in.

From up on stage, Maya heard an accordion and watched as the lead singer stepped into the crowd. He squeezed out a few notes, raised his arm, walked to the stage, grabbed a bottle of beer from his amp and took a long swig, and with an exaggerated gesture, sat it down. He then grabbed a unicycle propped up against the stage. With some rolling starts and stops, he played with the crowd who hooted and hollered. When he was up and moving on his unicycle he belted out an accordion riff while rolling back and forth.

Then he dropped into a Russian Cossack Folk rhythm. The band joined in, and people started stamping their feet on the floor and clapping as he rode his unicycle. As the rhythm became faster, so did his movements on the unicycle until finally, in a crescendo, he leapt off the unicycle and he and the band transitioned into their next song.

Maya and Jaden jumped back up and started dancing again. This time joined by Connor, Reyd, and Burt. Burt had met a girl and was dancing with her like a crazy man. Jay, Elaine, and Anna were dancing together as they floated toward Maya and the boys. The band switched gears, and the next thing people were lining up and snaking around the dance floor, following the pied piper bandleader with his wild accordion. The floor shook with stomping as the snake of dancers wound inward and outward behind the singer. Finally, it disbanded, and the singer did his last hurrah on the accordion. Maya was enthralled. This was one of the best shows she had seen in a long time.

At the finish, the band broke for an intermission. Maya followed everyone back to the table. They were out of breath, laughing, and the old guys were slapping each other on the back. Joe exclaimed, "I can still dance all night! I'm not dead yet!"

"Just wait until tomorrow," said Steve. "You can still dance all night; you just pay for it longer."

"Ah, you're right, but I wouldn't miss out. I'll be dancing in my grave someday."

"You guys are amazing," Maya exclaimed. "This has been the best night I've had for a while. All of you are my role models!"

"We try to set a high bar," said Jay and smiled a devilish grin.

Maya excused herself and went to the bathroom. She

looked in the mirror. Her long reddish blonde hair twisted in a disheveled braid. Sweat causing wisps of hair to stick to the side of her face. Her cheeks were flushed. Her bright blue eyes looked alive. She wondered if this was what normal people felt like. Years of sleepless nights at work and the high stress of her job caused her and her coworkers to always have a tight edge to their expressions and dark circles under their eyes.

Maya smiled as a warm flush rose up her neck and into her cheeks. She was enjoying the attention of Jaden and his friends. She felt a little reckless and detached. Even though she knew she wouldn't act on it, she was enjoying the flirtation and dancing.

The band launched into their next set. They led with a song called Egyptian Lullaby. with a lilting storyline that hopped along, then broke into a keyboard solo, Maya and her friends sat and listened. After, an upbeat song that sent everyone out to the dance floor again.

Jaden and Maya continued to dance together, playing off each other's moves and creating new ones that fit whatever song was playing. She felt her brain melt into the music.

She opened her eyes and saw a man staring directly at her from across the room with an intensity that was unnerving. She noticed the way he sat back against the metal chair, adjusting the baseball cap on his head; his hard angular jaw slightly lifted, as if he was gauging something about her. It caught her so off guard. Why was he looking at her like that? Fear flooded her mind. She tried to reel herself back in, but her fear escalated into panic. Her vision narrowed and suddenly she was alone, and no one could protect her. Jaden watched as she ran out of the Grange and into the street.

She ran down the road in a panic. What had she missed? There was something important that she should know but it kept eluding her. What was it? She kept running from the panic and the fear.

She followed her path back to the American River Resort and made it to the cabin. The dogs barked as she let herself in and slammed the door. She crouched in the dark as Kali and Rio crowded around her, noses sniffing and tails wagging. She sat listening, for what, she didn't know. Finally, she curled up in a tight ball on the bed and the dogs snuggled in beside her. She covered her head and tried to be as quiet as she could.

23

TROUBLEMAKER

SHE AWOKE SOMETIME LATER in the night. She was
sprawled out with Kali tucked up under her left arm that was
draped over her neck. Rio was snoring away on her right side.
She stared up at the ceiling of the cabin illuminated by a full
moon. She was in her cabin with the dogs in... Coloma.

She sat up and the dogs sprang up, suddenly alert now that
she was awake. Something had triggered her at the Grange.
She'd been having the time of her life up until the point she saw
the man. Mid-thirties, short brown hair, and a stocky build. It
wasn't the way he looked; it was the look in his eyes that had
spooked her. He was intently watching her and it wasn't because
he was admiring her dancing. It was something else. She almost
felt that feeling of panic welling up again. She stuffed it down.

Well, she bet Jaden and her new friends thought she was a
crazy one. One minute she was having the time of her life, and
the next she was sprinting out of the Grange. Damn, she'd been
having so much fun, too.

She couldn't tell how she would react anymore. Someone

could shoot a gun over her head, and she'd barely flinch. Then one of her coworkers would complain because she'd forgotten to take the trash out in the morning, and it would send her into a tailspin.

A few months before, when she had been pulling a normal shift, one of the medics came in to relieve her. The minute he walked through the door, she suddenly felt like she was walking on eggshells. She never liked this particular medic. He'd always resented her because she got hired before him. She knew that if he could complain, he would.

She put her gear away and made sure everything was perfect before she left. He had left the living room and gone out to do his morning workout. She felt on edge, so she chose not to interact with him anymore than she had to. She left the pager on the counter in the living area and left for home. They'd been up all night, so she went home to sleep.

At 5 p.m. that evening, she got a call from the shift supervisor. He called because her coworker had called his supervisor and complained that she hadn't given him the pager before she left.. Maya explained to the supervisor her unsettled feelings in the morning, and that she left the pager on the counter because she was uneasy about approaching him.

The supervisor knew something was up too, but he simply sided with the coworker repeating that she should have given the pager to him. She sucked it up and apologized and said it wouldn't happen again.

Even after years on the job, she always had to walk on eggshells, never knowing when some ridiculous complaint would land on her. It was always her fault, never her male coworker's. She found out a month later that his wife was having an affair and they had split up, and that he was probably angry before he even walked in the door.

She decided to get her laptop out of the car. She'd left everything before leaving for the Grange.

The full moon illuminated the river, and the sound of the current echoed off the valley walls. She walked from the deck around to the back of the cabin where her SUV was parked. She felt pain erupt across the back of her head and then she was falling downward into darkness.

SHE WAS JARRED awake as something slapped her in the face. She couldn't breathe. When she opened her eyes, all she saw was black. Cold was radiating into her chest, and it felt like her lungs were going to burst.

Suddenly, she broke through the surface of, what, water? She took a deep breath. With lungs full of air, she realized that she was in the river, being pulled beneath the surface again. She felt like a leaf as she was tossed and twirled and pummeled in the whitewater current.

As the river pulled her downward her butt hit the rocks below her. She felt helpless to direct her movement as the river took control. She let go and relaxed. This is it, she thought to herself as her lungs reached their tipping point. In another minute she'd take that breath and then... water would fill her lungs and she would drown.

She gasped and water rushed in. Then her face broke through the surface as the river became shallow. She coughed as she expelled the small amount of water she had inhaled just before she surfaced.

She quickly pulled her feet up in front of her and faced them downstream. Then as she saw another wave, she took a deep breath before the water broke over her again.

She looked ahead of her but all she could see was moonlight on the river's surface. She tried to figure out where she was. The current was tapering off and now she was just floating along the surface. Her fingers and feet were numb. She was shivering uncontrollably, and her body seemed so hard to move.

As she looked up, she saw the bridge near the Grange, and started a ferry angle toward the shore. She hoped that the movement of her limbs would keep her warm enough and alert until she could get to the shore.

She finally hit the shallows. She pulled herself in on some rocks sticking out of the water. Beyond the rocks, willows pushed out from the shoreline. She pushed up with her arms and tried to find purchase with her knees but slipped off the uneven rocks. She dragged one foot up below her body and placed it on what she hoped was a solid rock. As she tried to put her weight on her foot, she had to put her hands down on two rocks and use them to balance. She was able to drag the other foot up beneath her, but her feet were so numb that she could hardly tell where they were.

Her shivering became more violent, but she knew if she quit shivering, that meant that her low body temperature was causing her body to shut down.

She steadied herself, and on the count of three, pushed up with her arms and both legs. She staggered forward, slipping on rocks, but she stayed up.

She slowly inched her way across the rocky shoreline to the willows. The slightest unevenness threw her off center and she almost fell flat on her face. At the willows, she stopped to catch her breath. Downstream she found a small break in the willows and a dirt track that led up a short, steep embankment. She must be in the park she stopped at yesterday after lunch.

She came out near another dirt trail at the top of the rise. She was under oak trees now and it was pitch black except for a few variations of shadow cast by the moonlight. Further out, she could make out the outline of the old millwork. The meadow surrounding it was illuminated and almost clear to the highway.

She saw headlights coming down the highway and became afraid. What had happened to her? She couldn't remember anything after she went outside to... get her computer.

She ducked back in the shadow of the trees. Had she been attacked? She reached to the back of her head. She felt a large bump that was very painful as she pushed on it. Why would someone attack her from behind at three in the morning? Was someone trying to break into her car, and she had caught him or her in the act?

She assumed they wanted her dead.

Then she thought of Don and how he had just happened to be on the same trail as she was a few days ago. She thought about the man looking at her at the Grange that had triggered her into running out.

She waited until the car passed, and carefully made her way up to the road, just skirting along the edge of the meadow near the trees where she could take cover if she needed to. She remembered there were state park buildings just down the road that looked like they could be housing for some of the park rangers. She didn't want to venture back to her cabin until she was sure she was safe. She hoped the dogs were okay in the cabin.

Maya crossed over Highway 49 and made her way toward the back of park housing. She looked for one with cars parked in front of it, walked up, and pounded on the door. Nothing. She pounded again and looked around to see if any of the lights in the houses went on. Finally, a light came on inside the house.

"Who is it?" a sleepy voice said from behind the door.

"Hi, my name is Maya. Someone just tried to kill me! Please, I need help!"

A man pulled back a window cover on the door and looked out at her. He must have felt she was the real deal, because he quickly opened the door.

"Come in. Are you okay? You look, well, you're soaking wet."

Maya collapsed into a kitchen chair and asked him to call the police.

The El Dorado County Sheriff arrived fifteen minutes later. While she was waiting, Tom, the park ranger, gave her a pair of his pants, a shirt, and jacket and had her go into his bathroom to dry off and change.

Maya looked in the bathroom mirror. Her skin was ghost white and her lips were blue. Her hair hung in wet strands. When she started to dry her hair, her towel hit a wet sticky mess on the back of her head. She carefully cleaned it. She'd need to go to the emergency room.

She put on the dry clothes and immediately started to feel some of the cold dissipate. She had some scratches on her feet and legs, probably from walking through the willows.

She returned to the kitchen just as the sheriff knocked on the door. Tom ushered her into a seat near the heater and handed her a steaming cup of tea. "You need to drink this. You're hypothermic."

Tom then grabbed the door, and the sheriff walked in. Tom knew him and introduced her: "This is Ryan. He is our local officer."

Maya shook his hand and then sat back in her chair.

"So, Tom said you say someone tried to kill you? Can you tell me what happened?"

Maya held the tea between her hands and looked up at him. "Well, I'm staying at the American River Resort in one of their cabins. I woke around 3 a.m. and couldn't get back to sleep so I went out to my car to get my computer. I was just getting to my car door. I felt an excruciating pain in the back of my head. Next thing I was aware of, I was drowning in the river. I believe I was being tossed around in the whitewater. Then I was dragged along the bottom. Finally, I was able to get to the shoreline at Marshall Gold Park. I came here to find help. I honestly don't know how I ended up in the river."

Tom interjected, "You swam Troublemaker?"

"I guess" said Maya.

"You're lucky to be alive."

"I used to be a river guide, luckily I fell back on what I knew, or I probably would have drowned."

The officer gave her an incredulous stare. Immediately she knew what he was thinking.

"No, officer, I didn't drink too much alcohol. I was staying in the cabin with my two dogs and just went out to get my computer."

He seemed to register that she wasn't messing around with him. "Okay, so do you know who might have attacked you?"

"No, not really. Today I met some locals and spent the evening with them. I did have a weird incident at the Grange. A man I didn't know was staring at me intensely from across the room. It was unnerving enough that I didn't feel safe and left. However, I've been involved in a murder investigation in South Lake Tahoe."

She then recounted everything that had happened: how she'd had visits from animal control, how the husband just happened to be on the same trail as she was a few days ago, and then seeing him again at a local brewery. "It all seemed like coincidence, but now this. I'm starting to think that it might all be connected."

"So do you think that someone involved in that murder is trying to kill you?"

"I don't know. It doesn't make any sense, but who else?"

Tom had retrieved his first-aid kit. "Maya, I think I should get your temperature, blood pressure, and heart rate so we can make sure you aren't too cold. Do you feel like you are warming up yet?"

"Yes, I do. This tea and the dry clothes are working wonders. The hot air from the heater is heaven. I don't think I've ever been so cold in my life!"

Ryan was sitting down in one of the kitchen chairs now. He asked her some more questions as Tom scanned her head to take her temperature. "Jeez, Maya, your temperature is ninety degrees. I think I should call an ambulance and get you to the hospital for more aggressive rewarming."

"I agree," said Ryan.

"Ok, but I'm worried about my dogs. I need to check on them before I go. I don't know if whoever attacked me went after them. Ryan, if you can take me to my dogs and we can put them in your car, I'd feel much better about going to the hospital."

"I have an idea. Why don't I follow you over with Ryan?" Tom suggested. "You can bring the dogs and we can put them in my truck and bring them here. Then Ryan can drive you to the emergency room."

Maya wrapped a warm blanket over her shoulders and left with Ryan. He called in his location and plan to dispatch. He cranked his heater on to high and pointed all the front vents at her. Tom followed in his white California State Parks truck. They entered the American River Resort. Tom had the key code and punched it in and then got back in his truck and followed them in. Maya thought about that. Whoever had attacked her had come by foot unless they had a code.

As they pulled up, they saw that her SUV was still parked in the front of the cabin. Maya jumped out of the car and ran around to the slider. Both dogs immediately started barking once they realized it was Maya. Their tails started wagging but Kali had a worried look on her face. She lifted her nose up. When Maya bent down, Kali immediately went around and started sniffing the back of her head. "It's okay, Kali."

Tom walked up behind her and a low growl erupted from Rio. Maya gave them the command to "sit". They sat with their eyes glued on Tom. "Friend," said Maya, and then released them. They padded over calmly and checked out Tom. She could tell he was comfortable around dogs. They would need to trust Tom if she was going to leave them at his house.

"Tom, would it be possible for you to take me to the hospital? I think if I ride with you and the dogs, by the time we get to the hospital, they'll be more comfortable with me leaving them with you while I get checked out."

"I can do that. I already called in to my supervisor and let him know what's going on."

Maya handed Ryan the key. "Here's the key so you can look around for any evidence."

Ryan said he'd follow up with investigating the scene. They'd need to treat this as an attempted murder and gather evidence.

"I'll come by the ER when I'm finished. I'll probably have more questions for you by then too. Also, I can probably give you a ride back to Tom's later."

"Thanks so much."

Maya told Tom she would ride in back with the dogs. She could use their body warmth to help her warm up. Kali was wedged up against her left side. She had Rio draped over her lap.

"I have almost been killed twice and have found a dead body off of a mountain bike trail," she said out loud.

"You what?"

She told Tom about the ambush and officer's shooting in Seattle and explained again about finding the dead woman on the trail.

"At this point. I'd put the whodunit on the husband. I'd also say there is a pretty good chance that he probably tried to kill you. I mean, who else do you have on your list of enemies that might try to murder you?"

"No one that I know of. As for motive, maybe the husband thought I saw him at the scene of his wife's murder. I saw something near the location when I started CPR, but I have no idea what it was, let alone who.

"Do you mind if I let Ryan know about the incident up in Seattle? He may want to follow up on that too. You never know."

"I didn't think of that incident as being related to this but, who knows.

Her feet and hands were starting to tingle and with that came the pain of cold limbs waking up. She could also feel a rip-roaring headache developing. She reached down and scratched both dogs on the head. "You guys will be fine. Tom is a friend." She leaned back on the seat and closed her eyes. She was feeling exhausted.

TOM SHOOK HER. She looked up into the bright lights under the awning of the entrance to Mercy's emergency department. "Wow, did I fall asleep?"

"Only for about fifteen minutes," replied Tom. "I'm going to run and get some help and bring out a chair."

She looked up at the lights again. Pain seared through her

eyes. She felt nauseated. She pushed Kali out of the way, opened the door and leaned out and threw up. She closed her eyes and waited.

Tom and the tech found Maya leaning over with vomit on the ground and sprang into action. They scooped her up into the wheelchair and directly into a room.

Tom gave the staff the details that she had told him. They quickly undressed her, started an IV, and the rewarming process. They prepped her for a CT scan of her brain to make sure she didn't have a serious head injury. She just surrendered to the care as she struggled with the severe pain in her head.

"We'll give you something as soon as we can. Right now, we need to get you rewarmed and into the CT. Once we've done that and a neurologic exam, we'll give you something to help," a nurse said.

Once they were set up, they started to wheel her out to the CT. Tom caught her ear. "I'll take good care of the dogs. I'll check in on you later. Take care."

Six hours later, as she lay staring at the ceiling, the nurse came in and gave her discharge instructions.

"As you know, you suffered a concussion and hypothermia," the nurse said. "Luckily, the scalp wound will heal on its own and wasn't quite as bad as we initially thought. Just keep an eye on it. Since you're a paramedic, I'll assume you know most of what I'm telling you, but I just need to go over it with you before I let you leave.

She just needed to get back to her dogs and her SUV and head back to Tahoe.

"Okay, take Ibuprofen for your headache. Other than that, keep your wounds clean and follow up with a doctor in Tahoe in a few days."

The nurse left her to change. Maya put on her own clothes

that she had grabbed on her way out of the cabin. Then she waited until Officer Ryan showed up.

"Let's get on our way. I will bring you up to speed on where I am at in the investigation. Then I can ask you any follow up questions when we get back to Tom's place."

On their drive back, Maya sat back and listened as Ryan said that they hadn't found much at the scene. It was dry, so no tracks. They looked to see if they could pull any fingerprints her the vehicle. He said there was a trail down to the river just upstream of her cabin and that may have been where the attacker threw her in the river.

"Also, I called Officer O'Brien and let him know what happened to you. They are going to go over and pay a visit to the husband. They'll see if he has an alibi for last night. It sounds like they think he is their prime suspect for the wife's murder, but they just don't have the evidence to arrest him yet."

They pulled into Tom's place. Maya was itching to check on her dogs. They knocked and the dogs started to bark.

"Well, they were nice enough, but you sure can tell you're the pack leader!" Tom said.

"I contacted American River Resort. Now that the cabin is a crime scene, it will remain empty tonight. You can stay here. I can sleep on the couch, and you can have my bed."

"You know, I'm really feeling okay. I'd like to get back to Tahoe. I'm going to grab my stuff and stay in a hotel tonight. I have another place, an Airbnb, booked, starting tomorrow night. So hopefully, I'll get some peace."

Tom looked at her. "Do you think that is such a good idea after you've had someone attempt to murder you? "

"Maya, why don't you take Tom's offer?" Ryan interjected. "We can go over all the info and additional questions I have for you. Then I can also check in with O'Brien and see if they are going to pick the husband up and keep him.

Besides, if the person who did this to you thinks you're dead, we may be able to flush them out easier. If you don't show up at the house it won't, hopefully, tip them off that you survived.

I don't think you are safe right now on your own."

Maya reconsidered. "Maybe the drive back isn't such a good idea. I may see if I can get someone to just pick my stuff up from the apartment tomorrow, too. That way I don't have to go back until they've arrested the person who attacked me."

Maya knew she needed to take care of herself. Sometimes her job made her feel invincible because she was the lifesaver, not the patient. Now she was sitting on the other side realizing that she needed to let go of some control.

"Are you up to answering some questions or do you want to rest first?" Ryan asked.

Maya and Ryan sat down in the kitchen. "So, the information I need you to expand on is who you had contact with last night. Did you leave the Grange with anyone?"

"No, I actually left in a hurry after that man kind of alarmed me," Maya replied. Then she described the man as best as she could.

"Did you see anyone following you from the Grange?"

"Not that I was aware of. As I said, I was alarmed and just wanted to get out of there."

"Okay, you said because of the look that he gave you?"

"Yes, but I can't explain exactly why it set me off. It was just a feeling."

"Is there anything else you want to add in describing him?"

"No, not really. I've told you everything."

"So, the people that you met at Marco's and went dancing with, do you remember their names?"

"Yes, let's see. The long-haired guy with the walrus mustache was Jay. Then there was Steve, Juan, and Joe. Elaine and Anna. Anna's son and his four friends: Jaden, Burt, Reyd, and Connor. Sorry, I don't know their last names."

"Did they all seem to be reasonable people? Any feeling that one of them might have been unsafe or odd in any way?"

"No, not at all. They were great. I didn't get anything from them that would make me feel unsafe. Jaden and his friends were leaving for Norway today."

She thought of Jaden. What a disappointment. She'd meant to get his contact info before she left so she could touch base with him when she came back down.

"So, did you run into anyone during the day that could have been a suspect?"

"No."

"Two more questions. Is there anyone in Seattle that would want to see you dead?"

"Well, not that I'm aware of. I did, however, have a horrible call, right before I left. A right-wing militia group ambushed my crew and other emergency responders. Did you hear about the officer who was shot up near Seattle?"

"Yes. I also looked into it more today after Tom told me about it."

Maya told him about the call and how she ended up down here. "As you can see, things weren't going great before I got here and now... let's just say, I'm a little overwhelmed."

"Well, I can understand that. I want to thank you for trying to save that officer's life. If you ever need anything, you just let me know!"

"You're welcome. I know I was just doing my job, but that one was personal."

After Ryan left, she felt fatigue sink into her bones but her mind buzzed. She replayed the day before, the evening, and she searched her mind for any recognition of the man who had been staring at her. Nothing. She wondered how she could have been knocked out and carried or dragged to the river without her dogs alerting everyone. Then she replayed the meeting she had with Don on the trail for any clues about his behavior. Finally she slid into a deep sleep.

SHE AWOKE to sunlight breaking through the slats of Tom's window. Both dogs had jumped off the bed and the blankets were twisted in knots around her. She felt like she had just awakened from a coma.

She checked her phone. It was eight in the morning. She had slept all night. The dogs must have stayed calm when Tom left because she didn't remember being awakened by their alarm barking.

Maya poured herself some coffee in the cup Tom had left for her on the counter and took the dogs outside. She could feel the warmth of the sun already heating up the day. It felt good on her skin.

She saw Tom up on a rise at the back of the ranger station and walked up toward him.

After breakfast, Maya felt like it was time to get going. "I'm feeling better. If you don't mind, I'll rest here until, Ryan and Officer O'Brien have more information about what is going on. Then I can go right from here to my new Airbnb."

"You are welcome to stay here as long as you need. Can you text me when you leave here and arrive in Tahoe, so I'll know you are safe?"

Maya felt genuinely grateful that she had knocked on his door. "I will, and again, thank you, Tom."

After he left for work, Maya made some phone calls. The first was to Todd, the firefighter she'd had dinner with. Time to take him up on that offer of help.

"Todd, hi, this is Maya. Hey, I have a favor to ask you."

"Anything," Todd replied. "What do you need?"

"Well, your discretion, which is most important. Someone tried to murder me last night."

She felt the silence on the other side of the line.

Then Todd asked, "When? Where?"

I need someone to go over and get all my stuff from the apartment including my bicycle and take it to my new Airbnb. Would you be willing to do that for me?"

"Maya, of course. Anything."

"Please don't tell anyone you talked to me. Right now, I'm unofficially dead. We don't want the killer to know that he wasn't successful.

"Also, make sure no one follows you. It's obvious I was probably followed from Tahoe unless this was some crazy random attempt to murder me."

"I won't tell anyone. Give me your address. Can you text me a list of what you want me to bring?

Maya ended her call and made a list of things she needed from the apartment.

Then she called Georgia and left a message.

Then she called Nick.

"Hey, Maya. How are you doing?"

"Well, not so great... Someone tried to kill me last night."

"What? You've got to be kidding me?"

"No, I'm not kidding."

Maya recounted the event.

"Where are you now?" She could hear the alarm in his voice. "I'll get a flight as soon as I can."

"Thanks. I really need you right now."

"I'm surprised to hear you say that, but I am glad you need me."

"Oh, shut up and get down here," she said jokingly.

"I love you."

Maya was caught off guard. It had been a long time since he had said that.

"I love you too."

She had wanted solitude to sort through her feelings, but since someone tried to kill her, she was feeling less like solitude and more inclined to surround herself with people that could keep her safe. She'd always prided herself on her independence and ability to go it alone, but this was different. To be alone could be deadly. She was happy Nick was coming down.

24

THE RETURN

SHE DROPPED down Highway 50 into the Tahoe Basin, having decided to conceal her identity as much as she could. She couldn't change her vehicle, but she put her hair up under her Aussie river hat and had the dogs lay down on the floor between the seats.

She quickly made her way through Meyers and turned onto Pioneer trail. She'd take the shortest route to where she was staying and avoid going through the main highway through town. She watched in her rear-view mirror for anyone following her. She even pulled off twice to let cars pass. She couldn't afford to lead someone back to her new hide out.

She looked in her rear-view mirror. She saw a white truck, and behind that was a black sports car. She hadn't seen them along her route from Coloma, so she decided to pass her turn off and go to Carson City for groceries before heading to her Airbnb.

Leaving Costco, she took a back road that was dirt. Well, this should weed out the stalkers, she thought. She didn't see anyone following her on the dirt road. From there, she drove along Jacks Valley Road. Then she climbed back up the face of the mountains to the top of Kingsbury.

As she descended back down Kingsbury, she made her turn onto Benjamin Drive. Then she followed her directions to Castle Rock Circle. She took the first turn into the circle. She felt good that there were two ways in and out.

Her Airbnb was on the left near the middle of the circle. The driveway was lined with aspens as it curved a short distance around granite boulders and up a short rise before arriving at the house.

She pulled up in front of the garage and got out. The dogs jumped out and immediately started sniffing around the driveway lined with native grasses and pine mat manzanita.

The walkway to the front door was flagstone that led up to a granite step on to a covered porch. She keyed in the code and the door opened. She walked inside to find an entry floor of flagstone that led to an open living room with a wall of windows looking out at the local mountains, forest, and Castle Rock off to the side with its large granite summit. The dogs came running in. They were excited too.

She opened large sliders and went out onto a large wooden deck that curved around boulders and created extra privacy. The houses next door were closer to the start of her driveway than the house. Kali ran up to one of the boulders and Maya called out "jump". Kali scampered up the front of a seven-foot boulder and posed on the top, looking satisfied with herself.

This will do, thought Maya. She saw the hot tub at the edge of the deck positioned to overlook the forest and Castle Rock. She thought how good it would feel on her sore muscles and bruises from two nights ago.

On the counter were two notes. One was from the owner or manager. There other note was from Todd. "Maya, your stuff is in the master suite. Your bike, helmet, and shoes are in the garage. I walked all around the house and perimeter. I'd make sure and lock the gate at the top of the stairs on the deck and all the doors, including the slider. If you have any problems, please call me. I'm on duty tomorrow but one of my coworkers, Jake, said he would come by if you needed help. Also, Brandi said she'd love to get together with you to go hiking in the next couple of days. Take care, Todd."

Maya already felt better. People were looking out for her. She loved that about the fire service.

Down the hallway, to the right of the front door, was a full bathroom and two smaller bedrooms. A stairway at the back led up along a granite wall to the second floor. The whole second floor was a master suite with a king-sized bed that looked out the expansive wall of windows.

As much as she wanted to go for a walk, it was getting late, and her head still throbbed from the attack.

She fed the dogs and then poured herself a glass of Chardonnay and went out to sit on the couch on the patio over-looking Castle Peak as the sun sank across the lake onto the ridgeline above the western shore. She took a deep breath, and it was answered by Rio who returned from dinner and sank onto the patio beside her feet.

She texted Tom and told him she was at her new place and was safe with her two protectors. Then she texted Todd to let him know that she had arrived safe. She followed that up with a text to Georgia. Georgia hadn't called her back right away, but that wasn't unusual. Then she called Nick.

"Hey, I've arrived safely at my new place."

What do you think? Does it look like a place you can stay for a while?"

"Definitely. It's better than the photos. It has all the things I love. Lots of rock, views, a hot tub, and a king-sized bed!"

"Sounds like a great place to stay. Do you think you'll be safe there?"

"I hope so. I didn't see anyone follow me. I was really careful driving through town."

"I checked in with work. I wanted to leave tomorrow but the big client is coming in and we have an in-person meeting on Friday. After that, I can catch a flight early Saturday morning and be there by 9 a.m. That was the best I could do. I'll have to do some work while I'm down there."

"Nick, that's fine. I know you're worried, but I really worked to make sure I wasn't followed.

Maya got off the phone and pulled up O'Brien's number. It rang and she got his answering message. She left a message and then texted him. "Any update on the husband?"

A few minutes later, her phone rang.

"Hello, Maya, this is Officer O'Brien."

"I have some good news. We went to the house this morning and brought Don in for another interview. Based on some other information we had, we came with a search warrant. We found an item of interest, which has allowed us to book him into the county jail. So far, we can't find anything that links him directly to your attack. Now I need to confirm his alibi for last night. He says he was with his neighbor, Kathy Baker. So far she isn't answering her phone and she isn't at her house."

Kathy's main residence is in... some town near..."

"Santa Rosa. Yes, we know. We dispatched an officer to make contact with her there. So far, she isn't there either. Do you know much about her?"

"Just that she was friends with Karen and Don. I had dinner with her a few days ago. She seemed friendly enough."

"Once we confirm her alibi, I will let you know. Call 911 if you think that you are in danger. We want to make sure you are safe."

"Thanks."

Maya hung up the phone. She called Nick back.

"Officer O'Brien has arrested Don. It sounds like, if he killed his wife, maybe he is the one who tried to kill me the other night."

"I'm relieved. At least now you can relax with Don in jail, and I won't feel so guilty not coming down sooner. I'm so sorry. It's just this client…

"Look, I know. You need to have business to get paid and build the company. Someday you'll be able to take more time off. For now, you have to put in that hard work to get where you want to be.

I know you're worried. Only you, Georgia, Todd and Officer O'Brien know exactly where I'm staying. Plus, I've got my two protectors. If I had taken them out with me the other night, there is no way that person would have been able to attack me and get away with it. No way.

"Besides, this week, I'm going to be recovering from the concussion and the near-death hypothermia. I just keep thinking that I'm lucky to be alive."

She shuddered as an internal feeling of panic threatened to engulf her. "I'll be safe. I'll be waiting for some quality downtime with you. Maybe now, I'll get that decompression I've wanted since I got here. On that note, I'm ready to call it a night, but first I'm going to soak in the amazing hot tub."

"Sounds nice. I can't wait to be in there with you."

MAYA GRABBED a robe and headed out to the hot tub. The dogs followed her. They explored the edges of the deck as she slid into the envelope of warm water. The heat sank into her sore muscles. It seemed every inch of her was sore from the other night. She gingerly laid her head back on the air pillow to avoid where she'd been clobbered.

She looked up at the stars and the outline of the darker mountains against the sky. She heard the familiar howls of Tahoe coyotes echo across the hills. The sky was mesmerizing as the heat swirled around her. Her mind drifted from thought to thought.

25

DROWNING

SHE AWOKE to a feeling of not being able to breathe. The water was filling her lungs. No, it was blood. Blood was filling her lungs and spilling out of her mouth. She could feel the warm stickiness as it flowed down her face. She was lying on the stretcher in the back of her medic unit. The blood flowed on the stretcher and then spilled onto the floor.

She tried to scream, but only bubbles of blood erupted out of her mouth. She looked up and saw the police officer looking down on her, his face twisted in anger. "You should have saved me," he spat at her. The doors of the medic unit flew open, and a river crashed in, carrying her, her partner, and the firefighters out into a torrent moving into the street. She was caught underwater as people and debris swirled around her in river water the color of blood.

She choked and then awoke to the sound of her scream. She was fighting the blankets that she'd twisted into knots all around her. Her heart was pounding as she caught her breath.

Rio jumped up on the bed and Kali soon followed. They

licked her face and Rio whimpered. Their closeness and breath on her face brought her back to herself.

She lay there hugging her dogs, waiting for her body to settle down. Her heart continued to race, and she felt like she couldn't get enough air. When were these nightmares going to end? Her mental armor was deteriorating, leaving her raw and exposed. Why can't I just let it be? She knew. She couldn't pile on trauma after trauma and disaster after disaster forever. Sooner or later, it was going to come screaming to the surface, demanding her attention.

She finally fell back into a restless sleep interspersed with feelings of panic.

26

IGNORING THE DOCTOR'S ORDERS

THE NEXT MORNING, she felt exhausted, but she resolved to get up and make the most of the day. She took her coffee out onto the deck to sit in a lounge chair. She knew she should rest and recover from her concussion, but she was so drawn to the local trails right from the house. Maybe she'd take a short hike. If she felt a headache or dizziness, she could just turn around and come back.

Maya was not inclined to follow rules meant to slow her down. She just couldn't suppress her curiosity. The dogs were also reminding her of the world of adventure that awaited them right from the back door. She decided that a short walk would be good for them.

After breakfast, she grabbed her pack and camera and headed down the hill from the house to catch the Castle Rock Trail. The open, high, alpine landscape made it easy to weave around pine trees and thickets of manzanita towards the trail.

Wildflowers were still popping along the trail. She took her time and photographed the variety of different wildflowers she discovered. The slower pace was good for her. As she focused on flowers, the dogs were scouting outward exploring holes in the ground and following scent paths left by squirrels that eventually ran up nearby trees.

They reached the base of the rocky accent to the summit. She put her camera away and they scrambled up some loose granite sand and she veggie-belayed up a couple of steep rocky sections.

They finally arrived at the top. Only two men were farther out on the rocky top, just below Maya's perch. There before her was Lake Tahoe, spreading out both north and south. The western Sierras carved a ragged edge above the shoreline. She followed the southern edge down to Mount Tallac. To the north, the peaks of the Granite Chief Wilderness advanced toward the Truckee River Valley. Below her perch, she could see the eastern shoreline. The cerulean blue water enveloped the granite boulders popping out of the water's edge. The color of the lake always took her breath away. The blue was unlike anything she'd seen anywhere else on her travels. It seemed to glow from its translucent depths. It reminded her of a giant fire opal surrounded by a crown of granite peaks.

AFTER HER HIKE, she settled out on the deck. She'd finished her previous book and started a murder mystery she found on Amazon.

She'd never had an interest in murder mysteries. Science fiction and travelogues were more to her liking, but this recent experience made her feel like maybe giving a murder mystery a try would help her understand her own predicament.

A few pages in she found herself thinking of Karen. She had a pretty good picture of her. A crabby old woman who harassed her neighbors, was terrified of fire, and was a mountain biker. What she didn't know was, what would drive her husband to murder her after they had been together for that many years? From what Kathy had said, they had planned a retirement living part time in Tahoe and part time in Hawaii. It sounded like a pretty good deal. Was she as mean to him as she was to her neighbors? Did she tell him it was over, and she was dumping him and leaving him penniless?

Maya figured she was probably the major source of income in that relationship, but she could be wrong. From what she had heard from neighbors, she had been awful for years. So, her behavior wouldn't have been anything new. So, what brought about a murder made to look like a mountain biking accident?

She realized that she would probably never know the inner workings of his mind, or Karen's, for that matter. Where did Kathy fit in to all of this? If he was the one who tried to kill Maya the other day, why was she his alibi? Why wasn't anyone able to get a hold of her? Did he murder her as well? She had more questions than answers.

After a couple of hours of some reading and mostly running scenarios through her mind, she decided it was time to turn to something else. She reached out to her coworker on the status of the militia attack.

She texted Jeff and waited for him to call her back. Today would have been their normal shift, so he was probably on a response. A few minutes later, he called.

"We've been a bit on edge. There are rumors swirling around about more militia attacks. As you have probably heard, they are treating this like an act of domestic terrorism. No one knows if this is an isolated incident or whether we need to be on high alert for more follow-up attacks.

How are you doing?"

"Well, Part of the reason I'm calling is that I had someone try to kill me on Saturday night."

"You're kidding, right?" Jeff said.

Maya filled him in on the details including the consideration by local law enforcement that her murder attempt could be related to the ambush up there. "Have you heard anything concrete that might point in that direction?"

"There really isn't any sufficient evidence that they are part of a larger plot. Besides, why would they single you out and then track you to Tahoe and then try to kill you and make it look like a drowning?"

"They are just trying to make sure to cover all possible motives, including that some random psycho or robber that has no connection to me attacked me in Coloma.

"They've arrested the husband for the murder of his wife and are investigating the possibility that he was the one who attacked me. He has an alibi, but he also had one for the day of his wife's murder, so we shall see."

"The chief was asking about you. He hopes you are doing okay and said to take your time. "

"Hey, Jeff."

"What?"

"I'm still having nightmares. Last night I was drowning in my own blood with the near drowning and the officer's shooting all mixed together. I barely slept last night. I shouldn't have called. Can we change the subject?"

"Sure Maya.

"Guess what? Your favorite medic is getting divorced. His wife left him for the guy she had an affair with. Now he is on leave. Daniel and Frank checked him into rehab a few days ago. Curt said he'd been drinking heavy for a while. Even before his wife left him."

"That probably explains some of the struggles I had with him. I think a lot of issues; divorce, drinking, absenteeism… grouchiness are because of unrecognized job stress."

"Well, anyway. It's good he is in rehab and getting help. On a more positive note, Kalie just had her baby. She gave birth last night. She's been off work for the past week and went into labor yesterday morning. It's a healthy girl. She had an easy delivery. Well, as easy as it can be."

"I have some good news too. Nick is finally going to break free from work, take some vacation time, and come visit me. He is arriving on Saturday morning. We are going to spend some time here and then drive back to Seattle together."

"I can't believe it. You've been begging him to take some time off for a while, haven't you?"

"Yes, but you know. I needed this time to myself, but with all that has happened I'm thrilled he is coming now. But, I won't believe it until I actually pick him up from the airport. I need the company."

"Do I detect a bit of neediness?" He poked fun at her.

She countered with, "No, it's just that I need a strong man to take care of me. I'm so helpless on my own!"

"Ya, right," Jeff said. "I'd never call you helpless. Recklessly adventurous at times, yes. Helpless, never!"

"Ha, I'm not recklessly adventurous. I'm just realistic. If it is your time, it is your time. You can die tripping over a crack in the sidewalk as easily as you can die climbing Mt. Rainier. Life is risky. You just have to decide how you want to live it."

"Great. Now you are getting all philosophical on me."

"Yah and I'm not even drunk yet." She laughed. Well, I'm going to get a start on that now.

"Lucky you. I'm stuck here at work and you're down in Tahoe swimming whitewater without a life jacket and drinking vodka."

"Hey, don't knock it until you try it. Swimming whitewater without a life jacket is about as risky as it comes unless you are walking across an uneven floor after a fifth of vodka. Now, that is even more risky!"

"Stay safe!"

"You too!" Jeff was one her favorite people to work with. Having someone with a sense of humor made work so much more enjoyable.

She had good intentions, but some part of her that wanted to mentally check out took over. At dinner, she started with wine and then afterward graduated to vodka. Again, she found herself drifting into thinking about Karen and the murder. She decided that instead of thinking, she'd do a little investigative work.

She entered the woman's name, 'Karen Winter' and the city. She found a Yelp listing that had Karen's name and the name of a property management company: Manages apartments and housing for remote owners in Berkeley. It looked like she was also a licensed real estate agent. Maya scrolled down to the reviews.

"She is the worst apartment manager I have ever rented from. She was all nice and helpful until she got my money. Forget trying to get anything fixed. It's too much for her to bother. All she cares about is money."

"Property manager threatened to evict me because I have temporary help living with me while I'm pregnant, because of a medical problem. Who kicks a pregnant woman out of her apartment?"

"Be wary. All they want is your money. They'll take your deposit and charge you for every little thing. You'd be better off renting from someone else."

The complaints went on and on. There was only one positive review.

She drunk dialed Georgia.

She sprawled along the couch, kicking the dogs off.

"Georgia, this is Maya, How's it going?"

"Hey Maya," Georgia replied. "Sounds like you've been having some fun tonight?"

"Ohh, yes, I'm a little hammered. I wasn't going to drink too much but apparently that didn't happen." She giggled.

I had a rough night last night. Nightmares. You know, more nightmares about that officer.

"We all have those calls. I haven't really talked to you about this, but five years ago I had a rough stretch too. I wasn't sure I wanted to continue to be a firefighter. You remember the warehouse fire where five of our guys died?"

"Sure."

"It changed everything. I attended 'Line of Duty' funerals for five men that had been an integral part of our department. It seemed so surreal. I really struggled with feeling vulnerable. I started second guessing myself on fire scenes. Up until then, I didn't think twice. I love fighting fire. But now it was a reality that we could lose our lives. I had my crew to think about. If I made a bad decision, we'd all go down.

"It was a rough six months of feeling like I couldn't make the decisions that needed to be made. I finally got some counseling. Then, over time, I started to enjoy my job again. I started to feel the excitement of initial attack, albeit it was tempered with a little humility. I wasn't invincible anymore. None of us are."

"I hear you. You know, Georgia, you are great. I love you. I'm so glad you're my friend."

"I don't think I've ever heard you this drunk, let alone so depressed. You've never even talked about the calls, like the little girl. I didn't even know this stuff was bothering you until now.

Why don't you take it easy and quit while you are ahead?"

"Oh, and I didn't tell you. Someone tried to murder me Saturday night."

"What?"

Maya took another swig of her vodka. "Ya, and I woke up in the river drowning and I had to self-rescue."

"My god, Maya. Why didn't you call me sooner? Where are you? Why did someone try to murder you?"

"I tried to call you afterward." Maya was getting sleepy and drifting a bit. "It's a long story. I'm not up to telling it right now. I'm safe. I'm in my new Airbnb. Don, the husband of the woman, Karen, who was murdered, is in jail. He's being held for murdering her and they think he was the one who tried to kill me, too. So, I'm safe. I'm safe. I'll be okay. I'm going to say goooodnight now, okay?"

"I must have missed that you called. I would have called right back if I had known. Maya, I'm worried about you. Please call me tomorrow and let me know you are okay. I want you to tell me more about what happened."

Maya drifted off and passed out on the couch.

SHE AWOKE to Rio licking her face as she hung half on and half off the couch with her head buried into a cushion. "Rio, jeez. Leave me alone!"

She lay there not wanting to move. She kept her eyes closed. Two hours later, she awoke again, this time on her own, and realized she had out slept her hangover.

She got up and made herself some coffee and then took a shower.

She called the dogs. They had kept their distance after she had scolded Rio earlier. Her phone rang. "Hello, Georgia. How are you?"

"Well, I'm fine. The question is, how are you?"

"I'm great. I drank a little too much last night but managed to dodge the bullet and don't have a hangover this morning."

"Maya, do you remember our conversation from last night?"

"Not really," she said.

"Well, you were pretty drunk and depressed. I've never heard you like that. Then you started to tell me a story about almost being murdered. What happened? I got worried when you didn't call me this morning."

Maya looked at the time. It was eleven in the morning.

She told the story again. I feel much safer knowing that Don is in jail. Also, Nick is coming down here Saturday morning. We'll drive back to Seattle together."

"That's great Maya. I'm glad you aren't going to be alone. No wonder you were so distressed last night. Will you be all right until Nick gets there? I can come right down if you need me to."

"Georgia, no. I was just a little drunk last night. Yes, someone tried to murder me twice. Yes, the job is getting to me, but I'm not going to do anything crazy."

"All right. Yes, you did scare me last night. Now that I know you were almost murdered, I feel so much better," Georgia said sarcastically.

"Look on the bright side. My river rescue training came in handy. I bet Don didn't know I could swim a whitewater rapid while unconscious with a head injury. Gotta laugh because it's just too over the top!"

"Please call me tonight and try not to drink too much. I like you better sober."

"I promise. No drunk dialing tonight!"

The rest of Maya's day was low key. That night she decided to drink the mixer sans the vodka. She took a hot tub and then went to bed.

27

SINGLETRACK

WHILE SHE WAS MAKING BREAKFAST, she received a text from Todd. "Want to mtb w/ Brandi n I today?"

Maya thought about it and it sounded like a great idea. She texted him back. "Sure, where?"

"Can ride from your place, Kingsbury Stinger."

Maya quickly got on Trailforks and looked up Kingsbury Stinger. It was at the top of Andria Drive. They could leave right from the house. It looked like they'd need to shuttle, though.

"Should I meet you at bottom and we can shuttle? Where?" texted Maya.

"Sounds good. Meet at Kahle Park at 9:30?"

"OK, then we'll load bikes and drive back here?"

"Yes," Todd replied.

Maya was happy. It would be great to do a mountain bike ride with some locals. She quickly ate breakfast and got her bike and gear ready. She left the dogs at the house and headed down to meet Todd and Brandi. She reminded herself that she needed to take it easy on the trail. She'd had a concussion.

She pulled into Kahle Park and found them already waiting. Todd's Blue Toyota Tacoma was parked near the ball fields. Bikes ready to load onto her rack.

"Hey, thanks for the invite."

"We thought you might enjoy going for a ride today. I did forget that you recently had a concussion. Are you sure you're okay to ride?" Todd asked.

"No worries. I feel great."

"Todd told me about the attack. That sounds terrifying. Did they confirm that it was the woman's husband?" Brandi asked.

"Still waiting to hear, but who else would it be? It's not like I have a list of enemies who want to take me out. At least I don't think so."

"That is probably true!" Todd said.

"So, have you ridden Kingsbury Stinger before?" Brandi asked.

"No," said Maya.

"It's a fun trail. After a small climb, it's just fun, fast downhill," Todd said. "This ride is one of my favorites for a quick downhill shuttle run. We'll see how you feel. We could add another trail to make it a longer ride."

Back at the house, they unloaded their mountain bikes.

"I'm going to leave the dogs today. I took them on a hike yesterday. It's going to get pretty hot, and I need a day off with just humans." She laughed.

"Too bad. I was looking forward to seeing if they could keep up. Your Malinois looks like she is pretty fast."

"She is, but miles of fast downhill in the heat is tough on any dog. When my boyfriend, Nick, arrives, we'll all have to go riding together. I'll bring them then."

"Your boyfriend is coming down?" Brandi asked.

"Yes, this Saturday. He's worried about me."

"I'd be worried about you too," said Todd. "I'm glad he is coming down to protect you." He winked, knowing that she probably didn't really need protecting under normal circumstances.

They left from the house and worked their way down the loop to Andria Drive and then rode past the parking area. Todd led the way as they climbed up a jeep road toward the trail intersection. The climb was a short and steep granite sand road. It climbed up an open hillside before curving into the forest to the start of Kingsbury Stinger trail.

Both Brandi and Todd were strong climbers. It was easier for them since they were living at elevation. For them, this was everyday riding. She worked to keep pace with them to the top. Then they dropped down onto the start of Kingsbury Stinger and the fun began. They rode over rocky outcrops and along the hillside on fast flowing singletrack. Todd was leading with a fast pace. He stopped at the intersection of Kingsbury Stinger and the Kingsbury to Spooner section of the Tahoe Rim trail.

"Hey, since we don't have your dogs, do you guys want to ride up to The Bench?"

"I'm in!" said Brandi.

"I don't know what that is, but I'm in. I've been looking forward to doing some longer rides and I feel great today," Maya said.

They diverted off Kingsbury Stinger and started to climb up along the side of the ridgeline toward Genoa Peak. She met the challenge of shifting her weight above her wheels and using speed to loft her tires up and over rock obstacles. Her legs and lungs, at times, pushed to the limit as she ratcheted up the power to clear the technical areas. She loved that feeling of pushing her limits.

Except for the slight headache where she had been hit, she

was feeling great. Nothing like a good long ride to clear her head and put her back in control of her life.

Todd yelled back, "This trail is a lot more technical than Kingsbury and climbs fourteen hundred feet."

"I love this challenging uphill!" Replied Maya.

They turned in and out of drainages along the front ridge. Occasionally, the forest would open, and they'd get previews of the lake far below. She caught glimpses of the sun and blue of the lake contrasting against the towering presence of incense cedar, ponderosa and lodgepole pines.

They continued working their way up and around rock outcrops. In one place, she realized that she wasn't going to be able to ride up the steep steps. She jumped off her bike and carried her bike over her shoulder up over the rocks. Todd and Brandi hike-a-biked as well.

As the trail turned inward, it crossed through a flat plateau in the forest where they crossed a dirt road that descended towards Carson Valley. The trail leveled out through the forest saddle.

Their last push was for The Bench. As they emerged out of the forest, they found themselves in a large, open meadow of tufted grasses, wildflowers, and rock.

Lake Tahoe spread out below. Blue sky opened above them. They rode out into the meadow and then turned onto a short track that led down to a rocky outcrop. Between the rocks was a wooden bench facing towards the lake.

They sat on the bench and admired the beauty of the wide-open view of the surrounding ridge lines and the lake. A reward for their hard climb. A gentle breeze of dry mountain air quickly dried Maya's sweat. She looked outward and let the moment sink into her mind.

"Todd, this is amazing. What a view! I keep being blown away every time I go for another ride or hike.

"We figured you would enjoy this little detour. There are so many sections of the Tahoe Rim trail that lead to great viewpoints like this. I've ridden from Big Meadow to Tahoe City. It has section after section like this. This summer, Brandi and I are going to hike sections of the trail that are closed to mountain biking through Desolation Wilderness on the west side of the lake. There are some great high alpine lakes to fish and swim in up there."

"I hiked up to Echo Lake a while ago. What an incredible place. It's literally carved out of the granite."

"You should see Aloha Lake that sits at the base of Pyramid Peak. Just water and solid granite from lake to peak," said Todd.

"You guys have such a great home base. I'd never get bored, given all the adventure out your front and back doors!"

"We like it. What makes it even better is having a good job in town. Not a lot of them, but between the two of us we'll be able to get a small starter home that we can fix up."

"You are already thinking about buying a house together?"

"Just thinking about it," said Brandi and smiled at Todd.

They sat and talked about life in Tahoe. Todd loved being a firefighter in town.

"The tourists and recreation keep our job interesting," said Todd. "The skiing in winter is incredible. We usually get a season pass at Heavenly, Kirkwood, or Sierra at Tahoe. As soon as Brandi finishes up nursing school, we'll be able to figure out a good plan for our work schedule so we can play together on our days off."

"You guys are lucky. I'd love to live in a place like this. But Seattle is great. There is so much to do and so many beautiful places that would take a lifetime to explore. The city, itself, is also beautiful and has fun places to visit. The only drawback is the weather."

Todd took out some trail mix and handed it to Brandi who then handed it to Maya. They sat and talked. No one was in a hurry to get going. They had all day. Todd was on his second day off, so he was feeling rested.

"Maya, how do you deal with not getting sleep when you work?"

"Well, I usually make sure that if I have anything really important to do, I don't schedule it the day after a shift. Then, depending on whether I've gotten enough sleep or how I feel, I may go home and sleep right after my shift. That is usually after a rough night where we were busy. If I feel okay, which sometimes even happens if I've been up all night, I'll go for a ride or a hike. Anything physical that keeps me going until evening. Then I crash early. It's tough but I've learned how to deal with it over the years. The hardest thing is just the constant undercurrent of fatigue. The only way that I don't feel that way is if I take an extended vacation, like a month or two to travel. Then I get a taste of what normal life is like."

"Good advice. I'll see how I adapt over the years. For now Brandi and I still do everything we want to do even after I've had a rough night. The busy times are seasonal here. We can get a lot of tourist-related calls, like drunk driving accidents, overdoses, fights, mountain bike crashes, etc. It keeps it interesting but sometimes we are running from one call to another all shift long. The Fourth of July week seems to be a big one for us. That and the Snow Globe Festival at New Year's."

"We have seasonal fluctuations too. When the first warm weather hits, suddenly, our recreational accidents go up. We get calls for accidents involving kids as they venture outside on their bicycles or head to the rivers to swim. Then, in summer, we see more violence like gang shootings and fights. Just after Christmas, we tend to see more critically ill elderly patients.

They hold on through the holidays to be with family and then their bodies give up afterward."

Brandi asked Maya her favorite place that she had traveled to.

"New Zealand. I can't wait to go back. That is the land of adventure! I did a solo bike tour on the South Island a few years ago. I did some sea kayaking, glacier climbing, whitewater river rafting, and hiking too.

"I've traveled some, but once I get through school and start working, I'm going to definitely do much more during my vacation time."

"Definitely take advantage of traveling, especially before you have kids." Maya said.

"Should we go?" Todd quickly changed the subject.

"Now, let the fun begin. Downhill from here on out!" Brandi said.

They turned to ride back down the way they had come. What was work on the way up was now fast and fun downhill. They crossed over the road and descended the technical climbs and the hike-a-bike they had walked up. Todd missed one of the moves and almost rolled off the side of the narrow, rocky descent. He jumped away from the bike and came out unscathed.

Maya rode between Brandi and Todd. Both Brandi and Maya were strong riders, but Brandi was definitely more acclimated to the high altitude. Maya was a little better at riding the technical stuff.

The trail along the ridge line was fast and before long they were back at the turn off to the Kingsbury Grade. By Maya's estimate, they had already ridden about ten miles. Now they had six miles of downhill to the bottom of Kingsbury Stinger.

Todd took off and Brandi followed him. Maya waited a

minute or so for the dust to settle and then she launched down the trail. It was fast and furious. There were rocky sections, but also long stretches of smooth singletrack that snaked through the forest.

She let off her brakes and flew down the trail. Her mind completely focused on the line her front wheel followed along the river of dirt. She could see dust hanging in the air from Brandi's wheels.

There was one climb towards the bottom. Climbing after so much descent was always a little deflating. Her legs felt tired from the previous climbing and her mind had shifted to the gravity assisted downhill.

After they descended to a neighborhood, Todd navigated the streets and social trails through small meadows and stands of aspen until they arrived at the back of a ball field at Kahle Park. The trail skirted around the field to the parking lot where Todd's truck was parked. They had big smiles on their faces and their cheeks were flushed from an amazing ride.

"Good riding, Maya," said Todd.

"Thanks," said Maya. "What an amazing day! I'll ride with you guys anytime."

"I'm going on my regular shift tomorrow, but we'll have to get together next week when Nick arrives."

"He arrives on Saturday morning. I'm going to drive to Reno and pick him up at the airport. Maybe we can all get together and ride, then get dinner in town next week?"

"Sounds like a plan."

"We are meeting up with friends for dinner or we'd offer to have you over for tonight. We'll definitely get together next week, the four of us." Brandi said.

"You guys have fun. I'm probably going to make an early night of it anyway. I can feel just a little of my headache coming back. I probably overdid it a bit today, but it was so worth it!"

"We'll give you a ride back up the hill. We'll come in and say hi to the dogs."

"Absolutely. I have some great beer at my place. I found a local brew when I was in Coloma. A place called Barmhaus Brewing Company. They have a great Belgian ale."

"Sure."

They drove back up the hill to her place. Todd unloaded her bike. She put it in the garage and then upon opening the door, two housebound dogs came running out to say hi.

As Maya walked into the kitchen from the garage, she noticed that her Chaco sandal was sitting at the entrance to the front door. "Kali, are you a little unhappy that I left you today?" Maya gave her a look of admonishment. Kali slunk down. She turned away with a look of tragic guilt and acted as if the next thing to happen to her was that Maya would beat her. Maya ignored her instead.

"Kali always grabs one of my shoes and places it strategically in front of the door when she isn't happy that I left her. Pretty innocent, but she gets her point across." Kali slid behind the couch looking scorned.

Maya went into the kitchen and pulled three bottles of Belgian ale out of the fridge. Then Rio followed Todd, Brandi, and Maya outside to the deck. Kali stayed behind the couch.

They sat down and opened the beer. Maya gave it another minute and then called Kali to her. "Kali, come." Upon hearing her name, she bounded out to Maya, her body wiggling with joy at being invited back into the pack. "She loves to work me. She isn't worried that she is in trouble. She just fakes it so that she gives me the impression that she is sorry. I've never had such a smart dog. Half the time I think she is smarter than me!"

Brandi and Todd laughed. Kali came up and pushed her head into Todd's hand.

"Your turn to get worked," said Maya.

"Hey Kali," Todd said and started petting Kali.

"She'll never leave you alone now," said Maya.

Rio was taking advantage of Brandi's free hand and walking back and forth and playing keep away with his ball as Brandi reached down to try and take it.

"Dogs. They do keep you entertained," Brandi commented.

"Yes, they do."

"What are your plans for tomorrow?" Brandi asked.

"Hmm, I don't know. I'm just taking it one day at a time. I usually just wake up and make my plans in the morning. Why, do you have anything planned tomorrow?"

"Well, I was thinking about going on a hike. Are you interested in going?"

"That sounds like a great idea. Do you have one in mind?"

"Well, there is actually Daggett Loop trail. We can leave from here again. The route is about six miles long. The views up at the top are worth the effort."

"I'm up for that. I can bring the dogs and get them out since I didn't take them out today."

"Does 10 a.m. sound good to you? I have a few errands in the morning and then I'll be ready to head out and meet you here about then."

"Sounds perfect to me. Too bad Todd has to work tomorrow." Maya said.

"Sure, sure. Make me jealous. I'll be mopping the bay and waxing the rig while you guys are out enjoying another great day in Tahoe."

"So do they make the rookie do all the chores or does everyone do them?"

"Depends on whether or not, there is a football game on. If

there is a game, I'm the one doing the chores. I don't mind, though. I'm paying my dues. Someday I'll be watching the game and some new rookie will be slinging a mop and scrubbing toilets."

"I remember my rookie days. I definitely don't miss them. I'm almost an old timer now," Maya said. "I'll have been a paramedic for fifteen years this September. I can't believe it's been that long."

"Yes, you said you'd been doing it a while. I heard the burnout rate nationally is five years."

"Yes, in most places, your career as a paramedic could be short lived. Between low pay, bad management, and high stress, five years is about the time that people start burning out. Luckily, in King County we are well taken care. We have good pay, lots of leeway to practice professional medicine, good benefits, and enough vacation to get a break occasionally. Most of the old timers I work with have been doing it for twenty-five plus years. One of the original medics has been working since 1977. Back when it was the Wild West!"

Rio jumped up and draped himself across Brandi's lap. Then he reached up to lick her in the face.

"Wow, Rio never jumps up into someone's lap. He must really like you. What a goof ball."

Brandi liked dogs. It was apparent. She was totally comfortable with Rio and his white hair draped over her lap. Rio was sucking up the attention.

"He's quite a large, lovable dog," said Brandi. "I definitely want a dog later when I get settled. I'm not sure I want one this big, though," she said, and gave Rio a big hug.

"He thinks he is a lap dog."

They bantered back and forth while drinking their beer. Maya really liked these guys. They were fun to be around, and they had a lot in common. She looked forward to hiking with Brandi tomorrow.

Finally, Todd and Brandi said goodbye and headed home to take showers before heading out to meet friends. Maya was left on her own. She was finally unwinding. She looked forward to another quiet night. No excitement, just a good night reading her book and enjoying another hot tub under the night sky.

28

GIRL TALK

MAYA WAS MEETING Brandi for a hike later. She decided to clean out the clutter in her car. As she was cleaning the car, she found a black Samsung phone lying on the floor in the back seat. Brandi was sitting in back when they were driving back up to the house to go mountain biking, but she was pretty sure she saw Brandi with her phone when they were sitting around drinking.

Then she sat down to check her e-mail before Brandi arrived.

Her second e-mail was from her chief.

Maya,

I hope you are recovering down in Lake Tahoe. I wanted to give you some resources that you can follow up with when you return. Our Employee Assistance Program has counseling available. Also, as you know, we recently secured the services of a psychologist that works exclusively with first responders. We did an extensive interview, and we feel that she has a good understanding of the inherent demands of our profession. Her name is

Julie Harrington. Her number is 360-987-5436. I've let her
know you may be giving her a call.
   Please call me if you need anything.
   Sincerely
   Chief

MAYA WONDERED if they thought she couldn't handle her job. That sense of foreboding settled over her. If they thought she couldn't do her job, they'd be watching, waiting for her to make a mistake. They'd lost a couple coworkers over the years. One had just slowly withdrawn from the job. He showed up to pull his shifts, but his mind was somewhere else. Then he started calling in sick to work side jobs. The chief intervened and convinced him that maybe the side job was a better choice for him at that point. He realized that his heart just wasn't in the job anymore.

The other coworker's implosion wasn't so subtle. After the death of a child in his care, he was angry and started to drink all the time. One morning, his wife drove him into work and dumped him out the door. He was stone cold drunk. His coworker immediately called the supervisor, who showed up and they did an intervention, taking him to treatment that morning. During this time, his wife left him. He stayed sober for a few months but then started drinking again. He started missing work all the time. Then, one shift, he failed to show for work. His friends called and called him. No one could get a hold of him. A week later, a hiker found him in a parking area near a trailhead with a bullet in his head. No one thought he was so depressed that he would kill himself.

Now here were these words from her chief and it scared her to death. She wasn't like them. She still loved her job and...

Brandi rang the doorbell. Maya was jarred back to the

world around her. She jumped up and grabbed her pack and poles.

"Hey, did you leave your cell phone in my SUV yesterday?"

"No, it's right here in my pack. Why?"

"Well, I found this cell phone on the floor of the backseat this morning and thought it might be yours, since you are the only one who has sat in the back since I got here."

Maya felt uneasy but pushed the thought aside as she leashed the dogs. They found the trailhead at the parking area going in the opposite direction than Castle Rock. Once on the trail, Maya let the dogs off leash. They raced out ahead. Unloading their pent-up energy as they catapulted up the trail leaving Maya and Brandi. They ranged outward, and then once they burned off the high energy, they came back and settled into an easy gait just ahead of them.

"Wow, they are excited to be on the trail," Brandi said.

"Yes, they are. I try to get them out frequently or they get restless and edgy. If I wait too long, they'll drive me crazy. The good thing is they keep me active. It's less work to take them for a run than it is to ignore them when they are restless."

They started climbing right away. The trail followed the ridge above Andria Drive. As they climbed, they started to get views into the valleys between Lake Tahoe and the ridge. They could see the last of the snow on the peaks to the south near Heavenly ski area. It had been a big snow year the previous winter, so there were still pockets of snow in the gullies and shaded areas at the top of the north facing peaks.

"Do you feel like you are safer out on the trails by yourself when you have the dogs?" Brandi asked.

"Definitely. For no other reason than they look intimidating to someone who might want to harm me. I also know that Rio, especially, would do anything to save me.

"One time I was hiking off trail through some deep ferns. He jumped into the ferns right by my left leg and grabbed a raccoon and shook it to death. I was horrified until I realized that had he not grabbed the raccoon, it probably would have bitten me. If he doesn't like someone, I listen. He didn't like Don when we met him on the trail. Neither did Kali, for that matter. I wish I had brought them outside with me that night I was attacked."

"I bet they would have protected you. I love hiking on my own too, but always feel a little nervous being out here by myself."

"Sounds like a dog is in your future. I think waiting until you are finished with school is smart. You'll have more time to train a new dog and that will pay off later down the road."

"I'm looking forward to being done with the schooling part of this process and finally working."

"So, where are you from?"

"I'm from Sacramento, born and raised. I moved here to go to nursing school and to live in Tahoe. Living up here is different. Sacramento's weather is hotter in the summer and warmer in the winter. It was a great place to grow up, but I was ready for something different. I don't really want to live in the city. Sacramento has grown so much. The farms have disappeared as the housing developments keep spreading down the Central Valley and into the foothills. South Lake Tahoe is such a great place to live. We have so many friends here. I used to come up here all the time growing up. We'd come up and ski at Sierra in the winters and go boating on the lake in the summer. I fell in love with it and moved here as soon as I was able. I met Todd here."

"Can I ask how long you've been dating?"

"We've been going out for about six months now. He's a great guy. I don't think either of us are ready to settle down.

For now, we just like hanging out together and getting outdoors."

He seems like a great guy. Always good to have a guy with a good job in a tourist town like this too."

"Definitely. A lot of the men here are just not into commitment or working too hard. It's Tahoe. Life here has a different rhythm. Priorities are different. If you get a powder day, everyone calls in sick and goes skiing. It's just a matter of what is important. That's not necessarily a bad thing."

"No, I guess not. I know guys who work eighty hours of overtime a week. They work all the time and then complain because they aren't happy. I guess everything is a tradeoff of some sort.

"I work quite a bit too. I also do search and rescue volunteering with Kali. All the training and requirements along with the job keep me busy. I'm thinking about ramping it down a little when I get back."

"Really, why?"

"Well, I was pushing pretty hard and then when I had the ambush call, it shook me up. I think maybe I need to have more balance in my life. Get my head outside of work more when I'm home."

"But you sound so passionate about what you do. Do you see yourself continuing to be a paramedic until you retire?"

"Not sure. Time will tell."

They kept hiking up the trail. Falling into silence for a while. Maya watched the dogs ahead of her. Kali checked in every so often to make sure they were still behind her.

Maya thought about what Brandi had said. Yes, she really liked her job but was that enough anymore? She had been so committed when she started and dove into everything she did. Now she wasn't so sure.

These past two weeks had been a confusing time for her.

Her feelings were all over the map, like the other night when she drank herself into drunk dialing. Then the other day she couldn't get out of the house because she was so overwhelmed. She knew she just needed to let things settle and give herself some time. However, that e-mail had heightened her concern that maybe things weren't all right anymore.

She pushed those thoughts aside as they crested the high point. There they could see the mountains around Heavenly. There were high-rise buildings along the upper base of a hill. Above that, were forested ridges and beyond that, the snow-patched peaks.

From there, they descended back toward Andria Drive. The trail became steeper as they stepped down rock in a series of random steps. The views continued to the south. Then the trail turned west dropping down to Andria Drive. There they crossed over it to the other side. The trail wound around a large granite outcrop before dropping down into a low spot where it connected into the lower section of the Castle Rock Loop, below where Maya was staying. The landscape changed to groves of aspen, willow, and tall grasses as they crossed over a creek and along the western edge of Kingsbury Village. Both dogs were walking just in front of them now. Brandi and Maya decided to stop by the creek and have their lunch there. They'd been talking so much and hiking that they had forgotten to stop earlier. Realizing they were almost back to the house, the creek seemed like a good place to stop. The dogs could drink from the creek, and it was cooler.

Maya sat on a sandy beach and leaned back against a boulder while the dogs wandered in and out of the water. Brandi sat next to her.

"I am actually starting to unwind. I love the new place and the privacy. I love how I have some view, but it's nestled in the forest and its private. In my friend's place I kept running into wonderful neighbors, but that horrible woman and her husband overshadowed it all.

MAYA AND BRANDI finished up their lunches. Slowly they got up and continued the short distance back to the house. They entered back into the forest of large pines until they arrived at the shortcut Maya had used to access the Castle Rock trail. They peeled off the trail and hiked toward the house, arriving at the back gate along the deck.

"Another great adventure, Brandi. You and Todd are great guides. You'll have to come visit Seattle and I'll return the favor."

29

THE VISITORS

MAYA LET the dogs out to relieve themselves as her night wound down. She'd had an amazing three days of unfettered freedom. The last two nights sleep had been the best she'd had for a while. She decided that when she returned home, she was going to go see the department psychologist. Maybe she needed to dig deeper to work on the toll the job was having on her. She genuinely felt like it was time for a change.

Maya looked forward to Nick's arrival the next morning. She was ready to spend time with him. She realized she had been pushing him away for some time. Sometimes the only thing that forces change is an even bigger force from the outside that makes remaining alone worse than accepting the support from someone you love. She knew all too well what could happen when coworkers pushed their spouses and family members away. Divorce, addiction, and even suicide were some things she'd seen during her career.

Years ago, when she first started working as an Emergency Medical Technician driver for an EMT / paramedic unit in a large town outside of Seattle, her first trainer had been a hard ass. When he said she wasn't experienced enough to do the job, she'd convinced him otherwise. He gave her a chance. He had been her trainer and a successful paramedic. Years later, he was working as a paramedic in another system, and she heard through the grapevine that he had committed suicide after a bitter divorce. On the outside, he appeared the epitome of success. She had several older coworkers whose lives had imploded because of job stress and PTSD. She needed to heed those warnings and seek help sooner rather than later.

Rio came trotting back in, with Kali right behind. From behind them, she could hear a chorus of coyotes singing across the ridge tops.

"Scared you guys, didn't they?"

She closed the door and headed upstairs to bed. The dogs lay on the floor next to her. She immediately heard Rio snoring. *Silly dog, he must be tired.* She drifted off, hoping tonight she'd sleep through the night again.

SHE AWOKE to someone's hand over her mouth.

"Shhh," spat out a male voice. "We don't want to wake up your dogs, do we?"

She was confused. Rio and Kali should be attacking. She struggled under his heavy hand until she saw the dark form in his other hand. She stopped struggling. He had a gun.

She heard a woman's voice behind him.

"Don't hurt her, Xavier."

It's Kathy. Kathy, what the hell?

He pulled her off the bed. The dogs didn't budge. She wondered what was wrong with them.

As he escorted her out of the bedroom, Kathy quickly closed the door behind them. They brought Maya downstairs to the living room and pushed her down onto the couch. He pointed the gun at her. Kathy stood on the other side of the living room, facing them.

"Kathy, what is going on here?" Asked Maya.

Maya looked at the man holding the gun. He was the man she'd seen at the Grange, only... his name was Xavier. He was the young man who she met with Kathy? She was confused. This guy had a shaved head. No man bun. No beard. The realization dawned on her.

"I saw you looking up at me!" Xavier interrupted. "Why did your dog have to find her? If you hadn't fucked things up, I'd have been home free, and justice would have been done."

Kathy started whining. "Xavier, she said she didn't see you. Don't do this. Maya just happened to be in the wrong place at the wrong time."

"Oh, and your solution to get back at Don and Karen was to have an affair with Don and break up their marriage. Only problem is, he wanted out. All you did was really give him what he wanted. A dead wife and a new sugar momma!" He said with a sneer.

"Hey, I'm still here. I'm confused, why did you want to destroy her life and why did you murder her? Kathy, you said they were wonderful friends."

Kathy threw a piercing look at Xavier. "Remember when I told you my sister had died, and my niece became like a daughter to me?"

"Yes." Panic threatened to engulf her as she realized if she didn't do something they were going to murder her too. She looked for any opportunity to bolt.

"Well, my niece, Nicole, was living in an apartment building in Berkeley six years ago. She and Xavier were seeing each other. Xavier was asked to transfer to London for his business. He asked Nicole to go with him, but she refused. She broke up with him. He left a month later and she stayed in Berkeley.

Xavier sat down and to Maya's surprise listened as Kathy went on.

"Later she confessed to me she had found out she was pregnant and wasn't ready to commit to Xavier. I told her I was there for her and that I'd help if she wanted to raise the child on her own. She seemed to pull away from me too.

"When she was about five months along, she was having some medical issues with the pregnancy. She asked a friend of hers to move in with her to help her out because she was on mandatory bed rest.

"The apartment manager was Karen. When Karen heard about the woman living with Nicole, she immediately notified her she couldn't have anyone else living there. Nicole told her that the woman was just staying with her while she was pregnant because she was having problems with her pregnancy. Karen told her the woman had to leave immediately or she would evict her for violating her lease. Nicole pleaded with her to let her stay because she was sick and needed someone there.

"Karen was so cold. She just told no. Nicole couldn't move and also couldn't be on her own. She was at risk of having seizures due to a condition called preeclampsia.

"The next day, Nicole was served a sixty-day eviction notice. Then a few days after her help moved out, Karen and Don called the police saying that Nicole was threatening suicide and needed to be committed. Nicole didn't know what to do other than leave."

Maya saw Kathy's eyes water up. Her voice wavered as she described the next day.

"The next day, I called multiple times. When I didn't hear from her, I her friend to check on her. She went over to Nicole's and knocked on the door. Nothing. She entered the the apartment and found Nicole lying on the living room floor; face down, in her vomit. She was dead.

A dark rage erupted in Xavier's eyes. He leaned forward and shifted the gun from the arm of the chair to in between his legs. He still had the gun pointed at her.

"Nicole's friend immediately called 911. The paramedics came but she had been dead for hours. She died from pregnancy-induced eclamptic seizures.

No one was there to call 911. If there had been, she might be alive today. She not only killed my niece, but she killed my only remaining family, including Nicole's unborn child. She took everything from me! I decided I was going to take everything from her."

Kathy laughed bitterly, tears dropped from her eyes. "How was I to know that nothing really mattered to Karen, especially not Don? He was just another person for her to use."

"Wow," Maya said. "I'm so sorry. Honestly, I wish you'd told me. Even if I had seen Xavier, I wouldn't have said a thing. From what I've learned about her, she was a nightmare. Her neighbors, everyone, had a run in with her. Maya did her best to show this man with a gun pointed at her that she was on his side. Maya thought about the fact that Kathy seemed to single out Karen for all the blame.

Xavier's jaw hardened as he spat out the words. "After Nicole died, I came back, and confronted Karen and Don. Karen said, 'Those are the rules. I can't help it if she didn't know the rules when she moved in and got herself pregnant.

"Then Kathy figured out how we could get revenge!"

Xavier shifted the gun again.

"So, what happened?" Maya asked. She was trying to get them to see that she sympathized with them. Perhaps it was a brutal thought but at this point, with a gun pointed at her, she could care less who murdered Karen.

"That was it for me. Years of waiting for Kathy. Finally, I took control. I would kill her and make it look like Don did it."

"So, how did you figure out that I was still alive?"

"Well, fortunately I was to Reno. I had to stop at Costco to get gas. It just so happened you were driving by the Costco. I have to say, if I hadn't seen you, I would have gone home and called in an anonymous tip that they could find Don's phone in your car. You'd be dead and the only evidence would be his phone in your car. When I saw you, I realized that I needed to finish the job."

Maya's heart sank. She had thought if she drove through a crowded area that it would make her less visible, not tip off her murderer that she was still alive. *Small missteps*, she thought. "So, you followed me here?"

She thought about the phone in her SUV. So, it was Don's. What a convoluted sloppily planned murder. Besides not being adept at murder, his emotions were driving him to make delusional assumptions. Yet he looked at her with a false assurance. His jaw firm, his eyes piercingly confident. She hoped she convince him she was an innocent bystander and an ally. She didn't need to die. She could help him.

"Well, you know Xavier, up until this moment, I didn't know you killed her and tried to kill me. I thought it was Don that attempted to kill me, but he had an alibi. They were trying to verify it while he was being charged for his wife's murder."

"An alibi?"

"Yes, it seems that Kathy here was with him the night that I was attacked. At least, that is what Don said." Maya let those words hang in the air.

"Kathy, did you know about this?"

They turned to look at Kathy who was looking right at them with a 9mm gun in her hand. Maya was floored. She didn't take Kathy for someone who would know what a 9mm handgun was, let alone have the resolve to point it at them.

"Xavier, I can't let you do this. You've gone too far! What I never told you, is that Nicole didn't want to stay with you. You were abusive and you were destroying my niece. I watched as the more involved she became with you, the less and less she seemed like herself.

She started acting different, dressing different. She pulled away from me, her only family. She said that you put her down and made her feel like you were doing her a favor by loving her.

"Now you want to kill Maya too. Well, I'm not going to let you. She didn't deserve to be a part of this. She just happened upon Karen. She doesn't deserve to die, and you don't deserve to go free!"

Kathy pointed the gun at Xavier, and as she pulled the trigger, he shot her twice in the chest, pushing her backward. She crashed through the sliding glass door. The glass shattered into a million pieces as she fell. Maya watched as Kathy's blood flowed across the floor. She'd never witnessed a murder before. She always arrived after someone had been shot or injured.

Seeing Kathy talking one minute and then lying there on the floor dying was, well real. Not just a body she started IVs on, bandaged wounds, and transported. This was a person she had talked with, paddleboarded with, and gotten to know.

She shifted from horror into action. Before Xavier had time to react, she jumped over Kathy and bolted over the gate and down into the forest. She heard a loud crash somewhere and then she heard growls. She turned around as Kali came bounding through the broken glass of the slider and launched herself into Xavier with a fierceness that Maya had never seen before.

She decided to take advantage of the attack and run around to the front of the house. As the sound of Kali bearing down on

Xavier echoed in the background, she searched for something to use as a weapon. She looked up and saw the second story master bathroom window was shattered. Kali had broken out of the window to get out of the room. As she moved toward the front door, Xavier opened it as he fled from Kali. She had a visegrip on his leg as a terrible growl rumbled from her throat. Maya could see that his gun was gone, without thinking, she kicked him in the groin and sent him reeling backward. He fell over Kali onto the floor and Kali grabbed hold of his scalp, trying to drag him away from Maya.

He tried to swat her off, but she grabbed his right arm and started to shred it. Maya grabbed a rock off the ground and ran over to him. Without hesitation, she smashed it into his head as hard as she could.

He lay motionless, blood trickling from his head wound and gushing from the wounds inflicted by Kali. Maya reached down and felt for a pulse. He still had one. She commanded Kali to "watch."

Maya stepped over Xavier and ran upstairs for her phone. When she opened the door to the master bedroom, Rio was lying motionless on the floor. She could see his chest rising. She reached down and scratched his head. "Rio, I'll be back." Then she ran down to Kathy, grabbed her gun and went back to where Kali was watching Xavier.

He was still unconscious. His wounds were bleeding heavily. She dialed 911.

Finally, she heard sirens in the distance, The first police car pulled into the driveway. He had his gun drawn as he came up to the open door. It was Officer O'Brien. He looked at her and said, "I heard that address and knew it was you. Are you all right?"

Maya placed the gun on the entry table.

Two firefighters walked in. One went to check on Kathy

and the other bent down to inspect Xavier. He started to stem the bleeding and bandage up Xavier's wounds.

"Thank god for Kali!" said Maya. "Xavier must have drugged the dogs, maybe when I let them out to go pee earlier.

"Shit, Andy, Rio is still upstairs. He couldn't get up. I need to go check on him and get him to a vet if he needs one." Maya turned and ran back upstairs.

Rio lay on his side with his eyes closed, drooling. She laid her ear on his chest and listened. He was still breathing. She yelled down to the firefighters.

"Any of you carry Narcan?"

"Yes" One of the firefighters called out as he came up with his kit.

"Good, can you call your medical control and get a dose for an 80 pound dog."

"Hey doc, I have a different request for an emergency here. We have a 80 pound dog that may have been poisoned or maybe sedated. Can we give him Narcan to reverse the effects of whatever he was given?"

He turned to Maya. "He's getting the dose for your dog now."

"Do you have some long IM needles and a syringe?"

"Sure, look in my kit in the orange bag."

As soon as he confirmed the Narcan dose, Maya grabbed the syringe and injected the two milligrams of Narcan into Rio. The other firefighter came running up the stairs with four more vials of Narcan.

"I'm going to need you guys to help me get Rio downstairs to my car so I can get him to an emergency vet."

The firefighters carried him down. More firefighters had arrived. Xavier was being loaded onto the stretcher. Gauze and 4 x 4s covered his arms, scalp, and legs. He was going to have a few reminders of this night along with a long prison sentence.

She glanced over at Kathy. The recognizable yellow sheet was draped over her body.

Officer O'Brien met them as they went out the door. "Maya, let the deputy take you in his police car. You'll get there sooner, and it will be safer to have someone else drive."

AS SHE SAT with him in the back of the police car, all she cared about was making sure that Rio survived. "Come on, Rio, wake up." As if he'd heard her, he lifted his head and reached up and licked her in the face. "Hey buddy, you're back with us."

They pulled into the emergency vet, and the officer and Maya carried him in.

The clerk immediately directed them to a room. The vet was a younger woman, about Maya's age. She introduced herself and started examining him and asking questions. Maya explained the situation.

Suddenly Maya remembered that Kali was still at the scene. She left Rio in good hands and walked out to the waiting room where the officer was waiting.

"Can you get a hold of O'Brien and see what happened to my other dog, Kali?"

"Sure." He returned a few minutes later. "They found her hiding under the upstairs bed. She was panting and pretty stressed. They said she has some cuts on her paws."

"Why don't I drive back and see if I can pick her up and bring her down her here?"

"I'd really appreciate that. Thank you."

She could see the sky starting to lighten. She looked at her phone. It was five-thirty. Nick would be in Reno in less than four hours. He'd have to rent a car and come to Tahoe.

She called Nick.

"Nick, are you at the airport yet?"

"Yes, I just arrived. I'm getting dropped off right now. What's up?"

"Well, you know how I thought Don was the one who killed his wife and attempted to murder me?"

"Yes."

Maya recounted her last few hours. Now I'm at the vet because I couldn't wake Rio up. Kali is on her way here too. This is such a mess. You're going to have to rent a car at the airport and meet me wherever I am."

"Whoa, whoa, slow down. I'm not going to ask for any more details, but this is unbelievable. I mean that. This just gets worse and worse every time you call me. I'm so sorry I didn't come sooner, but I'll be there shortly."

"I'm so tired. I think we are going to have to go back to Georgia's house or get a hotel at this point. The place I was staying is a mess and now a crime scene."

"Don't worry about that. We'll deal with it when I get there. Let's just take it one hour at a time. I'll call you as soon as I get to Reno, and we'll go from there."

"Okay. I wish you were already here."

"Me too!"

Maya settled into her seat in the waiting room. About thirty minutes later, the vet came out.

Maya followed her back to the room. Rio was lying on a foam pad, looking comfortable and awake.

"He is doing much better," Anna said. "We gave him some more Narcan. Then we gave him some activated charcoal for anything that was left in his stomach. We took blood and we'll run a tox screen. I think it would be good to keep him through the day. Are you okay with that?"

"Yes, also the officer is bringing my other dog, Kali in. She may have had some cuts on her paws from running over glass."

"We'll check her out as well."

"I'll just sit here with Rio if it's okay. When Kali arrives, I'll want to be with her. She was found hiding under the bed at the scene, which tells me she was pretty stressed."

"No problem. We'll leave you two. I'll tell the receptionist to let you know when Kali arrives."

30

KALI

MAYA FOUND the vet trying to roll Kali on to her side without success. Kali stood on the exam table like a statue cemented to the table. She knew how to make herself an immovable force.

When she saw Maya, her whole body trembled. Maya got her to lay down. Anna and Maya worked slowly and cleaned up Kali's wounds When they were finished, she had on blue vet wrap booties that made her look like she was wearing socks. It was quite comical, especially when she tried to walk and kept shaking her feet with each step. Finally, she gave up and started to walk gingerly with them on.

They placed her in a kennel next to Rio. He was completely awake and very ready to go.

"We'll need to watch both while we wait for the tox screen to come back."

"In the meantime, why don't you get some rest? It's been a long night for you and your dogs. It's already eight in the morning. You must be exhausted."

"I probably am, but I'm too worried to feel it." Maya realized that Nick would be touching down in Reno in an hour.

"TODD, I have another favor to ask. Well, a couple of favors. Would you be willing to pick Nick up from the airport? I'm going to get a motel room down here in Carson but don't have my SUV. I don't want Nick to have to get a rental car if we don't have to. I know you worked last night."

"Maya, no problem. Consider it done!

Maya called and left a message on Nick's phone that Todd was going to pick him up.

She sat in the corner of the waiting room and closed her eyes for a moment. Her phone rang. It was Brandi.

"Maya, it's Brandi. Todd told me he is going to pick up Nick. I called my mom and asked her if it was all right for you guys to stay in our house up on Fallen Leaf Lake. You can use it for as long as you'd like.

"Are you sure your mom wants to risk us staying there since I seem to attract murderers at all the places I've been staying?"

"I'm sure you won't have to worry about that anymore.

"Let's hope so. I'm just not cut out for this type of high-risk lifestyle!"

"Its good that you still have a sense of humor."

"I was thinking that Todd could come by the vet to drive you and Nick back to your SUV or to the Fallen Leaf cabin where you guys could rest. Depending on when the dogs are released, we could go get them for you or you could."

"You guys are so amazing. Really, where would I be without you two? I can take this time to spend with Nick and the dogs. Then hopefully, get some much needed rest."

Maya leaned back and closed her eyes. She awoke to someone gently shaking her shoulder. She opened her eyes and found Nick standing there. She jumped up and wrapped her arms around him and buried her head in his shoulder.

He stepped back and commented. "Maya, you are a mess. You're covered in blood." Then he paused, grabbed her, and hugged her tightly.

"I'm sorry. I didn't realize. I've been completely focused on the dogs and staying alive."

"Way to make me feel guilty," Nick said apologetically.

"I'll have to get some new clothes. I'll need a shower too. I don't even know if this is Xavier's blood or Kali's. I've never had this much blood on me from calls. I guess fighting to stay alive is a much messier business."

"You always have such a twisted sense of humor. Let's just get to the cabin and I'll loan you some of my clothes until we can figure out what to do."

"That will work. I need to call Officer O'Brien and see if I can pick up my SUV"

Maya and Nick went to check in on the dogs. Anna met them in a room. "It looks like they were given a combination of benzodiazepines and opioids. I'm comfortable sending them home with you if you are."

"Yes, we're comfortable taking care of them and bringing them back if there are issues."

They drove up to pick up Maya's SUV. Todd ran in and checked with the officer in charge, to see if it was okay for Maya to get her SUV and personal stuff.

She could hear the officer agree that Maya could get her things. "Maya did you hear that?"

"Yes, that's great."

Maya and Nick walked through the garage and into the house. The other officer was talking to the medical examiner.

The officer looked over at Maya. "Maya, we wanted to let you know that Kathy recorded the whole discussion last night, which is good news for you. Your testimony is basically on that recording. All we'll need is to fill in a few details which we can do this week, sometime."

"I have to say you handled yourself pretty well. You were so calm given that he had a gun pointed at you and he said he was going to kill you."

"Well, I knew that if I was going to get out of the situation alive, I was going to have to figure out a way to get him to see me as an ally and not a threat. I really didn't have too many options at that point."

NICK DROVE, following Todd, from the scene, as Maya stared out the window at the scenery. Maya watched as the gondola cars moved up and down the Heavenly ski mountain with tourists that were oblivious to the murder that had just occurred.

At the house, Todd opened the garage and took them inside. The whole downstairs was the living room and kitchen. The entire wall, on the lakeside, had windows with a view of the Echo Lake and Mount Tallac.

Nick went down and let the dogs out. They all walked outside to a small yard framed in rock and a series of stone steps that led down to a small dock. The shoreline was rocky but not too steep.

"I'll check in with you guys later and see if you want to go sailing on Monday." Said Todd.

31

FALLEN LEAVES

MAYA SAT in a chair looking out at the reflection of the mountains, perfectly mirrored, on the surface of Fallen Leaf Lake. Her mind and body relaxed. She and Nick had made up for lost time with passionate lovemaking that ended with the two of them spooning. He held onto her the whole night. She didn't mind. She felt safe and warm.

Nick came down the stairs. It was amazing he slept in later than her. He was usually the first one up in the morning making coffee but she'd beat him to it. He walked over and kissed her on the top of her head.

"Fresh coffee in the kitchen."

"Just what I was hoping you'd say." He walked into the kitchen and poured himself some coffee and then came over and sat on the couch next to her. "So how are you feeling today?"

"I'm feeling pretty good and even better now that you're here. I feel relieved now that no one's trying to kill me."

"Understandable. Let me make you breakfast. I'm not sure what we have here but I'll go look through the cupboards.

Nick returned empty-handed. Let's go out for breakfast instead. Then we'll go shopping for food."

"I suppose that is an acceptable alternative," she said, with a hint of playfulness.

Tonight, I'll cook up a chicken curry with rice. How does that sound?"

"Perfect! I could use some of your great cooking!"

Maya and Nick drove into South Lake. They found a favorite local breakfast place called 'Sprouts'. It was a laid-back café with organic food and great coffee.

They sat outside to enjoy the morning sun. The dogs sat under the table with them.

The waiter brought out their steaming lattes as they waited for their food. Down the street, she could see a glimpse of the lake through tall pine trees.

She felt like Tahoe was a different place. Gone was the cloud of murder and motives of crazy people. Now Nick was here. Even the dogs seemed calmer. With this shift, even the reason she came here to escape seemed like a distant memory.

She felt like it took a sudden shock for her to hit the reset button and put things into perspective. Feeling safe also helped her clarify events and feelings. How many times had she gone on vacation over the years and started to unwind, sleep, and find a rhythm to her days. Then she'd return to work and within a week she was right back into rotating shifts, unpredictable calls, and sleepless nights? She knew that day was coming when she didn't want to do that anymore. For now she could just forget about that and imagine that this was all that existed in her life, an amazing boyfriend, two adventure dogs, and a beautiful cabin to stay in on Fallen Leaf Lake. They were just a normal couple with dogs on vacation in California.

The waiter brought out their food.

"I always seem to be so hungry during this trip. I'll probably eat this whole thing." Commented Maya.

"Well, I guess surviving murder, changing residences every few days, and mountain biking a lot could be part of that. You've been pretty busy defying death and injury lately."

"You know, you're right. I think we should spend the day inside the cabin, making love, and taking naps. Wouldn't you agree?"

"You read my mind."

They finished up their breakfast and headed to the grocery store. They hurried through the aisles, scooping up enough so that they didn't have to leave the cabin for a week if they didn't want to. Maya grabbed a couple of beef bones for the dogs. They figured the dogs might get bored while they took lots of naps.

They arrived back at the cabin. They unloaded their groceries and then spent the rest of the afternoon in bed. There was absolutely no reason to be anywhere else.

IN THE EVENING, Nick cooked up a gourmet dinner. They sat down to dinner just as the sun was casting longer shadows from the west behind the mountains. Maya poured some wine in their glasses, and they settled in to eat. Even eating seemed to be more meaningful in his company. She had someone to share her meal with and talk to.

She decided to bring up the idea of throwing everything they'd worked for in Seattle and launch into an imagined new life. "I have an idea that I want to run by you."

"Okay. What is it?"

"Well, I've been entertaining fantasies of quitting my job and starting something new. I don't have any idea of what that would be, but I just want us to discuss ideas about where and what that might look like."

"Well, while I need to be in Seattle for major meetings, most of my work is online. That means I could pretty much work from anywhere. I could fly back for meetings or travel to clients. Seattle is a great home base, but I'm not committed to living there forever."

"For me, either I work as a paramedic there or quit being a paramedic. I've told you that to work anywhere else would be a step backwards.

"I love my job, but I'm feeling pretty burned out. I don't know if I want to do this for another ten to fifteen years. Like you, I could do something computer based. I could do online continuing medical education or consulting. Beyond that, I've always been interested in writing and photography. Maybe we could travel, and I could build a web-based travel blog using my skills.

"What about the dogs?"

"We could take them with us. You've wanted to get a Sprinter van for a while, which would work as our mobile office and home. If we travel internationally, we could find someone to care for them.

Those are great ideas." Here's another possibility I want you to entertain." Nick said.

He reached to the chair beside him and pulled something toward him. "Will you marry me?"

Maya was stunned. She had no idea that this was coming. She sat just looking at the ring he held up and the look in his eyes. He was genuinely all in, she thought. "Nick, I can't believe this. I had no idea."

"Well, will you?" he repeated.

She thought about it, and it was like she knew the answer. Yes, she really did want to marry him, which surprised her.

She'd always seen herself as an independent woman. She really hadn't seen herself as a married woman. Here was the opportunity to marry someone that she absolutely loved, who was not only her lover but her best friend.

"Yes, yes I'll marry you."

"Oh, thank god. I thought when you hesitated that I had made a mistake."

"No, silly. I just wanted to be sure that when I said yes, I was absolutely sure. Yes, yes, yes. I can't think of anyone I'd rather marry than you!" She got up and leaned over to kiss him. That kiss left their dinner half eaten as they carried that thought back upstairs."

MAYA LAY on the bed looking out the window at the stars and dark rim of the mountains. She suddenly saw new possibilities and all the events of the past month fell like fallen leaves from her mind and her thoughts bloomed from long arching branches, reaching in new directions. Tomorrow was a new day.

32

ENGAGED

MONDAY, Todd texted Maya and asked if they were still interested in going sailing. Maya texted him back, "Yes!"

Maya and Nick found their way to the Tahoe Keys dock where Todd's sailboat was waiting. Todd and Brandi were there along with a coworker, Ben O'Malley, she had met at the dinner at the firehouse. He was there with his wife, Anna.

It was a forty-foot sailboat and the smallest she had ever been on.

It was still warm as they motored out onto the lake. Maya sat and leaned against Nick.

Todd explained because there wasn't much wind so they were just going to motor out to a nice location for dinner. He headed east to hang on to the sun as long as they could before it dropped behind the western ridge lines. As they made their way out and across, Maya and Nick talked with Ben and Anna. Ben and Anna had been married for four years. They had a two-year-old who was with their babysitter. They were happy to have a night out with adults.

"How long have you lived here?" Nick asked Ben and Anna.

"I grew up here," Ben answered, "and Anna is from Wisconsin."

"Yes, I moved out here to work for Tahoe Conservancy after I finished up my environmental degree in community planning. I jumped at the opportunity to live and work in a place like Tahoe. Then I met Ben and ended up staying here. It's been six years now."

"Are you working for the Conservancy now?" Asked Maya.

"Yes, part-time as an Associate Environmental Planner. I was working full time, but since Ava was born, I've been part-time."

"That's great that you can do that. With Ben being a firefighter, you guys have more time to spend with your daughter."

"Yes, when Ben isn't working or teaching. He keeps pretty busy but still has a lot of time to spend with us."

"Nick, what do you do?"

"I'm building a cyber security company based out of Seattle. We manage the online presence and security for individuals and corporations worldwide.

"That sounds really interesting," Ben said.

"It has its moments. It certainly isn't as exciting as your job. Maya was telling me you guys have a pretty interesting clientele based on time of year and tourism, not to mention a few crazy transplants."

"Well, it's nothing compared to big cities like Seattle and San Francisco, but we see a lot for a small town."

Brandi came back up with some snacks to go with their beer. "Hey, Nick, glad you made it down here to Tahoe. We were getting concerned about Maya being on her own with everything that has happened."

"I have to thank you guys for taking good care of her and

myself as well. We really appreciated your help last weekend. It made picking up the pieces much easier. Brandi, your parent's place is beautiful. We enjoyed lying around and catching up on some sleep Saturday and Sunday."

"I'm glad you guys are enjoying it. My parents have owned it for as long as I can remember. They just remodeled it a few years ago. Before that it was a truly rustic old Tahoe summer cabin."

"Well, we're here. This is Skunk Harbor. Some wealthy San Franciscans built that building over there in the 1920s as a retreat. Now the Forest Service owns it. You can hike down to it from Highway 28, but I prefer to visit it by boat," Todd said.

"Let's swim and explore while it's still warm. The building is definitely worth checking out if you haven't been here," Brandi said as she took off her shirt and shorts and then quickly dove into the clear water.

Maya dove in next. Both Maya and Brandi urged the men to come join them as they swam towards the shore.

Todd and Nick followed.

Ben called out from the boat. "Hey, Anna and I are going to stay on the boat. We're tired and just feel like taking it easy. We'll save a beer for you." He took a swig of his beer and cheered them on.

The water was cold but refreshing in the warm evening air. They swam to the sandy beach in front of the building. Then walked up the beach to find a house that looked like it was made of the granite stone that you would find in Lake Tahoe.

An entry ran across the front with steps leading down on either side. In the front was a greyish blue door. On either side were wood framed windows. Two of the windows had black grates over them and the other had greyish blue wood shutters.

The landscape around the building was left to its own devices. They walked around to the right to a courtyard snuggled in between two extended wings at the back of the house. In the middle was a tall outdoor fireplace with a chimney that rose above the roof.

Maya and Nick admired the details of the building around them. It was like finding a window into another time when the shores of Lake Tahoe were the private retreats of early California wealth. Today, houses along the lake were owned by new wealth. Movie stars, professional athletes, Wall Street executives, and tech founders like Steve Jobs and Mark Zuckerberg. Would their houses someday be isolated relics from another great time in California history?

Maya started to feel the cold sinking in and decided to head back to the boat. Nick, Todd, and Brandi followed her after they finished exploring around a point of rock at the far end of the beach.

Maya found Ben and Anna setting up dinner on the table in the galley. Ben had a tabletop grill on the flat area above the wooden bench seats. He was grilling chicken.

They changed into warmer clothes. Maya grabbed a bottle of Tatoosh Bourbon out of her bag and brought it, along with two Odin Stouts, back up with her.

"Nick and I wanted to give you a little something to thank you for your incredible support the last week. We really appreciate being able to stay at your family's house too, Brandi. It's not much, but we thought you might enjoy some moonshine from Seattle.

"Well, let's crack this bottle and have some dinner. I'm hungry," Todd said. "Ben, is the chicken ready to eat?"

They kicked back on the benches and upper deck and ate their burgers. The sun was dropping behind the western peaks above Lake Tahoe. The light cast a warm orange across the calm water. Maya watched the color change and felt warmly satisfied as she ate. She thought about how much had changed in just a few days. Now she was out enjoying an evening on a sailboat with new friends and her fiancé.

"I almost forgot to tell you guys. Nick, do you want to tell them?"

"Sure. Last night I proposed to Maya and... she said yes."

"Wow, no kidding," Ben said. "Congratulations!"

"No way," Brandi said. "I can't believe it. That is so cool. Did you propose at the house?"

"I did, over dinner. Maya was talking about life changes, and it just felt like the right time to ask. I had planned to ask her while we were down here. I guess I just couldn't wait."

"That's great news. Let's have a toast. To the engagement of Maya and Nick, our new friends from Seattle." Said Todd.

"To Maya and Nick! Here, here. Let's party!" Ben exclaimed and took a long drink of his bourbon.

Brandi plugged in her phone and connected it to speakers to play some music. They ate the rest of their food, laughed, and drank more bourbon and beer.

"We can't wait to come visit you guys."

"Better do it soon," Nick said. "Mayas got an idea that she wants to quit being a paramedic and start traveling."

"You want to quit?" Todd asked. "You're working in one of the best places to work as a paramedic. You don't want to give that up."

"It's definitely an amazing place to work but I'm starting to feel burned out. I'm just toying around with the idea of making a change. I may or may not. This is a tough time. Lots of things in play."

"Yes, then you throw in that wacko neighbor. I'm surprised you didn't kill her yourself," Ben blurted out.

Maya could tell he was a little buzzed and the words were just tumbling out of his mouth. He was helping himself to another shot of Tatoosh.

Here's to your dog jumping through the air and taking down the bad guy." To Kali!" Said Ben as he stood up and promptly fell backwards.

"Dude you're drunk." Said Todd.

Absolutely! Cut me some slack. I have a two-year-old and this is our first free night in a long time. Besides, I don't have to drive, brother! Anyway, Maya, you and your dogs are bad ass!"

"Ben, thanks for the compliment." Replied Maya.

Ben got up and headed for the bathroom. Anna silently apologized, then said. "He's been so great. I think he just needed to cut loose."

"I don't mind. I'm having fun. This has been a beautiful night," Maya said. Then she quietly said to Todd. "I don't want to get serious again, but you know Todd, I have a good feeling that your generation is going to be able to handle the pressures of the job with more tools than we did. Just spending time with you guys is so different than when I started."

"I sure hope so," Todd said.

Ben came back up and brought some more beers for everyone. Todd declined. "I'm the DD. I gotta get you home so I have to stay sober until we get to shore. Speaking of shore. Let's just slowly head back. Maybe we'll get lucky and find some wind along the way. I love being out on the lake at night under the stars."

Brandi brought up some blankets and handed a large one to Nick and Maya. Then she handed one to Ben and Anna. She handed Todd his fleece jacket and she wrapped a blanket around her shoulders.

They fell silent for a while as the boat moved through the water. The soft chug of the engine moving them along at a slow pace. Maya snuggled into Nick's chest and wrapped the blanket tighter around them. They always joked that she was always cold, and he was a human furnace. That is why they were perfect for each other.

Brandi stood in the back with Todd at the wheel. Ben wrapped his arm over Anna's shoulder.

The sky was demarcated by the dark outline of the mountains as it transitioned from a lighter midnight blue to a night-darkened sky. The stars started to pop out of the darkness creating the illusion of a dark star-filled dome above their tiny boat on the lake. It was another of those perfect moments, made even better for Maya because the man she was going to marry was wrapped up in a blanket with her.

"Dude, check it out. A shooting star," Ben yelled as he jumped up. He teetered for just a moment before Anna grabbed him and pulled him down next to her.

"Wow, that was awesome. How cool is it that we are out on the lake tonight? I'm going to have to get us a sailboat. We could even live on one before Ava gets older."

"No way, Ben. You must be high! You want me to live in a forty-foot sailboat with a two-year-old. She'd have to live in her life jacket. I'd take my eyes off of for one moment and and she'd be over the side."

"I guess you're right. It would still be cool, though. Maybe we'll just own one and not live in it."

"Let's just buy a house first. Then we'll consider a sailboat."

"Hey, are you guys going to have kids?" Ben asked.

Maya and Nick looked at each other. "Probably not," Nick answered. "We haven't thought about it much, but I don't think either of us really wants that kind of responsibility. Dogs are enough responsibility for us."

"You know, you don't have to have kids these days. I always wanted to be a dad. I was so happy when Anna got pregnant. Totally stoked. I came from a family of five boys. I'm the youngest. I loved having lots of brothers to hang out with. We want to have at least one more kid. A boy, of course."

Ben continued talking about family and his brothers in the fire department. "They are my other family," he said.

Maya was so comfortable with these guys. They were so familiar. She'd been around guys like Ben her whole career. Good guys who loved what they did. They were solid family men and they liked to party too, especially the older firefighters. 'What happens at the firefighter convention stays at convention', her union president had told her. The new guys seemed a little less inclined to go overboard on alcohol but then they were still young and didn't have years on the job to haunt them yet.

They made their way under the star-filled sky and back to the dock in the Keys. Todd and Brandi dropped them off. They were going to sail back out and spend the night under the stars, anchored along shore somewhere. Ben and Anna waved goodbye and headed to their car. Nick and Maya walked back to their car at the far end of the parking area. As they did, they saw a coyote walk right in front of them, stop, look them right in the eye and then saunter off in no particular hurry.

"Coyotes here. They are so bold."

33

KAREN

MAYA MET with the detectives investigating her attempted murder for an interview. As she headed home, her mind swirled in different directions. She was so tired of dealing with this messed up series of events that had involved her. She had been hit sideways by the winds buffeting someone else's sails. Nothing made sense to her because this wasn't her story. She'd been caught up in a campaign that started long before she'd stumbled into the mess and she wanted answers. With that thought, she turned left onto Highway 50 and headed for Meyers.

She pulled up in front of Don and Karen's house. She hesitated, then opened the car door and walked up to the front door. She rang the doorbell and waited.

"Who is it?" A voice yelled from inside.

A few moments later, Don opened the door.

"I want to talk with you. For the last couple of weeks, I have been caught in the middle of a drama that surrounded you and your wife.

Fear crossed his expression. Genuine fear. She must have looked formidable in her determination to get answers.

"Oh hell, come on in," he said with a hint of surrender. He turned around and walked into his dining room.

Maya followed.

As she looked around the space, she realized that all the shades were open and filtered sunlight spilled into the open living/dining room and kitchen. Well, at least if he attacked her here, someone might witness it.

Then she saw that around the side and back of the house was a six-foot fence. On the side where Georgia's house was, there was an eight-foot fence. The yard was choked with aspens and cedar trees. The ground was filled with wildflowers that surrounded a small patch of green lawn making it seem like a dense jungle instead of an arid Tahoe landscape. It looked like a small, secluded green island in the middle of a neighborhood.

Don sat down in a dining room chair near the window. He had dark circles under his eyes. He looked as if he hadn't gotten around to shaving since he'd been in jail. He waved her to a chair across from him. "Do you want anything to drink?"

"No thanks," she said. She sat down like a cat on alert. Any sudden move and she'd be off and out of there. The tension she felt being near him was palpable. She realized she was scared. On the outside, she looked relaxed and hopefully, in turn, he would be relaxed or at least not aggressive. She needed him to be forthcoming. She needed him to tell her why!

"So, you want an explanation?"

"Yes, I do. I think I deserve one!"

"Well, Karen is dead, and you want to know why all this has happened?

"Yes!"

Karen... she was complicated and let's just say, you aren't

first person to get caught in her destructive web. Don looked down at his hands, avoiding her eyes.

"I was with Karen for twenty years. We met years ago on a mountain bike ride while I was on vacation in Crested Butte. I came back to Sausalito where I was living at the time and working on houseboats. A few months later, she called to say she was moving to Berkeley. Her father had died and left her some money. She was buying a house there.

"From then on, we were together. I continued to live on my houseboat, and she lived in her new house in Berkeley. We both liked to mountain bike and paddleboard. His eyes softened as he spoke of their shared interests. We used to spend our free time on our bikes or on the water, he said.

Then his face tensed up. "Everything was going well, but I started to suspect something was wrong with her reactions to people around her. She started complaining incessantly that her new neighbor was playing his guitar during the day. He worked night shift at a bar and would practice during the day. I'd met him. He seemed like a cool guy.

Every day when he was practicing, she would start to pace and become agitated. Pretty soon, she was telling me I needed to go over there and tell him to be quiet. So, I went over and asked him if he could play his guitar quieter. He said that he had a right to play it during the day. It was our problem if we wanted quiet. He told me, 'You already live on a busy street. If you don't like it, then you shouldn't live in the city.' I told her what he said. Karen called the police.

"During this time, Karen started working for a property management company. At first, the company she worked for loved her because she always got the rent on time and was meticulous in keeping up their higher end apartments. She also had no problem evicting people if that was called for. However, she started finding issues with just about everyone who lived in the building. We had multiple tenants move out the first year after she took over the Berkeley Heights apartment building. She started harassing the tenants for the slightest infraction. Some of them were well off and were not too happy to be told how they should live. By the end of the next year, the corporation that hired her had so many complaints, that they fired her.

"After that she got her real estate license for California. She did well at first until the brokerage firm that she worked for asked her to leave after disagreements with other agents.

"She used her real estate experience to find a place to buy in Lake Tahoe, this house, with the additional money she inherited from her father. We took the summer off and worked on fixing the place up. Then that next winter, we went to Hawaii. I had been going there for years during my slow season for work. We bought a condo there so we could spend part of our winters there. We loved to get out on the water and it is a quick flight from SF.

"Everything seemed great. Then the previous owner of your friend's house started to build that monstrosity and it was all out war from then on. She wanted to drive him out. In Hawaii, she started complaining that the neighbors were too loud and that there were people who shouldn't be there. She would constantly complain to the management company. They blew her off, so she started to call the police on anyone who she thought looked suspicious. She said that there were people spying on us. People in the complex started to avoid her as she marched around looking for things that were out of place. She'd call the police if their car was parked in the wrong spot. She'd knock on the neighbor's door if their child's toy was left out.

"When we returned to Berkeley, she decided to lobby the owner of the apartment complex across the street from her house in Berkeley to give her the job as manager. She had been angry with people coming and going at all hours of the day and night. She was convinced if she managed it she could clean it up and get rid of the troublemakers. She told him if he had us manage the building, he wouldn't have to give up an apartment for an onsite manager because we would be right across the street. He agreed and he fired the current onsite manager and hired us. He didn't know at the time that all the complaints the apartment complex had been receiving were from her.

I moved in with her in Berkeley. We started managing the apartment complex together. I did all the repairs and maintenance. She handled all the rental business. That was where the woman, Nicole lived, the one who died from her pregnancy. He paused. I had no idea that was Kathy's niece, until Kathy told me. From the day Karen found out that Nicole had someone living with her, she insisted that the friend move out.

"I mean, we told her what the rules are. It was not our fault that she was in the situation she was in. Besides, Nicole was mentally unstable. We had to call the police for her safety. Karen fixated on Nicole and made it her personal mission to run her out. She didn't want an unstable pregnant woman living with an unauthorized 'friend'. I knew she wouldn't quit until Nicole was gone. Finally, her friend left after Karen served her the eviction notice. We didn't know Nicole would die.

"After Nicole died, we didn't allow anyone with children to live in the complex. It was just too messy. What if we had let her stay? We'd have had to deal with a toddler running around causing trouble. Kids are so noisy and disruptive!"

Maya sat in horror. He seemed completely disconnected from the results of their actions in harassing Nicole out of her home. It seemed to be all about them, without any regard for what the people around them were going through.

Don, paused, looking down at his hands. A hint of sadness in him as he continued. "You see, I was in love with Karen. I knew she was difficult, but we really had a connection. Believe it or not, I was able to calm her down. Without me, she would have been worse. Once we drove the owner out of the house next door, we'd have the peace she and I wanted. If she was happy, I was happy. We went to Tahoe to get away and enjoy the mountains, not to hear the pounding of nails and saws buzzing the whole time we were here. That neighbor's house just kept getting bigger and bigger."

To Maya, it seemed that he was caught up in a rambling story he had told himself many times before. Maybe it was the story he told himself to justify staying with an awful woman. She wondered how she treated him.

He continued. "That winter, we went back to Hawaii for a month. While we were there, the condo association came to talk to us. They asked politely if we would consider selling our unit. What they really wanted was to get her out of there.

At first, she was angry. She recruited me to help her when one of the men started screaming at her, calling her a crazy bitch. I'm not a violent guy, but some of the men she ran into would call her all kinds of names. I stepped in to protect her. She just kept escalating the situation. She slashed the president of the Homeowner Association's tires. She dumped garbage on the doorstep of one of the board members that talked with us. She did it all under the cover of night so they could never prove it was her, but they knew.

"The following year, we sold the condo and bought a house in a quiet neighborhood, on a cul-de-sac. It was good for a while until she started going after the new neighbors. Within six months, three couples sold their homes and moved. I started to realize that it wasn't the neighbors or the tenants that were the problem. I thought that eventually we'd find the right place with the right neighbors, and she'd settle down, but it only got worse.

"I finally asked her mom about her. Her mom said that Karen had always been like that. Before she met me she had never had a relationship that lasted more than a few weeks. She'd start behaving bizarrely and they'd dump her. Her mother told me she couldn't hold a job. Initially, she would be a great employee and the employer would be thrilled with her, but then she would start having clashes with coworkers and eventually a run-in with her bosses. She had been forced out of another real estate firm in Colorado because the other agents threatened to quit if she didn't leave. That was the real reason she came back to California.

"I took good care of her, but it wasn't enough. When I met Kathy, for the first time in a long time, I was happy. She wasn't as intense or fun as Karen, but she was consistent and kind. She appreciated my work on her house. Karen was never happy with the work I did."

He had a genuine look of sadness in his expression. He was in love with Kathy, she thought. He'd had no idea, initially, that he was a part of a plan to get revenge for Nicole's murder.

"When Kathy told Karen that we were having an affair, I was completely taken by surprise. I was going to tell Karen, but I needed to find the right time. When I came home, Karen was livid. She had her fists and jaw clenched. I thought she was going to hit me. She was so mad. She threw me out of the house.

"I went and stayed with Kathy. That was the night before Karen was murdered. I was angry with Kathy for telling her, but at the same time, I was relieved. Finally, it would all be over. I could spend the rest of my life with Kathy. I knew that if I left Karen she would implode, but I was past caring. I had done so much to help her, but she just didn't want help. She wanted control. Control of me, the houses, the finances, and the yard you see around this house.

That is all we did when we were here and in Hawaii, work on the yard and the house. I built an addition on this house, just for her, because she wanted a view of Mount Tallac from the second story. She wanted a quiet mountain house in Tahoe. She just didn't want neighbors.

34

VULNERABLE

NICK AND MAYA sat on the lounge furniture out on the patio enjoying the sun. Rio and Kali were feeling left out and crowded around their feet. Maya was checking her e-mail on her phone. Nick interrupted her and suddenly asked her if she was okay.

"You seem distracted. Talk to me."

A sudden intense fear welled up inside of her. He was asking her to be vulnerable. "I'm fine," she barked. "I'm just tired. Tired and I need some time to myself."

"Maya, I wouldn't be okay if those things happened to me."

Maya didn't want to break down in front of him or anyone. Tears welled up in her eyes. They burned as she tried to keep them from spilling down her cheeks. Then she started crying and she couldn't stop. "I just need some time off. I've been so tired. Every time I've tried to get some sleep or relax something else has come at me. All I could see was the officer bleeding to death and we couldn't leave because we were under siege." Then she stopped speaking and just sobbed.

Maya cried until she couldn't cry anymore. She hated herself for being so weak.

Nick then reached over and grabbed her hand . "You know we are going to get through this together. You're not alone."

"I think I really feel that for the first time in years."

Maya's tears had dried. She felt emotionally raw and exposed but she realized that was okay. If she was going to have this breakdown, better here than on the front lines.

"I've been thinking. I'm going to go see the psychologist through work. I think it's time to work through some of this or it's going to continue to affect me in ways I can't even imagine."

"I'm glad you are going to see someone."You've got a whole lifetime ahead of you to figure out. Once you deal with the past, it will open up a whole new world of possibilities."

"I like the way you put that. It's not about being a failure or broken. It's about clearing the path for something better. I knew there was a reason I said yes to marrying you." She leaned over and kissed him. "Thank you so much for being you!"

They spent the evening talking over a quiet dinner. She didn't plan any big adventures for the next day or make any big life decisions, like quitting her job. She just let herself be completely in the moment with Nick and the dogs. That night, she slept for twelve hours. When she awoke in the morning, Nick was already up and the dogs were down with him. She lay there hoping that the sense of calm she felt after the storm of emotions yesterday would carry into today.

MOUNTAIN BIKING ON VAN SICKLE

MAYA AND NICK planned a ride from the top of Kingsbury down the Van Sickle trail. Todd told them it was a steep technical trail that ended at the Van Sickle Bi-State Park near the casinos at State- line. Their plan was to shuttle and ride from the top. Then they'd meet up with Todd and Brandi and go sailing again in the evening.

Nick was working on a project for work and Maya was settling in reading her book. She'd given up on the murder mystery and was reading a story about two women who bicycled through China. A much lighter read and as far as she could tell, no one was going to die.

After lunch, Nick continued to work. Maya took the dogs down to the dock to throw some balls in the water for them. They'd gone on a long ride up Cold Creek to High Meadow the day before, so this was their day off, but Rio still wanted his time in the water. Maya threw the first ball out into the water and Rio dove off the dock to retrieve it. Maya's phone rang. She answered it as she waited for Kali to bring her the ball.

"Hello Maya, this is the chief. I wanted to touch base with

you before you came back. We've had some developments around the ambush. We are working with the FBI counterterrorism task force. They believe the group that ambushed our first responders is a smaller cell that is part of a much larger group.

"They've got an indication that things are ramping up so we are now on high alert. I want to go over some changes, so you won't be surprised when you return. Things are not settled, and I don't want to put you back in the line of fire until you are feeling solid."

"Boy, you've just dropped some weighted information into my lap," Maya said. "My plan is to be back in a week's time for my shift on Friday. I don't know if the elevated threat is going to change how I feel about returning to work. I think that is going to be the nature of our job now. We're not the only region that is dealing with these types of groups. That's what we get paid for. As long as we're taking all the steps necessary to mitigate as much risk as we can, I'm all in."

"Okay, I'm glad to hear that. So, we've changed all our door codes and procedures for entering and exiting our stations. We are concerned that our facilities could be targeted. We're also going to contract with law enforcement to have a security officer at each of our stations. We want to keep our stations secure. We don't want to return to find them booby-trapped or our rigs strapped with a remote bomb. That happened down in Kentucky. A local volunteer department went out on a routine call and came back to find their station on fire after it exploded.

"We've also changed our protocol on when to dispatch law enforcement with our medic units. The threshold for an automatic dispatch will be based on a list of criteria and we're leaving some discretion in there for the dispatcher and crews to add law enforcement if they feel it is necessary."

"So, can I ask what has changed? Why are they more concerned than last time I talked to Jeff?"

"The FBI intercepted some communication that seemed to indicate that the event you guys responded to was a test. Now they believe they are planning something on a larger scale such as a remote bomb or high-profile target. We rush in, and boom, a second bomb goes off. It could be in our area, or it could be in Seattle. They don't know where yet. We need to be prepared for it to be anywhere. Seattle is also on high alert as is Bellevue, and the other cities in the region.

"I never thought I'd see this coming from our own citizens in my lifetime. Is this just the insanity we live with now? It's really sad."

"Don't I know it," Maya said. "So, what else can I expect when I return?"

"We're going to be replacing all the bulletproof vests that we currently have with a higher quality vest. Also, Craig will be going over cyanide and organophosphate poisoning at our monthly CME. We'll go over the new protocols for mass casualty incidents that delay an immediate response, so we don't end up as the secondary target."

"Okay, so not many changes, just a total reorganization of how we do business. Got it. I think I have the gist of what's going on." Maya threw the ball for Rio again. The unease that she had managed to avoid the past few days was inching its way up her spine again and settling into her neck.

"I'll call you, chief, when I get back to Seattle and revisit whether I'm ready to return. I'm feeling good now, but every day is different. Also, it will give me a chance to get any updates."

"Maya, I hated to call you with this while you are still out, but I wanted you to know what you are walking back into and make sure you are ready."

"I appreciate that. It's information I need to know. If we're lucky, it will be all for nothing. If not, we've got the best plans in place. Plan for the worst, hope for the best."

"Exactly. We'll be in touch in a week."

"Chief, thanks. I appreciate the heads up."

Maya threw the ball for Rio one last time and then headed into the house. It was two o'clock. She realized if they were going to get their ride in, they needed to get ready.

"Hey, Nick, if we're going, we need to leave soon."

Nick was focused in on his computer and didn't hear her. She repeated herself.

"Oh, what did you say?"

"I said, if we're going, we need to leave soon."

"That's right. Would you be disappointed if I didn't ride today? Were going sailing again tonight. I really need to wrap up this estimate for a new client. I don't have a lot of work left, but it would be nice to just get it done so we can have the next three days to enjoy before we leave."

"That's fine. I think I'm going to go, though. I'm feeling restless and need to burn off some energy. I can just ride up Van Sickle from the bottom and then come back down. I'll swing back. I can text you when I'm about thirty minutes out and then we can head to Zephyr Cove from here."

"That would be great. Thank you for understanding. At least one of us can get out for a ride."

"I'm going to go get ready. Can you feed the dogs before I get back? Then we can just go?"

"Sure," he said. Then he was gone, deep into his work, leaving Maya to plan the ride without him. Maya thought about it. It might be good to just go out by herself. She wouldn't have to worry about the dogs and could just focus on riding.

She packed up her cycling gear and threw in a change of clothes and shoes for after the ride. That way, if she was running late, she could just change when they got to Zephyr Cove. Then she headed out. Thirty minutes later, she was parked at the Bi-State Park. As she unloaded, she noticed there weren't any cars in the lot.

She considered the change in riding plans. If it was technical going down, that meant it was technical going up. She was going to burn off a lot of energy. She started her climb up a gradual valley that passed a couple of rocky overlooks. Then she continued up to where the trail became steeper, passing an intersection with another trail on the left. At the intersection was a tight turn and rock steps that were too high and tight to ride up but would be fun on the way back down.

Then the climbing really started. It was steep. Besides the grade, the trail had lots of granite obstacles and steps that she had to set up to loft her tire up and over. That just about took all her energy with each shot, leaving her breathing heavy and spinning while she caught up.

As she climbed, she could see the lake to her left. Climbing higher, she could see the casinos from above. Harrah's, Montbleu, and Hard Rock. Large blocks of buildings that seemed so out of place along the beautiful shores of Lake Tahoe. She wondered who came to such a beautiful place to sit inside and gamble?

The trail turned to the right and again the rock steps were too much for her to ride up and over, so she got off and walked. The trail came to a beautiful small waterfall and a strong wood bridge across the stream below the falls. She dropped her bike against the side of the steep slope and took a break in the shade of the surrounding aspens. All around this stream were the remnants of a wildfire. She had ridden up an open, treeless mountainside. She wondered when the fire had burned the area. It looked like it had been a few years ago because there were new green bushes starting to cover the ground below where trees used to be.

She got back on her bike and continued. Now the trail turned and entered an unburned forest and continued to climb. It was cooler in the forest and a little less rocky. She picked up her pace and made it up to the saddle that intersected the trail she and Nick had ridden with Todd and Brandi the other day. Maya hiked up to a rocky knoll that revealed a view down into Nevada. While she ate a snack, she marveled at the sudden change from mountainous forest to dry desert as the valley spread out and met the Pine Nut mountains to the east.

That was a tough little climb. It was going to be fun going down though. She'd have to be a little more cautious since she was riding on her own and hadn't seen anyone along the trail. She didn't want to crash out here on her own.

She finally had time to think about what the chief had said. There was an increased level of threat. Those changes in protocol suggested there was a significant probability that something might manifest itself. Those were some extreme measures. She hadn't seen these kinds of changes come down from above since her early days when they had a police escort when responding to a hostile apartment complex where tenants had threatened to shoot firefighters and medics who responded to the location. That seemed to pale compared to today's threats.

She wished her government would take these homegrown terrorism threats as serious as they did the gang violence. These new right-wing groups almost felt they were untouchable and perhaps they were until they started targeting police and firefighters.

Do I really want to walk back into that? It's one thing to have the level of risk inherent in the job, she thought. It's quite another to be entering a time when it almost felt like they were in a war zone. She didn't know how she should feel. She signed up to be a paramedic, not a battlefield soldier. Well, she had a week to think it over. No need to make a decision right that minute.

She got up and decided to head down. She'd be back with enough time that she could probably even get a shower in before they had to leave. The ride had been shorter than she anticipated.

The first part was smooth forested downhill with a few rocky sections. She pedaled up a short rise and turned along the side hill before descending toward the stream. She felt someone coming up behind her and kicked up her pace. Suddenly, she felt someone bumping her back tire. "Hey, back off, you're hitting my tire," she yelled. She couldn't look back to see what was going because she'd risk crashing. She couldn't stop because whoever was behind her was riding too close and hitting her rear wheel. She sped up to increase the space between her and the rider behind her when she suddenly felt a solid hit on the left side of her rear wheel. The next thing she knew, her front tire hit a rock and she was launched off the downhill side of the steep trail. She rolled down into a tangle of white thorn and hit her head on a rock. Fortunately, her helmet took most of the impact. Unfortunately, her right arm wasn't so lucky. She landed with her palm outstretched and felt the impact and intense pain shoot up her arm. She lay there dazed, expecting that whoever had run her off the trail would at least stop and make sure she was okay.

She suddenly saw Don standing over her as she lay on the ground holding her arm. A look of insane rage emanated from his eyes. She opened her mouth to scream as he reached down and grabbed her neck with both hands. His hands were huge and easily wrapped around her neck as he started to squeeze.

She realized that she was fighting for her life. She tried to reach up with her good arm and loosen his grip, but he was too strong. She kicked upward, hoping to make contact with his nuts, but she didn't have enough room to land hard enough to send him reeling backward. She felt the air leaving her lungs as she fought, and he tightened. She wondered if this was it. Instead of dying on the streets in some ambush, she was going to be strangled by this weird, twisted man.

She had one last move in her. She reached up with her good hand and buried her finger into his left eye. She jammed it in as hard as she could. He screamed and suddenly let go of her, reaching toward his eye. That distraction gave her a moment to twist free from underneath him and roll farther down the hill, before coming to a stop. The pain in her arm was throbbing as she tried to protect it.

She knew the injury to his eye wouldn't stop him. She just knew. He was a man with nothing left to lose and he had fixated on her. The rage welled up in her body and mind with a resolve so complete as she grabbed a thick old pine branch laying on the ground and ran up the hill just past him on his left. As he struggled to pinpoint her, she swung the branch like she was hitting a baseball. She swung it against his head so hard, it sent his helmet flying off into the underbrush. He staggered to the side but stayed on his feet. She came around and using the branch as a battering ram, she aimed for his throat. She knew if she could crush his windpipe, she'd put a stop to his attack. He swung around and knocked the branch out of her grip. She was now facing him without a weapon. His left eye was sunken shut but his right eye was full of crazy. He started toward her.

She waited. Right when he was bearing down, she put all her strength into her good arm and punched him in the trachea as hard as she could. He gasped and staggered backwards. She jumped down and picked up a rock. Before he could regain his footing, she threw the rock at him, the force of the impact sending him to the ground. She quickly reached down and grabbed another rock.

She saw terror in his eyes as he realized he had picked the wrong woman to murder. She brought the rock down onto his head and screamed, "I'm sick and tired of you and your goddamn dead wife ruining my vacation, you sick fuck!" She lost all semblance of control and brought the rock down over and over, obliterating his face. Finally, she didn't have any energy left to heave it back up and bring it down again. "I've had enough!" As she bent over looking at what remained of his face and skull, she said, "Good riddance!"

She sat down on the ground, dropping the rock. Her breath coming in heaving sobs as she realized that she had just killed this man. Something so contrary to her identity as a lifesaving paramedic. The irony is that the knowledge of anatomy she had as a paramedic helped save her life. She shook her head, 'Gallows humor', she thought.

Why the hell did he have to come after her? What did she do? Did she really do anything other than be in the wrong place at the wrong time and meet crazy head on?

She sat there for ten or so minutes catching her breath and settling her mind by taking stock of her injuries. Except for her arm and the throbbing in her neck, everything seemed intact. She had a lot of scratches on her legs and arms from rolling downhill through the brush.

She looked up at her bike above her next to the side of the trail. She saw Don's bike behind hers. He must have skidded to a stop and jumped off his bike right behind her. He'd been on her immediately. She had no idea that old, tired man had that much strength when she had talked with him last. Tahoe fit, she thought.

Now what? She paused, realizing that there was no way

she could ride her bike to get help with her injured arm. She looked back up the slope. It was steep all right. She wasn't sure she could just walk around the white thorn bushes and get back up without using her arms to grab branches to belay herself upward. That would be hard with only one arm. She searched for the best way to get traction to climb back up to the trail. If she skirted around Don's lifeless body and around the white thorn to the right, she could anchor her feet against some larger rocks. Then she could grab on to a lodgepole pine branch with her good arm.

She made her way up to the pine, carefully anchoring each foot against a rock. The loose granite sand had a habit of sloughing away, but the rocks held her weight.

After five careful steps around the pine, she was able to lean her back up against the uphill side of the tree and rest. Her forearm was starting to throb, especially after she let go of it with her other arm to grab on to the pine before hiking herself to her current perch. Five more feet, she could get herself up the five feet. Now that she looked further, she could see that most of her easy climbing had just happened.

Now it was loose granite sand. She used her sports bra to anchor her forearm between her breasts as a splint and as a cushion in case she fell. Not exactly the most glamorous splint she'd ever adapted, but definitely the most interesting.

Holding her forearm in place, she carefully used her free arm to steady herself by placing it onto the ground. As she stepped upward, her feet struggled to gain purchase on the loose granite. Dig in, wait, and then push off. Each step up ended up being a half step because the sand beneath her feet had to consolidate so she could gain purchase. Slowly, and with careful purpose, she made her way up the five feet to the trail. She sat for a moment on the side of the trail and contemplated the next plan of action.

She had to get to the emergency room and get her arm taken care of. She had to call the police so they could come get Don's body. She decided that the best course of action was to call the police first. She dialed 911. Then rolled her eyes. Of course, she was less than a half-mile from the Heavenly ski slope and she couldn't get cell signal. After fighting for my life, she thought, just kill me now. With that defeat, she stood up and started walking down the trail. Three miles, no problem, she thought as her arm throbbed and the scrapes and scratches from the white thorn started to burn.

About a mile down the trail, she ran into a fit couple in their twenties running up the trail. They took one look at her and asked her if she was okay. She replied that she was, but a man had run her off the trail and attacked her. Her arm was broken, and she couldn't get cell reception.

She felt like she was asking a lot, but she wondered if they would help her get down to the trailhead where she could call the police. They immediately stepped up. The man, Luke, asked if he could get her bike for her. She replied, "No, you don't want to go up there. There's the dead body. Besides, the police are going to want the crime scene as intact as possible while they investigate."

Luke and his girlfriend, Eden, walked down with her. Luke carried her Camelback to lessen the weight on her shoulders. Maya thanked them. Eden was very talkative on the way down, which helped distract Maya from the pain and the reality of what had just happened.

"Did you happen to see anyone on their way up?" Maya asked. "I don't want someone to stumble on that chaos up there."

"No, we didn't," Eden replied. "You're the first person we've run into since we started up the trail."

"Did you see any vehicles in the parking area when you arrived?"

Eden thought for a minute. "No, no vehicles. It's pretty quiet today."

They walked with her to her car. They said they'd wait with her until the police arrived. She was able to get cell reception and called the police. She told them to call an aid car to take her to the hospital. She felt like she could take herself, but she wanted witnesses and someone else to take charge of the situation.

Then she called Nick. "Hey, I'm not going to make it home in time to go sailing. In fact, I'm headed to the hospital... I think I broke my arm."

"Did you crash your mountain bike?"

"No, well yes, but. Remember Don?"

"Yes, the husband of the dead woman?"

"Well, apparently he wasn't happy with me. He showed up out of nowhere and ran me off the trail. Then he tried to strangle me."

"What the hell?"

"That's what I said. He had the eyes of a crazy man with nothing to lose. I knew he wouldn't quit until he either killed me or I killed him."

"What? Maya. What happened?"?

"Well, I'm still here so...." Her voice trailed off.

"Did you kill him?"

"Yes." It was all she could say.

I need to figure out how to get to you," Nick said.

"I'll meet you at the hospital. "

"I'll see if Todd can pick me up and then we'll meet you at the hospital. Todd will know where it is, right?"

"Yes, he definitely will." Maya could hear sirens getting

louder and figured that must be the police and the aid car. It sounded like more than one siren.

"Nick, text me when you get things figured out. I'm safe for right now."

"Okay. I should have gone with you. Please, stay safe."

"I think I will be safe now."

The first police car pulled up and unbelievably the officer was O'Brien.

"Officer O'Brien, imagine meeting you again under similar circumstances," Maya joked half-heartedly.

"No? What or who now?"

"Well, it seems that Don wanted me dead as well. Only it didn't go so well for him. He was bent on killing me, so I had to fight like hell to save myself. He's dead. It was he or I. I have no doubt about that."

"That is not going to be hard to refute."

"Well, I met with him a few days ago to get clear on what the hell had gone on that ended up involving me. I got a lot more information, but the takeaway was he had lost everything. So, he was alone and destitute. I guess he had nothing to lose and was out of his mind. Just another victim trying to find someone to blame."

"You should probably stop talking now. We'll investigate and hopefully we can close the book on this quickly."

Two other police cars came flying in. It must be a slow day, thought Maya. The aid car followed right behind them. She didn't recognize the two young firefighters, but they had already heard of her.

"You're the paramedic who was involved in the murder of the crazy women?"

"Yes, I was."

She insisted on walking to the aid car and stepping in

herself. No way was she going to let them carry her on a stretcher.

Inside, they put her arm in a splint and a sling, did their exam, and took her vital signs. She gave them a good review on their performance.

They transported her to the emergency department at Barton hospital. She had never spent so much time in the emergency room as a patient in her life. One thing she knew was that everything took forever to get done. She'd be spending the rest of the day and evening lying on a bed in a room. *At least I'll be safe here*, she thought.

Nick arrived in the emergency room an hour later with Todd. They rushed in to see how she was doing.

"They just finished up the X-rays. I'm waiting for the results and plan for my arm." She pointed at her right arm lying in a splint elevated on a pillow next to her.

"I'm so glad to see you guys. Nick, I think I should have stayed home and just gone sailing with you guys, but I just couldn't miss out on a little more Tahoe excitement."

"This is not the time for humor. What happened?" Asked Nick.

Maya recounted, yet again, another attempted murder. "I really had no idea that he was that crazy. I met with him after my statement last Monday."

"You what? You met with him? Why didn't you tell me about that Maya?"

"Well, I knew you'd think I was nuts. I just needed to understand why someone would go to so much trouble to kill Karen. During my conversation with Don, I came to understand that she probably had underlying mental illness that caused her to be extremely obsessive and aggressive toward anyone or anything she perceived as a threat to her control. That explains a lot. The bad news is that while I thought Don was odd and probably took part in her campaigns, I didn't grasp how desperate he was after losing his wife, girlfriend, and financial support.

"My guess is that he fixated on me to run from his own situation. I think he was completely out of his mind and was bent on taking it out on me. I think he and Karen fed off each other. They both participated in her campaigns."

"Did it occur to you that you might not be safe meeting with him? I get that you're independent, but these people have wreaked havoc on your life." Nick had an exasperated expression on his usually calm face.

"I wasn't thinking straight. You know that. We've been discussing this over the past week. I'm going to have to rethink many things."

"So, Don is dead?" Todd asked.

"DRT," she joked sarcastically.

Nick looked confused.

"DRT means 'Dead Right There'. It's a term we use when we walk up and someone is already dead, meaning nothing we can do will save them," Todd explained.

"I had no idea how strong that old guy was. I really thought I was going to die. Look at the bruises on my neck. The only thing that saved me was driving my finger into his eye. Even then it only stunned him. I punched him in the trachea. I knew if I could take out his ability to breathe, I might have a chance. It worked and then after that... she looked away. Her eyes lost in the image of his head turning to mush in front of her.

Nick put his head down. She could tell he was stressed. She put her hand on his shoulder. "Look, unless Don has some long-lost relatives or another secret psycho lover, I do think this is the last time I'll have to thwart attempted murder. Now, unfortunately I have a broken arm and another murder investigation to deal with."

The physician walked in. "Maya, luckily your arm isn't fractured, just a severe sprain . The X- rays of your neck didn't show any injury to your spinal column or trachea. Let's get a splint on your arm and clean up your scratches."

Maya recognized him when she first came in but introduced him to Nick and Todd. "This is Mark Hatch. You probably won't be surprised, but he is, well, he was Don and Karen's next-door neighbor."

"Does this ever end?" Nick asked.

"Look, we all want to support Maya and honestly thank her for putting an end to the nightmare we've been living with since we moved here. No one will miss those two. The fact that someone murdered Karen was no surprise to us. We didn't suspect that Don was quite as bad, but here you have it. He attempted to murder Maya. Luckily, he was unsuccessful. Thanks to her, our kids, dogs, and neighbors are safer now. I only wish that she didn't have to go through this for that to happen. We are going to take good care of her tonight." Said Mark.

EPILOGUE

MAYA AND NICK left after the investigation into Don's death. Luckily the evidence gathered at the scene confirmed her story.

With her sprained arm, Maya couldn't go back to work right away. She realized that she needed a safe supportive environment to work through her PTSD from the ambush and the new trauma of being attacked. It was time to work on herself. If anything, the whole Karen drama along with the militia attack had brought home to her how mental illness or dysfunction can ripple through a family, a community, a workplace, or a country. She had a personal responsibility to make sure she stayed healthy, and in return, she could be a support for her coworkers and community. How that would play out, she was no longer sure. That was a decision for down the road, after she found solid ground again.

As the long desert vistas spread out before them, her phone rang. It was Jeff. "Maya." His voice wavered. "Kalie and Brian are dead along with three of our firefighters. They walked into a call for an unconscious patient at Highline Community

College. He paused...and a series of explosions went off, killing everyone in the building, including them."

His voice ominously reverberated through her whole body. Maya dropped the phone and stared off into the distance.

Maya, Maya, her name echoed from the phone.

AFTERWORD

Like this Novel?

Please help others find it. Leave a review on Amazon, Apple Books, Google, Goodreads or other websites where you purchased this book. You can visit my website for direct links.

Love the Adventures?

Check out my blogs for more on great Tahoe and Gold Country adventures, links to trail routes described in the novel, bonus features: the map of murder, extra content, and more.

Resources for Emergency Service Providers

For pre-hospital healthcare workers, firefighters, police, and others struggling with the effects of the job, visit my website for blog posts and links to helpful resources.

Stay tuned for the next novel in the
Emergence Series

www.lisaparsonsauthor.net

ACKNOWLEDGMENTS

I'd like to acknowledge the people and groups that made this book possible. To my husband for the heavy lifting when I disappear to write. My two dog's, whose input were invaluable in developing the canine characters in this novel. To my alpha readers, Elise Forrer, Gloria Olson, and Georgia Daniels. You inspired me to keep going. To my beta readers for all the helpful input, corrections, and comments. Thanks to Bridjet and Joey Orr for the cover photograph of Bridjet mountain biking. To Darbi Delfiner Macy for editing my final draft. To Shut Up & Write for getting me online 2 days a week to inspire me to finish the publishing process and to keep writing. To my past coworkers at King County Medic One.

ABOUT THE AUTHOR

About The Author Lisa Parsons

Lisa is an adventurer, woman, writer, paramedic, conservationist, world traveler, photographer, and dog companion. She weaves her multifaceted, real world experience into her writing.

Her writing and photographs have been published in books, newspapers, magazines, and blogs in the Pacific Northwest and across the globe.

To learn more about this author visit her website at:

www.lisaparsonsauthor.net

CPSIA information can be obtained
at www.ICGtesting.com
Printed in the USA
JSHW050934260622
27344JS00003B/13